Pancakes & Handguns

A Hitman's Daughter Novel

Nala Henkel-Aislinn

LODESTAR
PRESS

Chapter One

If the Darwin Award existed as an actual trophy, I'd bet my favorite PS5 controller I'd win it. The dedication would read, *To Lena Kozek, for bravely—and idiotically—holding a mob boss at gunpoint in a public library.*

Because that's exactly what I'm doing, and it's making my upper lip sweat like a shot glass of Fireball on a humid summer's day.

I make it a point to avoid stressful situations like this one. It had been easy, back when I didn't have a clue about who I was, who the guy on the other end of my gun was, or who the other people in the room—all holding guns—were. But now that I'm in this situation, I feel myself hovering above it, as if someone knocked me out of my body to float above the library's reading room.

And yeah, I said library. Twice. It's a weird situation that I'd love to explain, but right now I've got a mobster to neutralize, should I ever return to my body.

He's a small-*m* mobster, although the weapon he has trained on me is a big-*G* gun. His eyes flutter from my gun to my face, then to

1

my legs, which are visible below the hem of the checkered sundress I'm wearing.

Why I'm wearing a dress is another thing to ponder if I live long enough to have a quiet moment of reflection.

Mobster guy's gun is on me, but there are two guys nearby—also pointing guns but thankfully at mobster guy.

One of them is a superhot FBI asshat. The other is a schlumpy, delusional dork of a police detective who got himself entangled in an outer layer of my heart. If you repeat the part about my heart being susceptible to someone like him, I'll hack your computer and steal your credit card info to buy myself several new gaming systems.

But I'm getting off track.

Behind me is a half circle of gray-haired grannies, their postures rigid like deruny that've been left on the counter overnight. That's a potato pancake, if you're not Ukrainian. They're best right out of the cooking oil.

The grannies think they're pointing their guns at the mobster, but since I'm standing between them and trouble, I can't see how I won't catch a few bullets should they fire. Their eyes are full of cold, hard malice (and maybe a cataract or two), but their half dozen hands are trembling like boiled cabbage.

My Auntie Korinna is the wrangler of this group of badass gray hairs. It's fifty-fifty on whether she's pointing her gun at me or the mobster, which adds a little unexpected spice to this whole situation, don't you think? She's my deceased mother's sister, may her soul rest in peace, but since I'm the blackest sheep of the Kozek family, it means our relationship is deliciously layered like a Napoleon cake minus any sweetness.

Was it only three days ago that this whole mess started?

Thirty-six hours ago, I was in New York, just another nobody at a boring job, doing mundane things like resetting forgotten email passwords and retrieving accidentally deleted files. And when I wasn't working my 9-to-5, I was killing my old college buddies in some dystopian computer game. I was a tiny cog turning inside the larger gears of a boring but gunless life. Tick, tick, tick.

Then my simple life went boom when I tried to exact revenge on my slimy boss, who was attempting to—

"Galyna," purrs the guy on the other end of my gun, and I snap back into my body. I gotta say, the dress feels nice. "Think about this," he reasons. He's calm. Friendly, even. "Killing is so final, family or not."

"Family," I repeat, the tone of my voice hinting that I'm open to contemplating what he's saying. But when his finger tightens on his trigger, mind does the same, and his pupils shrink to pinpoints.

"Tak, rodyna," he says with an ingratiating smile. "We have much to talk about, and I can't talk if you shoot me."

What a slimeball, thinking he can play the family-should-talk card so late in the game. Plus, he hasn't been juggling felonies or gangsters or ghosts like I've been.

I haven't mentioned the ghost yet, have I? Well, hang in there. It's coming.

"I don't need to think," I tell him as I let the sight of my gun hover over the space between his eyes.

He smiles. Then shrugs.

"So who will shoot first?" he muses, his gaze flicking behind me, then back.

If I shoot him first, it would solve a lot of problems. For my aunt and her friends. My hometown too. But mostly for myself.

They might arrest me for murder, but he's pointing a gun at me, so I could claim self-defense. And going to jail wouldn't be so bad. After all, they give you three meals a day in jail. Better than making nutritional choices based on which is the fastest-heating pizza pocket.

Sorry about all the food references. I've only had one decent meal since all this started.

Any or all of the grannies might shoot first, so if I hear any of them move, I'll have to beat them to the trigger. I would never deprive the world of their amazing varenyky and holubtsi.

But I'd be pulling the trigger for my father too. Even though I'm back home, he's still waiting to *go* home. He's also the only one who didn't side-eye my combination of sundress and army boots. For a grouchy, dead hit man, he's been very supportive. He's the ghost I mentioned, although he's nowhere in sight right now.

"What are you waiting for, Galyna?" coos the mobster.

It's a solid question. Thinking back over the last three days, I can see I *have* been waiting for something. A missing part of myself, perhaps.

Three days ago, I didn't think anything was missing. And I'd been excited to pull the trigger on something completely different...

Chapter Two

Lena, three crazy days ago...

There I was, in the cozy basement dungeon of the smallest New York City bank ever incorporated.

Aside from a cityscape of filing cabinets, I had the entire basement to myself.

I had just finished my cheese-and-pickle snack, and I was about to get some luscious vigilante justice.

I hadn't started out to be a crusader—it just kind of went that way.

My mom died when I was three, my father when I was ten. My mom died from cancer, but my dad's death had been a hush-hush thing, resulting in my banishment to my aunt and uncle in New York. Like any other kid with a martyr complex, I reveled in my status as an orphan. When it didn't win me any sympathy, not even a birthday card from my Auntie Korinna, the Banisher, I purged everything about my childhood from my memory. And when I said purged, I mean eradicated, burned, and incinerated in a magnificent furnace. Done. Gone.

"I'm going to do it," I said into my earbuds.

"You said that last time when the dude didn't give you that promotion," Brick scoffed.

"The last *three* times your boss didn't do what you wanted," JP corrected.

"This time is different. He's blackmailing Mandy," I explained.

"Who's Mandy?"

"Sinkhole's niece," I said.

Let's pause here, because this was unusual.

My slimy boss had done a lot of slimy things. Actually, hiring his common-sense-challenged, incredibly inexperienced niece was a nice thing. Shockingly nice. But then my boss exposed the slimy underbelly I should never have doubted.

"So?" Brick asked.

"I've got him on video telling her she owes him a personal favor for her promotion," I said, shivering in disgust and triumph at the same time. "And I'm paraphrasing 'personal favor.'"

"Video *and* audio?" Brick asked.

"And a clear shot of his face as he's saying it?" JP followed up.

"Microscopically clear," I confirmed.

There were about a million cool things about being an IT administrator at a small bank, but three stood out.

First, even though I had a glob-of-slime supervisor, I rarely had to interact with him or anyone else at the bank. With all the servers in the basement and me being the only IT person on staff, nobody ever came down there.

Second, my job was dead easy because I was absurdly overqualified. My biggest task was fixing email even though I was certified to handle server installations and network configuration. Hell, I protected the banking system from people like me, who hacked into it all the time just for fun. I could even requisition all kinds of equipment that nobody knew the bank didn't need.

Third, reasons one and two let me do the thing I love most—spy.

"Did you back your evidence up?" JP asked, breaking into my musing.

"Of course," I said.

"Good old Swiss servers, doing the job of the righteous," Brick laughed.

"You know it," I agreed, reaching for the black box under my monitor.

I'm going to pause again.

In hindsight, I missed a red flag. That morning my black box sat slightly askew from the monitor stand. I always lined the two up perfectly, and that morning it was skewed by a quarter inch.

My downfall was assuming that quarter inch was the fault of the cleaners even though we had an agreement that they'd never come close to my workspace. They were happy to have less work, and I was happy to maintain a pristine working environment.

But that freaking quarter inch... crap. Anyway, back to the story.

"Are you going to release the video?" JP asked. "Get him arrested?"

"No," I replied, pressing the Power button on the box. "Something better."

"Something sneaky," Brick guessed. "She's a very private vigilante."

It was true; I liked my secret, private life. With all the secrets I collected at work, I never felt lonely.

And holy *crap*, does my job let me gather the most ridiculous amount of information about the people I work with. It's the best kind of reality show ever.

I had the whole bank rigged with security cameras and remote recording devices. I could even turn the VoIP desk phones into recording devices. All of it was essential for security and signed off on by Sinkhole, but it meant I could tap into everything anybody did or said.

For example, I knew that our sixty-year-old, uptight assistant loans manager used her work email to subscribe to some pretty salty dating app stuff.

The bathrooms were the biggest gossip areas, though. Not in the stalls—gross—just near the sinks. You wouldn't believe the gossip I overheard. Affairs (a teller and a bigwig at corporate), fetishes (pro tip: don't ever watch a questionable video while you're sitting on the toilet), and Sinkhole's sexual harassment (the guy literally practiced in the bathroom mirror right before he met with Mandy).

I'll be honest, Sinkhole featured so predominantly on my secret server in Switzerland that I pretty much monitored him 24/7 at work. I always knew I'd get him fired one day, but threatening his own family with assault crossed some line in my psyche.

"Are you going to clue us in on this plan?" JP asked.

I cracked my knuckles, then accessed Beatrix.

Beatrix Potter was the name I gave my black box. She'd been fascinated by drawing fungi, which dovetailed neatly with my obsession for drawing dead plants. But that's another not-as-exciting story.

"I'm thinking bank fraud for starters," I said and started typing, entering my credentials into Beatrix. I never accessed my files until I was cloaked. I dug through the server to find my file on Sinkhole.

His legal name was Sinclair Whitmore. He hated women, people of color, and authority figures. His family was rich and, according to the confidential email I could access, had stepped in at the board level twice to avoid him being fired—once for discrimination and the other for showing up at work drunk. I have video of him peeing himself and had to talk myself out of posting that on YouTube. And despite his family stepping in to save his butt, he hated them too.

"Bank fraud is thrilling stuff," Brick interrupted, "but I've got to go to a meeting. Shoot me a text with the details."

"Good to see Google is wasting your programming skills with endless meetings," JP chided.

"Hey, we can't all luck in to gaming design jobs," Brick groaned.

"Gaming tonight?" I asked before he logged off. It was a stupid question. When didn't we game?

They both agreed and ended the call, letting me get back to the task at hand.

I riffled through Sinkhole's file until I found his home IP address. I set up a new path via Beatrix's VPN, found a friendly server out of Chile, and accessed his IP. Beatrix would keep my identity hidden, but Sinkhole's digital fingerprints would be all over the changes I was about to make.

First, via his home computer, I logged into his online banking and lowered his interest rate by .0125%.

Next, I uploaded a worm program to his computer, then deployed it to the banking system. That little beauty would scrape .01 percent from every account at the bank and funnel it into his savings account.

Last, I logged into his SpankBank.com account and changed his alias name to his real name. I then switched the billing to his wife's credit card.

Yes, somehow Sinkhole had found a woman to marry him.

I texted my achievements to JP and Brick, then logged out of Beatrix.

I had to admit, my hands were sweaty. I'd never taken action like this. The smart thing would have been to just sit on the information. Gathering secrets might give someone power, but revealing them was stupid. I don't think Beatrix Potter said that, but somebody did.

Anyway, the point of all this wasn't that I was getting even with my slimy boss, but that I had just committed a serious crime.

A bubble of nausea stirred in my belly, and a layer of just-committed-a-felony sweat coated my neck.

I was the girl who hid in the shadows. Even gaming with Brick and JP, I was the one in the background, making sure we didn't wander into a trap. Now, I was the one out front, doing the things.

The felony things, warned a strange voice in my head. A man's voice, which seemed odd at the time but would become obvious later on.

"Felony, schmelony," I taunted the voice in my head out loud.

Four hours later, my phone rang. It was the schmelony taunt coming back to haunt me.

Chapter Three

Lena

"Lena," slurped my boss's voice over the phone. Ugh, even the way he talked was disgusting.

"Yes," I replied. I clenched on the receiver even though I had no reason to think he'd discovered what I'd done. The man couldn't use the banking system, let alone stumble across my genius hacking skills.

But then he said something he'd never said before.

"In my office," he demanded.

I blinked, wanting to ask, "What?" except my tongue had instantly dried into a shapeless husk incapable of forming words.

Sinkhole never asked me to his office and rarely called me. He'd just done both.

I looked at Beatrix and thought about the quarter inch I'd smoothed away. She was the only way anybody could trace what I had done.

Every sweat pore on my body cringed, soaking my black jacket and pants with insta sweat.

Heavy breathing filled my ear, making me gag. Sinkhole hadn't hung up.

"No-ow," he crooned, then finally hung up.

I replaced the receiver, then pulled Beatrix from where I had stashed her. I felt around all her surfaces until I found a raised bump on the bottom. Turning her over, I saw a small foil patch. I picked at the corner until I could peel it back, revealing a microscopic silver circuit.

Crap and crap and *crap*.

My body broke out in another wave of perspiration. A rivulet ran from my scalp and down my neck, and I flailed at it like it was a spider crawling out of my hair.

I had committed a felony, and the only thing I could cling to was the hope that Sinkhole was about to lay me off. The problem with having access to so much information, though, was knowing everything that was going on. There was zero chance I was being laid off.

The only thing I didn't have access to was who'd put that data collecting circuit on Beatrix. The single camera in the basement didn't show my desk, as it just covered the stairs up to the main floor.

Wasn't that some hubris?

I took my time going to Sinkhole's office. Several curious glances followed me, like I was the monster from the basement lagoon, letting herself be seen by the people of the blue-collar village.

I avoided attention as a rule. I was so good at staying under the radar, I was almost at the Earth's core, but with every step, my breakfast threatened to projectile out of me. Trying to breathe more slowly, I looked around for a handy garbage can just in case I couldn't hold back the vomit.

After what felt like a year, I stood in front of Sinkhole's door.

"Come in," he burped after I knocked.

I did.

The cheap excuse for a man stood in the corner of his office pretending to look at some paper. As I walked further into the room, his pasty, round face rolled into the smile a slug would make. He jabbed a finger at the chair opposite his desk.

"Sit," he demanded.

I crossed my arms and wandered to the chair.

"I'd rather stand," I said, proud that my voice didn't sound as rattled as my nervous system was.

This could be nothing, I told myself. *Game face.*

I put on my mildly concerned expression and angled my head as if I was ready to help him solve some big mystery.

I rested my sweaty hands on the back of the chair. This was a good move. My words were respectful, and my demeanor reeked of pure innocence.

His eyes wandered down to look at the concert T-shirt I wore under my black jacket, and a blaze of hope shot through me. Maybe this was a reprimand for breaking the dress code. Then his eyes snapped back, full of disappointment that I didn't have much of a rack. I'm not being judgmental—I just know his SpankBank.com history.

His lips clamped together so hard, they didn't even look like lips anymore.

"I have to say, you've shocked me. I can't believe you'd betray your Heritage Savings and Trust family like this."

I kept my expression neutral, though I wanted to laugh at the word "family." Unlike him, if I got into trouble, I had nobody ready to pay my way out of it.

"I don't understand," I said and made sure my words curled up at the end like I was an innocent waif trying to understand the big important man in front of her.

Sinkhole stared at me, his lipless mouth curling up at the corners.

"I think you understand." The words slithered out of him. "What have you got to say for yourself?"

Only a dummy would reply in a situation like this. You never talked until you knew which way the wind was blowing, and some-times not even then.

I frowned, molding my expression into one that said I was concerned but confused. It just made him chuckle, which was annoying. I wish I'd sent off the evidence of his interest rate change so he'd be the one being questioned.

"They're coming in from the van, and then everything will become clear," he murmured, using one hand to smooth back the fringe of hair that encircled his pink scalp.

Crap. Crappity-crap crap!

People coming in from a van sounded suspiciously like surveillance. I concentrated all my efforts on keeping my face relaxed. I projected calm interest and hoped the sweat I could feel beading on my top lip wasn't too obvious.

"Mr. Whitmore" came a silky voice from behind me, and I turned to face a slick stranger filling Sinkhole's doorway with smug confidence.

If Sinkhole chose his clothes based on how closely they made him resemble a polyester sausage, this man chose them to win a Bruce Wayne impersonation contest. And speaking of Bruce Wayne, his looks were a major problem for me and anyone who had a Christian Bale crush.

Never in my life have I looked at anyone's face and thought, "That's a strong forehead," but it's the very thought that ran through my mind. That, and how his wide shoulders made me want to jump up and hang off them, which should prove how little guy game I had.

This stranger was the first person who made me understand descriptions in novels of "chiseled cheekbones" and "a piercing gaze," to which I would add "an entitled mouth."

"Ms. Kozek," Batman Look-alike greeted, angling his head toward me.

I raised my eyebrows but otherwise said nothing.

He glided into the office with negligent grace and came to stand between Sinkhole and me. A thought occurred to me as he tapped a folder against his leg. Getting busted by a gorgeous male model posing as a cop seemed like a practical joke my friends might play on me. Would they be this clever, though? Unlikely.

"Ms. Galyna Kozek," Batman clarified.

He sounded cultured, his smooth inflection curling around the letters of my name like a cat napping in the sun.

"Uhhh," I responded cleverly.

Damn him. Was he using his sexiness to knock me off-balance? Because it was totally working.

"You caught her at something, didn't you?" Sinkhole's voice intruded the way finding a slug in your romaine could put you off enjoying Caesar salads ever again.

Batman's eyes swung from me to Sinkhole, letting me breathe. I saw Batman hide a flare of disgust as his eyes moved slowly to Sinkhole's bulging stomach and back up.

Now he's making me like him! This had to be some textbook CSI-investigator-level trick.

"You can leave us," Batman said, disappearing behind me and offering a clear path for Sinkhole to head out the door.

"I think I should be here for this. It's the bank's policy—" Sinkhole attempted, his flappy face turning pink.

"This is a federal issue that supersedes any corporate policy," Batman said, his steely tone cutting through Sinkhole's words.

Shiiiiiiiiiiiitt, I groaned internally. I almost asked Sinkhole to stay in the room, but the worm shuffled away, the click of the closing door sounding like doom.

The hot grim reaper took his time strolling to the other side of the desk, looking as stiff as the metal door he was about to shut on my freedom.

As sweat broke out on top of the sweat already covering my body, I wondered if it was less embarrassing to pass out or vomit. Probably pass ou—

"I'm Agent Palmer," Batman/Palmer said, tapping that folder on the desk. "I'm with the Federal Bureau of Investigation."

Then, in slow motion, the corner of his mouth curled up in a sneer and my vision went two-dimensional. Batman was gone. Instead, the Road Runner stood in front of me holding a cartoon sign that read "Bye-bye!"

Chapter Four

Thomas

Thomas stared at the girl on the other side. Not a girl. According to his information, she was a lot older than that. But looking at her, he wouldn't have thought she was old enough to drink.

With her short black hair on a head that looked too large for her body, she could barely pass for nineteen, let alone twenty-two. The baggy suit didn't help, with her skinny wrists sticking out beneath the cuffs of the jacket. Underneath it she wore a T-shirt that read **blur PARKLIFE**. She looked like a teenager pretending to be a bank employee.

He reached into his inside breast pocket, pulled out his ID, and flipped the leather wallet open on the desk.

Her eyes shifted to it, and then she leaned in and examined it. Really examined it. As if she was looking for signs of a fake.

"Do you know why I'm here?" he asked in his serious I'm-a-Federal-Agent voice.

She didn't flinch the way most people did. Her body didn't stiffen in fear, either, although he swore he saw perspiration on her upper lip.

Her eyes just kept moving, absorbing every detail of his ID, not acknowledging that he'd said anything.

"What you just did was a felony. Tampering with your employer's system software is bank fraud."

Goddammit, even the word "felony" didn't get a response. She just kept eyeballing his credentials. With a snap, he flipped the wallet closed and returned it to his pocket.

Her eyes shifted to him, her expression bored. He didn't like that he was tense while she wasn't.

"Galyna Kozek," he drawled, wondering if using her full name would solicit a reaction. The slight twitch of her mouth was a small reward.

"Tommy Palmer," she echoed, narrowing her eyes at him as if she knew the name Tommy would annoy him.

"I prefer Thomas," he said and gestured for her to sit in the chair in front of her.

She stepped around and dropped into it. Then she folded her hands on her stomach and rested an ankle on her knee. The heavy leather boot distracted him for a second. It looked like an old army boot creased from years of wear.

His gaze snapped back to her pale face, but he couldn't find any signs of the stress he was looking for. No shifting eyes or rapid blinking. No parted lips or shallow breathing, and definitely no tightened or shaking fingers. She sat calmly, innocently, as if grateful for the break in her day.

"I bet you do, Tommy," she replied, that eyebrow still raised.

His smile covered his annoyance.

"Your little tweak to Mr. Whitmore's interest rate could get you a minimum ten years in prison," he said casually. He took a seat in the office chair, trying not to grimace at the clammy feel of the lumbar cushion. He could picture his suit soaking up Whitmore's second-hand sweat.

He kept his eyes on the girl—woman—who, maddeningly, now looked amused.

"Ten years of no rent and free meals doesn't sound *so* bad," she said, her eyes drifting upward as if imagining something wonderful.

He stared at her, matching her pose but not crossing his legs.

He was so close. He'd given up on finding her until his sister had come through with a name. Mike Kovalenko. An uncle the Kozek woman lived with in New York. After that, he'd just exploited a few government contacts to track her down. All of it under the table, most of it as illegal as what she'd done.

But here she was, a computer nerd working at a struggling bank off Wall Street. The daughter of the hitman who'd murdered his father. The last tangled thread to a past that he needed to snip.

"Jail life isn't a free ride, trust me," he said, grimacing as he sank further into the sweaty chair. He wanted to get out of the disgusting thing, but pacing would make him look weak. "But there's a way you can avoid it."

"Really," she muttered, the skepticism thick.

"We need a way into the Olynyk family. It appears your father used to work for them," he said and opened the folder on the desk. Inside was a single piece of paper. He used two fingers to spin the file and push it toward her.

He'd hoped mentioning Olynyk or her father would get a response, and it did—but nothing more dramatic than her body going completely still. Her eyes stayed focused on his for long seconds, and then her body recovered. Either she was relieved about something or she could channel a cosmic level of self-control. Whatever caused it, it wasn't the paper he'd laid down. She didn't even glance at it.

"What Olynyk family?" she asked, her demeanor shifting again. Now she was the picture of confusion.

"The family run by Oleg Olynyk, also known as Legs. In case you've forgotten, Legs ordered your father to kill people."

A lot of things flitted across her expression, but he couldn't decipher any of them. He just had to hope the result was fear. Fear of not doing what he was about to tell her to do. If her fear of Legs was greater than her fear of jail.... Well, he'd deal with that if it came up.

"According to my aunt, my father was a consultant for a business executive," she said, her confusion momentarily flashing scorn.

He saw it and made a mental note of it.

"That's all I remember about my past." The tiniest shimmer of moisture reappeared on her upper lip.

She was lying. Goddammit, she was lying! She *had* to know Ilya Kozek killed his father! He dug his thumbnail into his palm to hide the triumph that shot through him.

"Memory's interesting like that, isn't it? Burying things we'd rather not remember," he said, keeping his words measured. If only his own memory acted like that instead of amplifying the past to impossible levels. Levels that forced him to work long hours so he didn't have to remember. "But I digress. We caught you in a felony, and you can get out of it by completing a simple task for us."

She smirked now, but her upper lip glistened even more. Her pinky twitched too. Just once. But he knew she was dying to brush a hand over that top lip. To hide her only outward sign of unease.

"I bet any task the FBI needs would be the opposite of simple," she said, her voice still calm. "Besides, if it has to do with my father, you're out of luck. He died a long time ago."

"I'm aware of that. The task involves Legs. We need you to contact him. Face-to-face."

She made a sound that was between a snort and a laugh, but she drilled into him with black eyes. He'd never seen truly black eyes before, and he knew it wasn't dilation causing it. The striations of her irises were one shade lighter than the emptiness of her pupils.

"Sure, I'll just fly out to the West Coast and grab a coffee with one of the Odessa Mafia. Do I need to find out where they buried a couple of bodies?" she asked, her words prickly with mockery. "Sounds totally doable. I expect you'll get my estranged aunt to identify the shovelful of what's left of me in an alley when coffee time is over too."

"I don't think the daughter of Ilya Kozek would necessarily wind up dead," he surmised. "You might have inherited some of his... skills."

"Do you mean his skills at getting himself killed? I have a vague memory that my father didn't live to an old age," she said, her voice airy as if she didn't have a care in the world.

He shrugged and smiled back at her, refusing to say anything further. The next one to speak would be the loser in this conversation. He checked his watch. He had about twenty minutes before he had to lie to his boss about why he was in New York.

In the end, she waited an impressive seven minutes before speaking.

"This contact you need me to make," she said, flicking a speck of something off her boot. "If word on the street is that he wants to assassinate the president, forget thinking he'll tell someone like me something like that. Ten years of Salisbury steak and instant potatoes is way more attractive to me than politics or doing something for my country."

He twirled his thumbs as he stared at her. Should he tell her he knew she was there the day her father shot his? That he'd judged her guilty by association, despite her being a kid at the time? The sooner he put her in Legs's proximity, the sooner justice would shut the last door on the painful memory of everything he wanted to forget about Steeltown and his life there.

"We have that in common. I hate politics," he said. "No, we need you to do something even your father might approve of."

He gestured toward the paper, and for the first time, she leaned forward to look at it.

Her eyes moved feverishly over Ilya Kozek's police record. Her face paled, and he finally saw the shallow breathing he'd been waiting for.

"We need you to meet with him and ask him for a job," he said. His hands clenched into fists, and then he slowly loosened them. "For old time's sake. For old daddy's sake, you might say."

"Yeah, right," she scoffed in a breathy voice before leaning back. She swallowed before she spoke again. "I was ten years old when I left Steeltown. I don't think Olynyk would remember me."

"Trust me, he'll remember once he hears your last name," he said. "We're sure he'll give you at least one meeting. Tell him about your computer skills. He'd probably love having someone with your skill of hacking into banks."

"And commit another felony? I guess if I do it for the FBI, it's okay, then, right?" she asked.

"All I need is for you to get close enough to name check him on his business partners," he said, touching his fingertips together.

"Business partners," she murmured, her eyes looking glassy. If she coughed up a few names right now, his plan was screwed.

"Drug partners. The Danchuks. I can't tell you more than that," he said. "All we need is for you to get close enough to get more specific names."

"And that's it?" she asked, her voice heavy with doubt.

"That's it."

"Is this a new FBI strategy, blackmailing innocent citizens into doing your job for you?"

"You're not innocent. You're a felon," he reminded her with a kind smile.

"I'm not a qualified FBI guy like you. If you don't know who this guy is working with, how do you know Olynyk's doing anything wrong? And if you have evidence, shouldn't you give me a dossier for this or something?" she asked, derision clear in her eyes. Derision and enjoyment. It was the enjoyment that rattled him.

"We don't.... A dossier isn't.... Look," he grunted, frustrated that he had been about to make up what was sure to be a flawed cover story. She was quicker than he'd anticipated, and he hated it. "You need to make one decision. Either you help us, or you go to jail."

"I choose neither," she stated, glaring at him.

He didn't think she was testing him as much as she was hiding something. Since she'd been staring at her father's record, it had to be something about him. He reminded himself that nothing about her mattered beyond that she got on Legs's radar and the Ukrainian gangster snipped this loose end for him.

"Either way," he continued, "you're fired from the bank. Pack up and go home. I'll have a car outside your Uncle Mike's place at 8:00 a.m. tomorrow. It's up to you where the car takes you."

Something loosened the tightness of her features.

"Don't involve Uncle Mike in this," she murmured, folding up the paper on the desk and jamming it into her jacket pocket.

"Hm, good old Uncle Mike," he said, giving her a small smile. "Thanks for giving me more leverage."

Chapter Five

Lena

I sat on the sticky seat of the M103, staring out the window as the bus took me up Broadway. It would loop around Harlem before coming back to Little Ukraine, giving me plenty of thinking time.

And crap, did I need to think.

I hugged the router box full of my meager office possessions against my bulging backpack. The god-awful August humidity made the ride juicy, which didn't allow for the clearest of thinking.

My first thought was *Had I really been fired?* Followed by *Wait, had I really been caught in a felony?* And then *WAIT—had I really buried horrific details of my childhood so deep that just looking at a photo of my father burst my brain open like Pandora's box?*

Yes, yes, and YES.

My brain started jabbering, so I turned to the only thing that soothed me. I pulled the small sketch pad out of the side pocket of my backpack.

Remember Beatrix Potter? Well, sometimes I channeled her and drew dead flowers I found on my way to the bus stop. I was pretty good at it too.

I flipped to the last page, where a dead buttercup, just a generic *Ranunculus*, lay in the top corner. Underneath was a flattened dandelion, labeled *Taraxacum officinale*, and to the right was my work in progress—the crushed head of *Monarda fistulosa*, or wild bergamot.

Why dead flowers? Good question. I guess living things are just too complex.

Anyway, as the bus trundled along, I added a little detail to a crushed petal. In my mind it became my father's crooked nose. I erased the line and tried shading the underside of the petal. Instead, I saw his flat stare boring into me from the paper now in my pocket.

I looked away and out the window.

Building fronts slid by as my chest tightened. I waited for numbness to slide down my left arm, because a heart attack had to be coming. Finding me sprawled on an uptown bus, soaked in my urine, would be the perfect way for me to finish this day.

But the tingling didn't happen. Instead, twelve people got off at Bowery and Hester, and a new group of people filled their spots.

To put off the anxiety attack I could feel bubbling behind my eyes, I decided to reflect on my next steps.

Not that there was a lot to reflect on. Go to jail, or go back home. To Steeltown. Just the thought of that place made me shiver. I had buried the first ten years of my life so deep, seeing that word on the paper was like sucking poisonous snake venom out of my brain.

"Whaddis that? Some kinda flower?" asked a curious man directly over me, swaying among the bodies crammed in the aisle.

I snapped my notebook closed.

"Yeah, it's a none-of-your-business flower," I replied, squinting at him until he shrugged and looked away.

I might not have been born in New York, but I'd adopted its persona like a stray cat stealing someone's lunch.

Not born in New York, repeated a voice in my head. That seemed like a safe thread to pick at.

I ended up in New York after being shoved on a plane. By who? By my disapproving aunt. Uncle Mike had picked me up and driven to his apartment building to live with his similarly disapproving wife, but it was a home.

To be fair, Uncle Mike wasn't mean as much as he was grumpy. Same went for my Auntie Stazzi. She'd worn a perpetual pout ever since I decided I wouldn't call her by her full name—Aunt Anastasia. She liked the glamor of it.

I slipped the notebook back into my backpack and felt the paper in my jacket pocket crinkle.

I remembered the image of my father's face on the paper. Back in Sinkhole's office, it had been a shock that I tried to hide. I'm sure FBI Batman picked up on that.

Ilya Kozek. Good old Dad. Long forgotten until just thirty minutes ago.

Something else bubbled to the surface. Smooth fabric and a book about ducks. It was a nice memory, though. *My mother,* I thought, and it felt right.

She used to read to me, but she died when I was little. Toddler little. Then I heard her voice in my mind, high and scolding, saying, "Don't show her how to do that." And the tickle of her long hair. I leaned back into the sticky seat. It wasn't much, but it was something. Something safe, at least.

My father was a different story.

I shifted my body away from the nosy guy who smelled like gym socks and thought as far back as I could remember. There wasn't a lot —mostly... glimpses of memories.

The gruff image of him looking down at me, disapproving of something. The smell of BBQing meat. Then a presence that smelled like industrial cologne. Salty and oily at the same time.

After that, there was only a blank space. It wasn't the absence of memories, but more like an empty footprint. Something was there, leaving only a giant ball of gravity in its place. It tugged at me, but my mental heels dug into the now, refusing to go back any further.

Oh well.

As far as the choice I had to make went, while I didn't want to go to jail, I absolutely didn't want to go back to Steeltown. It was dangerous back there, and not just because of this Olynyk guy—another person who I didn't remember but had a menacing feeling about. My gut told me I had done something wrong. Something that got me sent to New York.

"I could leave," I mumbled, then coughed loud and long so nobody would catch that I was talking to myself like a total freak.

I could, though. I could just peace out to one of those middle states, like Ohio. Or Iowa. JP could help me create a new identity, although telling anybody about my plans was exactly how plans got discovered.

That thought straightened my spine.

Little sayings like that popped into my brain all the time, but now my gut told me they weren't mine. That they were my father's. That he'd filled me with all kinds of warnings about people and situations, and that I'd incorporated those into my psyche.

I hugged the box against my chest, feeling the paper in my pocket crinkle again.

The face on that paper, along with his name... that had caught me. It was like my father's likeness had illuminated a door, and behind it was the tsunami.

Batman telling me he was a hitman didn't bother me. My father working for a crime family didn't seem far-fetched. No, the paper held back a more sinister weight. What was waiting to crush me in that tsunami?

The bus looped up into Harlem and headed back along its return route. Every intersection that brought me closer to my apartment building raised my blood pressure another notch. When glowing letters out the window caught my eye, I almost got off the bus.

Bar flashed the neon light.

I could delay the inevitable if I got off the bus here. Have a few or ten Blazing Fireballs, hook up with a stranger, and wash away this heart-attack-inducing anxiety I couldn't shake.

The bus stopped at the light, then chugged away, the flashing **Bar** sign going about its divey business without me.

It was just as well. This wasn't the kind of stress I could sex away.

I watched the people get on the bus, hating every one of them. None of them were facing what I was, and a few times I imagined changing places with them. Going home to their partner in their tiny apartment, complaining about their workday. Or finding the sink overflowing with dishes or having to take their dog for a walk.

Those were things I'd laughed at. Adulting things that JP, Brick, and I swore to never get sucked into.

I sighed. I was stuck in this mess, and no amount of sex or Fireball or daydreaming was going to drown out my past or help me decide between jail or Steeltown.

But there was one person who might clarify things. I just had to hope he was in a good mood.

Chapter Six

Lena

"What the hell is this?" Uncle Mike yelled at me before I even crossed the street. "You never come home early, not even on a Wednesday."

He was right—I never came home before six on any night. I spent exactly two-thirds of my life at work and one-third in my tiny apartment in his building. Monitoring and organizing all my spying took time, and since I lied about why I was staying late, I got paid for it too.

Correction. Used to get paid for it.

Anyway, if you're wondering why Uncle Mike singled out Wednesday, don't. He liked to emphasize all kinds of random things that were meaningless. He once gave his son crap for adding peanut butter to the grocery list "especially this week." One time he told Auntie Stazzi, "Don't put the empty mayo jar in the recycle bin before lunch." He pronounced all of this from the stoop of his apartment building, which was his unofficial office.

"You got something goin' on with that face?" he asked me after I trudged up the stairs.

"I got fired," I told him when I was close enough that I didn't have to shout.

He almost dropped his foil-wrapped sandwich. That was another thing. Uncle Mike always had a sandwich with him. If it wasn't in his hand, it was in his sweatpants pocket. Again, don't ask.

"Fired? Why the hell'd you get fired? You need me to talk to someone?"

"Bank fraud," I blurted. Why not get it all out at once?

He smirked.

"No. Really. Why'd you get fired? You do nothing all day but mess with computers. What can they fire you for?" he demanded.

I sighed. Uncle Mike had a kind of street IQ that could help me out, but I wondered if I should wait until he'd eaten more of his sandwich. Food usually chilled him out, and things not following their usual course got under his skin.

"We in a staring contest or what?" he demanded, his sandwich now completely forgotten. Damn.

"Actually... you got a minute?" I asked and dropped my bag.

His two buddies walked out of the lobby door, glaring from me to Uncle Mike to see if they needed to sort me out. It didn't matter that I was Mike's niece or that I'd been living in the building for more than half of my life.

Uncle Mike waved at his two buddies. "She's my niece, screw off," he told them, then pointed me to the illustrious metal railing across from him. He jammed his sandwich into his pocket and folded his arms.

I got right to it.

"I think I'm going to jail," I said, the words falling between us like lead as the reality hit me. *Jesus, I might really go to jail.*

"You think? You don't know?" my uncle demanded.

"The FBI guy said either jail or—"

"FBI guy? You sure about that?" he asked, jamming a finger at me.

"Yeah, his credentials were legit."

He squinted and nodded. I couldn't tell what he was thinking about. He just looked pissed. Then he cracked his neck and nodded at me.

"You won't make it in jail, no matter how hard you are," he declared.

"You think I'm hard?" I asked, feeling the tiniest bit of pride.

"Hard as in coldhearted, not hard as in tough," he explained.

In my opinion, it was an even better compliment.

"You said 'either jail or.' What's the or?" he asked.

"Or I go back to Steeltown. The guy wants me to get information on someone—"

"Who's this someone?" he demanded.

"Legs—"

"Olynyk?" he grunted, his eyes popping out at me. "Jesus, jail might be the better option."

"What if I just took off and went to some middle state? Isn't one of your friends from Philly?" I asked, gesturing to where the two hulking men leaned against the wall inside the lobby.

"Jesus Christ," he said, ignoring my go-on-the-run suggestion as he hauled out the sandwich and jammed it into his face. He ripped off a bite and chomped it like the shark in *Jaws*, his eyes going black.

He chewed so intensely, sweat popped out on his forehead.

He swallowed and repeated, "*Jesus* Christ," before ripping off another bite.

I'd never seen him think-eat with so much focus before. I was relieved that Uncle Mike understood my situation. He was wired to every criminal element in Little Ukraine. He was the guy who could fix problems, but the more he chewed, the more I worried that maybe he didn't see an easy fix.

"When you gotta decide?" he asked, a stray piece of lettuce clinging to the side of his mouth.

"Tomorrow morning," I answered.

He nodded. Then he went still and looked thoughtful.

Thirty seconds later, he wrapped up the last of his sandwich and shoved it into his pants pocket.

"You're not smart enough to make it on the run, especially in the South. No offense."

"None taken," I said, ignoring the fact that Philadelphia wasn't in the South. He was probably right about the smarts part, though. I had never been on the run, and even if I wanted to try it, I didn't have enough time to get my digital crap together to be successful.

"I'm gonna be honest with you," he said, folding his arms and sweeping his eyes over me. "I think it's time you knew something."

Jesus, this was exactly *not* the time to tell me something I didn't already know. I'd had enough of that to last a lifetime.

"Uncle Mike, can we just focus on—"

"You're not my niece," he announced, his voice rising in a half yell.

I froze. Wait... *what?*

"Your Auntie Korinna.... She ain't my sister. She's no relation to me. I knew a friend of your aunt's, and she got my name when everything blew up back there."

By the sweat on Unc—Mike's face, I knew this was the truth and not one of his nonsense generalities.

"When what blew up... exactly?" I asked.

"All I can say is, this Olynyk is a bad guy. He's small-time but only because the big bosses don't want nothing to do with him. He's that mean," Mike explained. "I looked into him when your aunt asked me for help."

"My father worked for him," I said, then shook my head. He probably knew that.

"And he probably had your dad killed," Mike added and put out his hand in a warding-off gesture. "Don't go back there. Go to jail. At least you'll have better odds at staying alive."

I looked at this man that I'd always considered family. Not the loving family that everyone else had—definitely not. But someone who knew me and accepted me. All that had been a lie.

"Is Auntie Korinna really my aunt?" I asked. The world had tilted, and now everything I thought I knew about my life was up for grabs.

"Yes. She's really your mother's sister. I looked into that too," Mike claimed, pointing a finger at me like I'd accused him of a crime.

I tried to adjust to a new reality.

The only family I had didn't want to raise a hitman's daughter, so they found the slimmest connection as far from her as possible and shipped me away. To strangers.

My uncle wasn't my uncle, and my cousins weren't my cousins. The cousin part wasn't too much of a blow because Jordan and Dallas were a pair of Neanderthals. But still... they'd been *my* Neanderthals.

"Look," Mike said, holding his hands out in reassurance. "The feds'll probably give you five years upstate. It's easy time if you stay out of dark corners." He dug the sandwich back out of his pocket, then shook it at me. "Just don't get admitted on a Tuesday."

Chapter Seven

Lena

I'm not proud of it, but I had an anxiety attack on the elevator.

I didn't cry or anything like that, but I started hyperventilating and got dizzy. The doors opened and closed on my floor while I leaned on my knees, trying to get normal.

When I got into my apartment—was it even my apartment? Was anything real anymore?—I went right to the freezer and heated a pizza pocket.

I nibbled at it as I looked out the window. Everything outside, from the brick laundry building across the street to the light posts and garbage cans, looked different. That didn't make sense, because I was the one who'd changed. I was the one detached from everything I thought I knew.

I was halfway through my dinner, poking the microscopic pieces of ham to the bottom of the pastry to savor in the last bite, when my phone buzzed.

Uncle Mike's text thread popped up, something I'd have to change to just "Mike" now.

Feds are here, his text read, and I pressed against the window to look down at the street.

A dark sedan inched down the road and pulled to a stop in front of the laundry. My heart dropped like a pebble into my stomach to roll around with the half-eaten pizza pocket.

Had it been following me while I was on the bus? Maybe. Probably. I was a felon, after all.

I expected Not-Uncle Mike to walk over to it and give the driver a hard time, but he'd merely taken up a position on the sidewalk outside the apartment, glaring at the car.

I guessed since I wasn't family, he didn't feel obliged to harass cops on my behalf. If I'd been the kind of person to feel sad, having my brash, opinionated uncle not stand up for me would have done it.

I watched for a time, but nobody got out of the car.

I backed away and put another hot pocket in the microwave. I poured myself a healthy glass of Fireball and dropped onto the couch to fire up JP's game.

I was twenty minutes into it when my headset buzzed.

"Hey, Rook, are you playing solo, or can I join in?" asked Brick, annoying as usual. But at least this was something that hadn't changed.

I gripped the controller and fired another ten rounds into the corporate zombie that lurched through a curtain of sparking electrical cables.

"I guess you can join," I said, feeling some of my old self coming back. "I cleared out this floor, so you're clear from the elevator to the west office. But if you're just going to kill me in a gun sweep that *never* works, wait until JP logs on."

"They work sometimes," Brick whined. "And why do you need JP to protect you?"

"He's not for protection. He's my personal bullet shield."

"It's not like you need one," Brick replied. "You're too good at this game. Even with me shooting at you."

"It's probably all the self-defense practice I get whenever you log on," I joked.

I heard the telltale beep of his microwave in the background.

"What's up for dinner tonight?" I asked.

Brick and JP were the only people I came close to befriending in college. We had to share a table in Linear Algebra, and they promised me endless online gaming credits for tutoring them through it. I could play games into my nineties for free after all the help I gave them.

"They have this new meat pie at Trader Joe's. Stout and steak, or something," he said, a fork clattering against a plate in the background.

"Living in California has damaged your taste buds," I told him.

"Whatever, Rook—you're stunted in pizza-pocket land," he chided.

"Stop calling me Rook, Noob."

"Don't call me Noob, Geek," he laughed.

I laughed back. A genuine laugh. Screw family. I had my friends and my game for at least one more night.

"Loser. Geek is a compliment," I said, then yelled when his character ran into view and immediately shot me.

"Brick, Jesus," I complained, going back to my last save. I made my character shove his character forward, then thought about the car outside.

"I've got a hypothetical for you," I said as our characters pulled at a pile of twisted metal that covered a hole in the wall. Outside the high-rise, digital snow fell.

"Let's hear it," Brick said as he aimlessly wasted several rounds of ammo on widening the cement hole.

"Would you rather go to a jail with three meals a day, or—"

"A chick jail? Because my answer is yes."

"Yes, probably a *women's* jail," I corrected. My friend was smart, but he could still be an immature jerk. "But don't answer until you hear my other option."

"Doesn't matter. I want in on being locked in a prison full of girls."

"It's women, and I'm pretty sure none of them will want to have sex with you," I said, pausing before adding, "Kind of like your life now."

"That's harsh, Lee. And thanks for spoiling my fantasy, but okay. What's the other choice?"

"Going to your hometown where a crime boss will probably kill you."

"Ooooh, crime boss kill. That's cool. Why will he kill me?"

"The why doesn't matter. All you need to know is, the odds of it happening are high."

"How high?"

"Who's high?" burst JP's scratchy voice into my headset. "I thought we weren't doing Weed Wednesdays anymore."

A new green diamond glowed on the map as JP's character started moving toward our location.

"We're not high," I sighed, rubbing my eyes. I never got high, something they used to hold against me. "I'm giving Brick a hypothetical situation, but as usual, he's an idiot."

"Give it to me, then. I got the highest mark in Multivariable Calculus," JP said.

"Like that means *anything* once you're out of school," Brick complained.

"It means my dimensional thinking is more advanced than yours. That makes me the most qualified of the three of us to consider a hypothetical."

"God, you always say that like it's some magical talent," Brick complained.

"It is. You should see the ladies drop like flies when I use it at the bar," JP bragged.

"They're dropping because they're climbing over each other to get away from you and suffocating under their own weight," Brick muttered.

"Guys, shut it. JP, the hypothetical is this. Given the choice, would you go back to your hometown to get shot and probably killed, or go to a fairly safe jail for ten years where you might only get beaten up a few times?" I asked, internally questioning my choice of friends.

"Is it one of those all-female prisons?" JP asked.

"Forget it," I said and pressed the button to switch weapons and blasted my buddies with my flamethrower.

"Geez, I was just asking," JP said as his character regenerated. "My answer is jail. Duh. Plus, if you have time before you're locked up, you could take some self-defense classes and put a beatdown on anyone who tries to pick a fight."

"What if there's no time to take any classes?" I asked.

"YouTube," they both intoned.

Geez.

"Wait," JP said. He turned his character to look at mine, which was a little startling. "Is this really a hypothetical? Does this have to do with your vengeance today?"

I hesitated. If I told them what was really going on, could it implicate them? Were they already implicated, and Batman was waiting to use them as final leverage to get me to Steeltown?

"Of course it's hypothetical, moron," Brick answered. "Why would Lee be going to jail? She's got a cush job where nobody would ever suspect her of hacking. As long as you're not tampering with the bank code, Lee. Cuz that's a felony."

The word "felony" dug into my gut.

"Of *course* it's a hypothetical," I assured them, but I heard the catch in my voice.

I'd never told the guys about my aunt shipping me away or my dead father's association with crime. As far as they knew, my only family was Not-Uncle Mike. The folded paper with my father's old arrest record in my pocket pulsed like the timer on the explosive JP's character had just set.

"Setting detonator for ten seconds, but it's only going to take out the first ten or so zombies coming up the stairs," JP warned. "Geez, whose idea was it to set this game in an office tower?"

"Yours, idiot," I reminded him. "You programmed it."

I thumbed over to my machine gun and checked my ammo.

"It's in beta. Just add a way for us to get a helicopter to the roof," Brick suggested, and then his character swung a grenade launcher off his back.

"Ready for a sweep—" Brick yelled, causing me and JP to scream, "No!" and dive for cover.

Ahh, friends. If only we could have played all night. If I'd been awake, I would have avoided the nightmare that came next.

Chapter Eight

Lena

I woke up.

I wasn't slumped on the couch like usual after gaming until 2:00 a.m. I was flat out on a lumpy mattress. Since my mattress was pretty incredible, I knew I had to be dreaming.

A sharp blue flash pulsed behind my eyelids, then pulsed again. Probably my TV reminding me to save my game. But there was a smell too. It was familiar, but not something I could describe except as... dusty. Maybe musty was a better word. Whatever it was, I didn't ever remember smelling things in a dream.

I splayed my dream hands against the dream mattress, feeling a thin blanket instead of my luxurious quilt or the rough fabric of my couch. It should reassure me this wasn't real, but then the light pulsed again, and the musty smell got stronger.

I could have opened my eyes, but underneath that weird scent was a metallic machine odor. A smell had never scared me before, but that one did. The dusty metal combination scraped every hair on my body into a standing position.

You're being stupid, I said to my dream self and pushed myself up.

I squinted my eyes open, bracing in case I found myself in some Terminator-style nightmare. Instead, I saw a small room. And I wasn't on some old blanket—I was under my old *Star Wars* quilt, with the gray-and-white schematics of the Millennium Falcon right on top of my crotch.

It *was* a dream. Just a dream.

Obviously the stress of choosing between being a felon and being dead had affected me. Or was it realizing that I was truly an orphan in a world that didn't want me and I was totally alone?

Cue the 😵 emoji followed by the 🫠 emoji.

I ran my hands over the Falcon's outline. I might as well enjoy the dream while it lasted, and man, did I love that quilt. Being a *Star Wars* nut hadn't won me any friends in school, especially one girl bully in particular. She'd shoved me one time, and the last science project I ever did—

"Hey," I said into my empty childhood room. I'd just had a new memory pop into my head! Not a great memory, but as long as my past trickled back slowly like this, maybe it wouldn't drive me crazy.

"Galyna," grated a voice from the darkness beyond my bed.

And just like that, my trip down memory lane had me stumbling into a pothole.

I knew that voice. I'd buried it, but not so deep that I didn't recognize it.

"Galyna," the voice said again, but sharper, as if frustrated that I didn't recognize him.

The darkness where the voice came from separated from the wall and drifted closer, thickening as it moved to the foot of the bed. It took the shape of a man's body.

This is a dream, a dream, a dream, I chanted to myself because my brain couldn't rationalize why I was hearing the very real-sounding voice of my father. My *dead* father.

The more he took shape, the more my body started to sweat. I was unlocking a new level in a game I didn't want to be playing.

Strange thoughts started flashing through my mind like road signs.

Where is my weapon? Where are my exits? Did I hit my target or is the job incomplete? They were almost like thoughts I had when I gamed. Almost.

"Wake up," my dead father grunted.

No way. This was a dream, and I was sticking to that.

"I'd rather stay in the dream, if that's okay with you," I replied, not liking how very real my voice sounded.

His body snapped into full focus, his glare nothing like the sullen, dangerous eyes the police rap sheet portrayed.

Oh, his face was gaunt like in the photo. He had high cheekbones and hollows underneath, but his eyes shone like silver, and his posture was more welcoming than threatening. He wore a long-sleeved shirt and his blue suspenders, like always, and—

Like always?

—his favorite gunmetal trousers with the narrow cuffs. He was the picture of a thirties gangster, which, now that I was old enough to appreciate it, was a pretty cool look.

He sat the way he always did, left leg crossed elegantly over his right, with the knife-sharp crease in his pants highlighted by a blue light streaming in from my dream bedroom window.

However, he looked dead. Corpse dead. Sunken eyes, pointy chin, bony fingers DEAD.

I pushed myself away from him and against my dream head-board, my childhood drawings crinkling against my back. I didn't have to look to know my sketches of plants and flowers covered the wall. It triggered a memory the way an ammo cartridge snapping into my AK47 did in a game.

My father, standing at a sink, washing a plate. Little-kid-me showing him a drawing of a dandelion. Not the yellow flower, but the white puffy one. The one that was full of promise before it became the weed the world hated.

"Drawing is good," he'd said in his unsmiling way, not even looking. "It relieves the stress of the work."

Sounds nice, right? Except he'd said, "the work," which made me think he meant some very specific kind of work. Now, what kind of work was little-kid-me doing that I needed a way to relieve stress?

"Why am I here?" asked the gravelly voice of my corpse father.

"Why are you where?" I blurted. Stalling was a reflex that gave me time to fight back my dream panic.

His body shifted in a familiar way, and I knew before he said anything what his answer would be. A *tsk* sound, and then—

"Ne bud' durnym," he said in Ukrainian. Don't be stupid.

I bristled, just like I used to as a kid. *Click.* Another memory of a forgotten childhood slotted into place. My dad annoyed me.

Wait, back that up.

I understood Ukrainian?

"I'm not being stupid," I replied, relieved the words came out in English.

I took a steadying breath. Since I wasn't sure how to wake myself up, I'd just have to push through this conversation.

He tsked again, then said, "Why did you bring me here?"

"I didn't bring you here," I said.

"Of course you did."

"You're just in my head. A dream," I insisted, gripping the quilt.

"*Tsk*, this is no dream," he scoffed and leaned forward.

Suddenly he was inches away from me, and I knew what that musty smell was. It was his drying, decaying skin. Leave it to me to conjure my dead father as a corpse instead of a living—

Killer

—parent.

"It has to be a dream. It's not possible that we're back... at the apartment and I'm talking to a dead man," I said, hoping my dead dream dad didn't notice I'd stumbled, almost saying home instead of apartment. I'd excised the concept of home and all my memories when I'd stepped off the plane years ago. I'd do it again once I was out of this dream.

"We're not there—we're here," my corpse father scoffed as if I was an idiot. "Where is this place?"

The fabric under my hands dissolved, and the nubbly texture of my couch rose behind my back. The lingering smell of microwave pastry floated by my nostrils, telling me I was still in my New York apartment. I wasn't back in my childhood home, yet for some reason, my corpse father hadn't vaporized along with my Millenium Falcon quilt.

No, no, no. I didn't want to be going insane and talking to corpses right before I went to jail.

"Galyna!" he barked, making me jerk. "Where are we?"

"In New York. In my apartment in N-New York," I stuttered.

"What did you do to bring me here?" he asked, anger making the words crisp.

"I—well," I mumbled, feeling guilty. But maybe he was on to something. "I must be conjuring you because I might have to go back to Steeltown."

"Go back to Steeltown?" he asked, leaning back as if surprised.

"Or to jail," I continued. "I have to decide by tomorrow morning, and I still don't—"

"To jail?" he interrupted, leaning forward with interest. "Did you kill somebody?"

He sounded hopeful, maybe even proud. Other than while gaming, I didn't get a lot of compliments. Not that I needed any. I was a loner and proud of it, but I appreciated his reaction all the same.

"No, I didn't kill anybody. How is that your first guess?" I asked.

He shrugged. "You're my daughter. It was a reasonable question."

I thought about his arrest record and what Batman had told me. I hadn't believed it when I read the various murder charges, but something about my corpse father's dangerous aura told me everything on his record was true.

I was the daughter of a hitman. I knew it the way my hands knew a gaming controller.

There was a lot more that the cops didn't know about him. I knew that, too, although the knowledge squatted in the back of my mind like a demon, hoarding those dark secrets in a sack. Hopefully he'd only release them one at a time to protect my psyche.

"Well, there was no killing. I tampered with a banking system, which is a big no-no at the federal level," I explained.

"Did you steal money?" he asked, a lesser amount of hope in his posture.

"No, I shaved interest off my sleazy boss's mortgage."

He scowled at me, his eyes shiny and nothing but pupils. "Shaved off. You mean you lowered his rate? If he's sleazy, why would you do him a favor?"

"So I could anonymously report him. Then *he'd* be the felon." I waited for a grudging respect to shine from his sunken, dead eyes. My plan had been a solid one. How could I know the FBI was spying on me?

"Durnyy," he huffed. Stupid. "Why not just have somebody break his leg, since you are so against my training."

"Training?" I said, trying to match the level of scorn in his voice. "What kind of training?"

He moved forward, bringing his horrific features into sharper focus.

His cheekbones were sharp, the skin under them hanging in vertical, papery lines. His sunken eyes shone like mercury pooling out of a broken thermometer. But the smell....

More memories flooded back, and I closed my eyes to brace for them.

Instead of witnessing a hit or seeing more corpses, cold air blew against my shoulder. The rustle of trees filled the room. A weedy berm appeared behind my closed eyelids. This was nice.

My hands, resting on my lap, now felt a metallic hardness between them. Even with my eyes closed, I could see myself gripping an AK pistol. I felt the smooth metal of the barrel in one hand, the stock pressing into my armpit.

It wasn't just any AK—it was *my* AK.

"What the hell," I muttered, my eyes jerking open. The sensations of the memory were gone, but my corpse father wasn't.

"I trained you to kill, not get petty revenge on office workers," he declared, disdain sharpening his accent.

He was right. He had trained me. But there was something else that lurked deep in my memories. Something that made my mouth turn to cotton.

I'd done something back in Steeltown. Something bad. My lungs emptied, and I couldn't draw in any air.

This was definitely a nightmare, and I was spiraling into a panic.

At least my scream will wake me up, I thought—if my body let me draw in enough air to scream.

"Why did you *really* bring me here?" he demanded, his wrinkled corpse mouth gruesome in its demand. But behind the anger, I sensed he was as confused as I was. It was enough of a comfort that I could finally breathe.

"If I did, it wasn't on purpose," I said.

In a blink he was at the end of the couch, giving me a little space.

"Unless it's because I saw you on this."

I reached into my pocket and pulled out the wrinkled arrest record. I opened it and pressed the creases out as I flattened it on the coffee table close to where he sat.

He looked away, though, tweaking the knee of his pants, then leaning on it. He looked like he was deep in thought, and I tried to ignore the way his ear seemed ready to fall off his body.

"Look, I really think I'm dreaming you. I'm sure you're fine. I'm going to wake up, and you're going to go back to whatever afterlife you came from—"

He interrupted me with a papery snort. "You have to go back," he stated, sitting back to uncross and recross his other leg with a horrific creak of dried bone and sinew.

"Go back?"

"To Steeltown."

"I'm kind of leaning toward jail, since I won't have to cook—"

"Ya ne znakhodzhu spokoyu!" he shouted. *I do not find peace.*

"You're not real—"

His arm shot out, the wiry sinews of his bony hand gripping my right wrist like a manacle. His moldy smell enveloped me, making me gag. I didn't look away, though. I looked straight into his silvery eyes. He pointed in the vicinity of my neck, which was not reassuring, but I didn't flinch.

"Go to Steeltown. Vy povynni diznatysya, chomu ya ne mozhu pity," he growled. *You have to find out why I can't go.*

I woke up on the couch, the game controller slipping from my fingers and clattering to the floor.

The TV screen showed my character standing in a giant hole in a wall, the scarred and snow-covered landscape stretching fifty floors below her. The digital background pulsed a blue light over my plate of pizza pocket crumbs in front of me. I tapped my phone, and it showed me the time was 2:37 a.m.

It was a dream. All of it—right down to my father's bony hands.

Relieved, I bent down to pick up the controller... and saw red scratches around my wrist.

Chapter Nine

Lena

Four mini pizzas and five hours later, I trudged to my bedroom and started packing. Well, started and finished.

I still had my work clothes on, so I packed some underwear and socks and a pair of sweats. I spent a minute debating which Radiohead T-shirt to bring and settled on the white *OK Computer* one. My backpack still had my laptop in it, so I just added a few cables and connectors, then looked at the clock. Packing had taken a whole six minutes.

I'd been flip-flopping about what to do all morning. When the red marks on my wrist faded, I'd thought, "Screw corpse Dad. I'm going to jail." When I had a quick chat with Brick about Google looking for AI developers, I thought, "Go on the run to California? Hell yeah!" Frankly, nothing had come up to make me think I should listen to a ghost and go toe-to-toe with a mobster.

I took one last look around at my sparse apartment. So long, gorgeous 85″ Sony TV and kick-ass gaming system. So long, lumpy thrift-store couch and freezer full of frozen delicacies. "Do pobachen-nya!" I called out, then slapped a hand over my mouth.

I'd just said goodbye. In Ukrainian.

I dragged my bags to the elevator, refusing to think about all the memories of my father that swarmed like bees in my mind. All the way down, I fought it, sweating with the intensity.

By the time I dropped my bags on the front stoop, the sun had cleared the buildings across the street. The black sedan that had been parked there was gone, and I realized if I was going to make that run for California, this was the time to do it.

I didn't. I guess I already knew that I wouldn't, though.

I took in the sounds and smells of New York. I loved this city with its anonymous bus drivers and oblivious people. You could do your own thing here, and no one cared. No one even knew you were alive unless you walked into them. I always liked flying under the radar like that.

That was all going to change now. In that moment, as the sun hit the garbage bins in the street and I caught the resulting whiff, I knew I wasn't going to jail like my uncle... like Mike thought I should do.

I was going back to Steeltown.

There was a metric crap-ton of things to sort out—such as what was a good conversation starter should a person run into a mafia guy? —but I told myself I'd have a long airplane flight to figure it out. Or who knew—maybe Batman would have some meet-up all arranged?

The door rattled behind me, and two arguing voices and shuffling pairs of feet spilled onto the stoop. The Neanderthals. Perfect. I needed the distraction.

"Hey, Dad said we should get your key from you," said Dallas.

He was the oldest at eighteen, although his thinning hair and gut would make you think he was closer to thirty. He already wore the velour tracksuit uniform. All he was missing was a sandwich jammed in the pocket.

"Yeah, you didn't take any of the furniture, did you?" asked his younger brother, Jordan.

Jordan was a huge contrast to Dallas with an athletic build, thick black hair, and a New York Jets jersey he wore constantly. I was secretly pulling for him to resist the velour tracksuit, but it was probably a vain hope.

I dug in my pocket and pulled out the key, dangling it from the string it had been on the whole time I'd owned it. Dallas stepped forward to swipe it off my finger with a huff.

I looked at my bags, then at Jordan, raising my eyebrow to see if anything would sink in. Finally, I said, "Does it look like I took any furniture?"

His expression remained suspicious until his brother punched him in the arm.

"Hey," Jordan yelled in complaint.

"Don't be so stupid," Dallas jeered. "She knows a lot of that furniture belongs to Dad. He'd be pretty pissed if anything happened to it. Ask her about the TV, though."

"What about the TV?" Jordan asked.

"Whatever's up there is staying," I replied, not wanting to add grieving my prized possessions on top of everything else. Again, I could do that on the plane.

They stood around as if unsure about how they should act around me. I wondered if Mike had told them we weren't related. Then I realized maybe they'd known all along.

"So, you're going to jail, huh?" Jordan asked, backing up to lean against the metal railing.

His brother did the same, keeping one hand on his stomach while the other one swung the key around his finger.

I squinted up at them, wishing I had a good comeback. The eagerness in their expressions just depressed me.

"Which one of you will get the apartment?" I asked instead of answering.

"Me because I'm older," Dallas replied.

"Me because I already asked Mom, and she said yes," Jordan gloated, shooting his brother a look.

Then the shoving started, and they ended up down on the sidewalk, slugging each other repeatedly in the shoulders.

Ah, the simple life they had. Arguing over an apartment I doubted either of them would get. Not when their dad could make triple what I was paying him. *Had* been paying him.

"You should know something about the apartment," I called down to them when the punching slowed down.

"What's that?" Dallas wheezed, leaning on his knees.

"It's haunted," I said.

Dallas shook his head in scorn, but Jordan's eyes widened.

"For real?" he asked, climbing on the bottom step.

Down the street slid a familiar dark sedan creeping toward me. I stood up, regretting waiting outside. I was already sweating through my clothes in the muggy air.

"Haunted, like, by a ghost?" Jordan asked, taking another step closer to me.

"Don't be stupid. What else would haunt something but a ghost?" Dallas asked. "But you're an idiot because ghosts aren't real."

Now it was Jordan's turn to scoff.

"On *Paranormal Adventures* they show a ton of apartments in the city that are haunted. Those guys—"

"Are total scammers," Dallas finished, shaking his hands at his brother like he wanted to strangle him. "You paying for their livestreams is another reason I'm getting the apartment and you're not. Because you're *stupid.*"

"Am not," Jordan argued and jumped off the step toward his brother. He pulled on Dallas's waistband when the bigger boy curled away in self-defense.

"Ow! Ow-ow-ow!" he yelped as Jordan gave him a wedgie.

Usually those two buffoons made me feel nothing but derision. Instead, I felt something different.

Sad was not the word for it, but knowing this was the last time they'd put on this show for me had me feeling... heavy.

The sedan rolled to a stop at the curb, and any emotion I'd been analyzing drained out of me. The door opened, and everything shifted into slow motion.

Batman-Tommy stepped out of the back, buttoning his suit jacket as he went. When he saw me on the stoop, his chin jutted out. He stepped to the side and angled his body toward the open door, then folded his hands in front of himself and waited.

The two buffoons stopped fighting. Dallas peered into the dark back seat from his stooped-over stance.

"Anyone want to take my place? You'd be going to jail in style," I suggested, and the two of them backed away, clearing the pathway from me to the open door.

I expected a comment from Tommy, but he remained stone-faced.

I stood up, hauled my backpack and bag onto my shoulders, and walked down to the sidewalk. Now that I was closer, I could see the smug press of Tommy's lips as he knocked on the roof of the car. The trunk clicked and then opened.

Nobody moved to help me with my bags, so I sighed and marched to the back. I threw my bag into the trunk but hugged my backpack close.

"Let's go," I enthused, like this was one big adventure instead of a death sentence.

Tommy didn't comment, just stood by the door and waited for me.

"Which jail are you going to?" Jordan called after me as I climbed into the dark car.

"Shawshank. Did you know it's real?" I called back, watching his eyes widen.

"That's so cool, I didn't think—" he exclaimed, but Tommy had climbed in and shut the door.

Jordan's gullible shock was the closest thing to a going-away present I was going to get.

Chapter Ten

Thomas

Thomas was screwed. Oh, so screwed.

"Let's go," he told his driver.

Galyna Kozek, right there beside him. Choosing jail, if her comment about Shawshank could be taken seriously.

Just breathe, he told himself. Panic would get him nowhere.

Her relaxed body language was odd, for one thing. Definitely not the posture of someone choosing to go to prison. He thought back to everything that had happened since yesterday.

He'd really thought she would try to run, but other than taking an inordinately long bus ride home yesterday, she hadn't attempted it. Or called anyone at headquarters to check on his credentials. Or stalled when he got out of the car moments ago.

"So. Jail," he said, keeping his tone as bored as she looked.

She continued to stare out the window for a full block before swinging her gaze to him.

"Nah, I guess I'll go to Steeltown," she said.

He had to force himself to breathe normally to maintain his composure. His whole body wanted to collapse in relief.

"Are you sure?"

"Pretty sure," she replied and looked back out the window.

Now that he wasn't screwed, he looked her over to where she sat slumped against the door. She wore the same clothes she had on yesterday, even the T-shirt. He'd looked up Blur and listened to the album *Parklife*. He didn't get it.

The album was almost thirty years old, and none of the lyrics made sense to him. It was an odd, insolent selection of songs that curiously matched her life.

She'd been in and out of various public schools since arriving when she was ten. She got her GED and then—surprisingly—a technical degree in computer programming. All her school photos showed a surly, unsmiling face.

She lived in the same place and had been at the same job for years. Other than her actions yesterday, she hadn't been caught breaking any laws. She had a clean record.

None of that mattered, though. Anyone with her level of calm when being accused of a felony was hiding something. She'd go back to Steeltown, and either Olynyk or his people would mete out their own justice.

It would close the loop for Thomas.

Hands washed, he'd move on.

"Call this number tomorrow," he told her, pulling a card out of his pocket. "I'll expect you to have made contact by then."

She ignored him.

He tapped her shoulder with the card. She glanced at it but didn't take it.

"If I don't hear from you, I'll have one of my field office agents pick you up on a warrant," he continued. Her face still didn't move. "A federal warrant means I have jurisdiction—"

"I get it," she muttered, snapping the card from his hand and glaring at it. "You want me to talk to Olynyk by tomorrow. You might as well send your field office dude to come and get me with a body bag."

She turned back to the window, ignoring him as the car merged into Queens Tunnel traffic toward JFK.

"Does the FBI have some kind of safe house for me to stay at?" she asked, surprising him.

"No," he replied.

She looked at him with the first genuine emotion of the morning —scorn.

"I need someplace to execute your plan from," she replied.

"The plan is, you meet with Legs and ask him for a job," he replied and flattened his hands on his legs. They were sweating, and he battled the urge to wipe them. He wouldn't fully be at ease until she was on the plane. No, had landed in Seattle. No, was reported dead.

"So... no plan," she said, sarcasm in her voice.

"It's enough of a plan," he replied. "Don't you have family in Steeltown you could stay with?"

All emotion fell from her face, almost as if she'd gone unconscious. Except for her black eyes. They'd gone cold.

"That's none of your business."

She swung her gaze back to the window.

"You're the felon smart enough to hack into a banking system. I'm sure you can find a way to get into Olynyk's email and get us some names," he said.

Her jaw clenched.

"For an FBI guy, you have a pretty simplistic idea of how criminals operate," she muttered. "He'll probably just kill me on sight."

He could only hope.

"That's... possible, I guess. But unlikely in a small town like that."

He wished she'd stop talking. Wished the traffic would magically lighten so they could get to the airport and he could wash his hands of this.

Instead, she turned and fixed him with that black glare of hers. His hands sweat even more.

"Okay, Batman, it's time to come clean," she stated.

"Batman?"

"There's more to this than some case you're trying to sell me on. Tell me your angle on this, because it all feels super off the FBI books to me," she said.

He half smiled at being called Batman. She wasn't wrong. He *was* seeking some personal vengeance like the cartoon character, just without the cool gadgets. Unless one considered this girl-woman a gadget.

He pondered whether to outright lie or give her some glimpse of the truth.

"Will getting Olynyk's connection get you a promotion?" she asked, narrowing her gaze at him. "Or is it personal? That would make more sense. What evil thing did the Olynyks do to you?"

He decided to give her most of the truth.

"You're right. It's personal," he said. "Legs had my father killed. My father was a cop in Steeltown."

She didn't hide the surprise on her face, and it was a small win for him. He never thought he'd get past her cynicism.

"Shocked?" he asked.

"I guess," she allowed, leaning back with a thoughtful expression. "But I still think there's more."

"Lucky for you, thinking isn't anything I require of you," he replied.

"Huh," she grunted. "Son of a beat cop turned FBI agent finally gets revenge for his father's murder. I didn't think you could be any more like a movie cliché, but you did it!" She slow clapped three times.

He looked straight ahead. He wouldn't let her get to him, and he was pretty sure that was exactly what she was trying to do.

They rode the rest of the way in silence until the car pulled up to the airline the FBI used for its flights.

"Let's go," he said, but she was already climbing out of the car. He scrambled out on his side.

She waited by the trunk until the driver popped the lid. After jerking the bag out, she faced him with an icy expression.

"Where's my ticket, Agent Buttwipe?" she demanded, holding out her hand.

He pulled a paper out of his pocket and handed it to her.

She moved to breeze past him, but a flash of uncertainty in her gaze made him reach out and grab her arm.

"Don't," she warned with a grunt, trying to jerk her arm out of his grasp. He just tightened his hold and nodded at her.

"The number I gave you. Call it when you're done. But also call it if things get... difficult," he said, letting her go.

She stared at him for several seconds, the uncertainty replaced with surprise. Which quickly changed to sarcasm.

"If things get difficult between me and the head of an organized crime family, you want me to call that number? Wow, thanks for the lifeline," she gushed.

Then she punched him in the shoulder, forcing a high "Ow!" out of him.

"See ya round, Batman." She marched away, humming, "Na-na, na-na, na-na, Batman!"

"Don't think about running," he called after her, grimacing when she merely flipped him off, her middle finger over her head and directed at him.

He reassured himself that he could track her flight when she landed and make sure that she'd gotten on the bus. His gut told him she was really doing it. Maybe for reasons of her own, but she was returning to Steeltown.

He looked at the driver, who stood in the open door.

"Back to your office, sir?" he asked.

"To LaGuardia," he replied. He needed to get to the Feds' direct flight and his ass back to Virginia before his boss asked too many questions.

"You got it," the driver said, and they both got into the car.

Thomas rubbed his forehead as they pulled into traffic.

He'd plotted his moves and executed his plan. He just hadn't counted on the emotions that would come along with it.

Best-case scenario, the woman was killed. Two days ago, that had been the logical outcome in his mind. Now, the reality made his hands even sweatier.

Worst-case scenario, he'd lose his job. Worst-worst case, he'd lose his job and go to jail for misappropriation of federal resources.

Shit.

His phone bleated a familiar ringtone from his breast pocket.

"So?" asked the voice on the line.

"She's at the airport. In twenty minutes, give or take, she'll be on the plane."

There was a sigh, a pause, and then, "What if you underestimated her? If she's Ilya's daughter, like you say, her father was Legs's next in command—"

"Her father was a killer, an enforcer. Nothing more. His daughter's not some mastermind criminal," he said, thinking about the scruffy tomboy whose biggest defiance was sarcasm and a childish gesture.

"That doesn't mean Olynyk will see her as—"

"He'll see her for exactly what she is. A loose end that needs to be eliminated. You know what I say. The daughter—"

"Inherits the sins of the father. And you know what I say. It's a stupid saying."

He sighed.

"I thought out of anyone, *you* would be on my side," he said.

There was a pause before she replied.

"I am—even though you're landing a mess in my lap."

"No. She'll just be the victim of a senseless crime that the police will have to sort out. If Olynyk is sloppy about it, he'll be arrested and his drug empire will crumble," he said.

"Anything to do with the Olynyks makes my life a mess," she

groaned. "And there's no way Legs will see her as anything but a threat."

He thought about the card he'd impulsively given the woman. If she used it, which he doubted, as he remembered her flipping him off, it would definitely make his sister's life a mess.

"I'm counting on Legs feeling threatened," he said, relaxing his hold on the phone. He looked at the driver, who was busy navigating the car through heavy traffic.

Thomas lowered his voice and murmured into the phone, "I want him seriously, hard-core, life-and-death-level threatened."

Chapter Eleven

Quinn

Quinn shook his old boss's hand and accepted the letter the grizzled man thrust at him.

"I'm sorry to see you leave the department, but you've earned it," Seattle Chief of Police McCallum said, twitching his walrus moustache at him and beaming. "And don't worry about the investigation. That's just a formality."

The chief's misplaced pride, along with all the back slaps he'd been getting since the incident, made Quinn grateful he'd had a shot of scotch before dropping by.

"Right," Quinn said noncommittally. He opened the envelope and saw the word "Steeltown," then tucked it in his pocket and grabbed his cardboard box off the chief's desk. He pushed the head of the Han Solo figurine out of sight with his thumb, not in the mood to endure any parting jokes about his *Star Wars* obsession.

"What does your family think about the move?" McCallum asked.

"They're fine with it," he lied.

His sister in Minnesota wasn't fine with it. She wanted him in St. Paul, but fortunately his boss only had the authority to transfer him within the state.

McCallum frowned as if he'd heard Quinn wrong.

"They're excited for me," he tried again, and McCallum's expression smoothed into a smile. He strode around the desk to slap Quinn on the shoulder.

"Not as much organized crime up north," the chief lamented. "But if a shooting breaks out, you're the man to handle it."

Quinn gave him the expected smile of agreement as the man jerked open the door.

"Surprise!" yelled a crowd of uniformed and non-uniformed personnel gathered in a semicircle. He tried not to jerk back at the loud greeting and kept the smile steady through the wave of nausea that hit him. The sound, the crowd of people.... Everything was triggering these days.

"You're going to hate working up there, out of the action," groaned Pete, his old partner. "Just the Olynyks up there, and they stopped the serious crime years ago."

"Will they even issue you a weapon?" joked Clark, another officer.

"He'll get his shiny detective badge and just ride a desk of prowler reports and watering violations," laughed another.

Quinn's smile was genuine at that comment. It sounded like his idea of perfection.

"Leave him alone," scolded Jenny, the dispatch operator. "Maybe he wants to start a family in a place where a bad day at work doesn't include shooting anyone."

Jenny turned to look at him coolly, speculatively.

He'd had a drink with her once, their idle work chat sliding into prickly questions about his personal life. He'd alluded to someone without admitting or denying he had a significant other. It had been the last time he'd had drinks with anyone. He did his drinking with his cat now. Cats and a geographically removed sister were all the family he needed.

"If this geek has a girlfriend, I'm Tom Brady," Pete said and reached into the box of Quinn's belongings to grab the Han Solo figure. He made the classic quarterback motion and tossed it to Clark.

"Hey," Quinn said, laughing to cover his annoyance. He'd gotten good at never showing his true feelings. "That's a collector's item."

Clark tucked the figure under his arm, pretending to rush for the end zone, then tossed it back to Quinn.

He caught it and settled it back in the box with a stiff smile. In the three years he'd been there, he'd never fit in. Not until he'd killed a man—then he'd become a celebrity.

The other irony was that it would have made his dad proud too. Police officer had been a job suggestion on a career printout in high school, and following the steps to apply had been the only way to get his dad off his back. His loathsome, abusive dad had been a cop, and Quinn still didn't know why he'd followed his career path. Wasn't that something you did to honor your father?

"...for a piece of cake," Jenny suggested, looking at him inquiringly.

"Sure," he agreed and followed the crowd to a side table where a slab cake sat beside a stack of paper plates. The cake read "Congratulations on your promotion!" and included a black-icing outline of a service pistol. A red dotted line extended from the barrel to a yellow bullet on the right.

Great. Let's celebrate one of the worst moments in my life, he thought, accepting the knife from Jenny with his best fake grin, and cut into the bland vanilla cake.

An hour later, he merged his loaded SUV onto I-5. Solo mewled despondently from the carrier beside him. He'd angled it to face him so he'd know right away if Solo threw up.

He'd only had the cat in the small cage once before—the day he'd brought him home. Solo hadn't been all that happy to find his "forever home" as much as the shelter staff had assured Quinn he had, and he threw up twice on the way to his apartment. Then he'd been a howling banshee when Quinn tried to get him out.

He'd pulled his SUV behind a semi, content to stay well under the speed limit, when his phone buzzed. He thought about ignoring it for two more buzzes, then answered.

"Hello," he muttered, bracing himself.

"You didn't call me back," his sister, Patricia, whined.

He loved her and all her quirks, but there was a reason he kept a lot of miles between them.

"I was busy packing and... everything," he replied.

"Are you heading to your new home?" she asked.

Home, he thought. He didn't really think of it like that, but he supposed she did.

"Yeah."

"So, what's this Steeltown like? Is it anything like Pittsburgh?" she asked.

He knew she was just curious. That she didn't *mean* to draw a line to their childhood, but his hands tightened around the steering wheel all the same.

"I hope not," he mumbled.

There was a beat before she replied, "I didn't mean it like that."

He sighed. "I know. Sorry. I hope Steeltown isn't like any city I've ever been in before," he said, injecting a false cheer into the words.

She went along with it.

"Well, since I knew you wouldn't do it, I looked it up on the Internet. It started as a town built around a steel foundry back in the forties, which, duh, is how it got the name Steeltown," she recited, the clicking noise of her mouse sounding in the background.

"Even more exciting than I thought it would be."

"'Steeltown has just under fifty thousand people, is right on the main interstate, and ranks eighteenth for the US city that gets the most rainfall,'" she said.

"I guess that confirms that this was the right move. I like rain."

"Butler is better, ranked sixtieth for rainfall and only ten minutes from my house."

He sighed again. "Did I say like? I meant I love the rain," he replied, not wanting to get into the usual circular argument with her about how they should live in the same town.

"Liar. Also, Butler doesn't have a crime family like Steeltown does. Did you know *that*?" she asked in a smug voice.

"I doubt Steeltown has any kind of crime family like Seattle does. I bet Butler does, though. They probably own the newspapers so it doesn't get reported on," he suggested.

She sighed.

"Let's talk about you," he said before she could argue about whether crime families controlled media. "What's going on in your life? Have you met anybody?" he asked, imagining her eye roll.

Her grunt confirmed it.

"Relationships are overrated. No offense, but *men* are overrated. I wish I was attracted to women," she grumbled. "I wish *you* dated. Then we could compare notes."

He chuckled.

"I agree with you that relationships are overrated."

"How else will I become an auntie if you don't date?" she asked, like she often did.

"You're an auntie to Solo," he said, looking over at his unhappy long-haired cat. "And he loves being your nephew."

She was quiet for a moment, and just when he was ready to hear another plea about transferring closer to her, she surprised him.

"We're a pretty messed-up family, aren't we?" she asked unhappily. Then gave a little laugh. "Except for Solo. He's chill."

"I think most families have some level of messiness in them," he replied.

"Do you ever think that our family name is going to end with us?" she asked.

"No," he said, and it was the truth. It would end with them, but he never thought about it.

"I do. I think how pissed dad would be that neither of us will pass on his genes."

"Dad always called me a bastard, and I took that to heart," he said.

"He always called me a slut, and for a long time, I took that to heart too," she murmured.

He clenched the steering wheel.

His only physical fight had been when their father had called her that after she got home from a date. She'd cried, and when he grabbed her, yelling "Slut," at her over and over, Quinn lost it.

"Look at us now, though. I got a promotion for shooting someone, and you're a wannabe lesbian Googling crime families on the Internet," he said, forcing a cheerfulness into the words.

She laughed. Not a polite chuckle, but a deeper sound that came from her gut. At least he could make her laugh.

"You're a goof," she said.

"*You're* a goof," he countered.

She sighed again. "Do you have any free time before you start your job? Maybe you could fly back for a visit," she asked.

"No, I start right away," he lied.

"Poop. I wish you were closer than twelve billion states away."

"It's only eight driving states," he corrected, like he did every time.

"They're looking for an officer at the Butler PD. I downloaded the application, and—"

"Oops, Solo looks like he's getting carsick," he said, glancing at the drowsy but content cat. "I'll text you when I get to my new place."

"Hold your phone so I can hear him gagging, you liar," she accused, but he laughed, said goodbye again, and ended the call.

He turned his thoughts to the passing scenery. He didn't know why he wanted to keep a few thousand miles between the only family he had. He only knew he did.

Chapter Twelve

Lena

Twenty-seven sleepless hours later, my comatose brain registered that the airport shuttle bus had arrived in Steeltown. I'd been too paranoid to sleep, positive my corpse dad was lurking in my mind, ready to pounce as soon as I dozed off.

The thing about going so many hours without sleep is that you start to make bad decisions. Like the one I made as I stepped off the bus.

I was going to visit my aunt. She'd either let me stay or kick me off her property. I don't know if I really hoped she'd give me a free place to crash, or if I just wanted to see the only living family I had in the world, but it just seemed like something to do. Like I said, sleep deprivation equals bad choices.

"I don't think your flower is going to make it," commented a gray-haired woman in a pantsuit. She stood at the side of the bus, waiting as the driver hauled baggage from the bus's cargo hold.

I dazedly followed her stare to the dead plant I still clenched in the same hand as my backpack strap.

"It's a guzmania bromeliad, from the Bromeliaceae family...," I babbled before my overtired brain snapped me out of it. I wasn't used to strangers striking up a conversation out of nowhere, which was my excuse for why I kept talking. "I... got it at the airport."

She raised an eyebrow as she looked at the crushed thing in my hand again.

"You should get your money back," she said and laughed.

"A little late now," I replied.

I didn't tell her I'd ripped it out of a planter in baggage claim, then was yelled at by security when I stomped the life out of it.

"Are you visiting family—"

"I gotta go," I blurt-yelled and walked in the opposite direction of the woman.

Strange people talking to me, my exhaustion, and the worst thing —not being able to draw to smooth out my sleepless anxiety—put me in a panic.

Coming back to Steeltown had been a huge mistake. I could be in a cozy, concrete jail cell right now, sleeping on a paper-thin mattress before spending a luxurious afternoon fighting off a street savvy woman for jailhouse supremacy. Instead I was drowningly out of my depth. I bet pantsuit lady back there loved everyone in her family and made instant pudding on Saturdays.

I should just ask someone if the Olynyks still hung out on Main Street, then go right there and get shot.

Instead, I walked to the far end of the depot where there were fewer people. After pretending to read the wall of notices, I calmed down. I'd just have to adjust to sticky small-town friendliness until my visit ended with me free or in a casket.

"Hey, Flower Girl!" called a too-jovial voice from the direction of the station office.

Jeez, not another friendly local.

I ignored the man's greeting, faking absorption in a faded lost cat poster. Buttons had gone missing a very long time ago, based on the overlapping notices. Buttons's face was what grabbed my attention.

He or she looked like a furry like Bruce Willis. Actually, that *was* kind of absorbing.

"Yo! You look like you're about to commit an *act*," called the voice again. The body attached to the voice stepped in front of me. "Another one, since you already committed something that resulted in that dead flower there."

A tall man with an impressive burst of dreadlocks tied behind his head towered over me, the bronze-tinted ends dancing around his grinning face.

Everyone here was annoying. Especially him. Not only was he friendly and talkative, but he had that kind of demeanor that seemed perpetually cheerful. But I registered the blue of his Steeltown Transit shirt and breathed a sigh of relief. He wasn't a psycho local, just a psycho bus driver.

"I need to go all the way up Arthur Avenue," I told him, sounding all business and no chat. "Is that the 521—"

"Naw, first you gotta tell me what the deal is with that flower," he said, then bent over to look at it more closely. "What did you do to it?"

"What makes you think I didn't find it this way?" I asked, curious despite myself.

"Well, something flattened that thing like a pancake," he reasoned happily. "Most flowers die regular, not flat."

"I found it like this," I lied.

"You found it that way," he said, lowering his head to give me a disbelieving scowl. "And you just decided to walk around with a butt-flat flower?"

"I... sort of draw them." Who was this guy? The flower police?

"Sort of? What does a sort-of drawing look like?" he asked, raising a curious eyebrow.

"Like a dead flower," I replied.

He just stared. Then his head snapped back, and he let out a bark of a laugh.

"Tell you what. You show me your drawing, and I'll tell you that the 521 goes through town and up Arthur Avenue all the way to Copper Ridge," he said.

The name, Copper Ridge, clanged in my mind like a ding-ding on a game show, but I pushed that niggling feeling aside. I wanted total privacy from prying eyes before I faced any new memories.

And something that might distract me was placating this guy who was too likable for his own good.

I yanked out my notepad and flipped to one of the pathetic bromeliad sketches. I sighed heavily to make sure he knew how annoying he was being.

"It's not finished. It's not really started, even, but—"

"Well, look at that!" he exclaimed, peering closer at the sketchbook. Then he grabbed it and flipped to a different page.

"Hey!" I protested, half scandalized, but half sort of liking how impressed he was as he looked through the pages.

"What's this one?" he asked.

"*Asclepius incarnata.*"

"What's that mean?"

"Swamp milkweed."

"Swamp milkweed?" he asked. "Looks nice, sounds disgusting."

I gave him a non-smile. I liked it for the same reason.

"It's a flowering perennial back where I used to live."

"Used to live. Does that mean you're moving here?" he asked, flipping through a few more pages. He was careful to thumb the edges and not touch the pencil strokes, which sneakily made me like him a little bit.

"No. I mean, I don't think so."

"So you don't live somewhere else, but you don't live here? Are you homeless?"

"Technically, I guess so," I said, the reality of it rolling a lump in my throat.

"Huh," he said, flipping the notepad closed. He handed it back to me. "Nothing but old neighborhoods and corner stores up on Arthur. You got family up there?"

I tucked the notepad and the flower into the side pocket of my backpack, trying to read his expression. It was never smart to tell anybody too much.

"Is this some questionnaire I have to answer before I can get on a bus?" I asked him, and it prompted another loud laugh that startled me.

"Sketch Girl, you're growing on me," he said, then laughed again. "But *not* like one of your flowers. I'm going to give you the nickel tour. Come on, now."

He waved an arm at me to follow and spun to walk ahead before stopping at the door to a bus. I stopped as well, looking at the number on the reader sign—521.

"This is your bus?" I asked, lifting my eyebrow at him.

"Arthur 521, at your service," he said, circling his hand and sweeping it toward the bus like an unveiling.

"You're not like any bus driver I've ever known, and I've known a lot," I commented, climbing onto the empty bus. I sat in the nearest side-facing seat and dug out my wallet to find bus fare.

"Where have you known a lot of bus drivers?" he asked, dropping into the worn driver's seat and facing me.

"New York."

"New York the state, or New York the city?"

"City."

"Well, I'm honored you're sitting this close to the driver's seat, then."

"I'm surprised you're not surrounded by bulletproof plexiglass," I replied.

I dropped a couple of bills into the fare container and sat back. I should have gone all the way to the back, but I was obviously in a weakened state from the long trip west.

"What are New York City bus drivers like? Not talkative like me? Not friendly like me?" he asked, folding his arms and looking very smug.

"They sure don't ask a million annoying questions like you," I said, and he barked out another of his signature laughs. It was a mix of a hoot and a shout. I guess you could say I liked it.

"I'm Damon," he announced and shoved his hand out at me.

I looked at it like it was an alien tentacle.

"This is where you shake my hand, tell me your name, and we engage like the friends we're going to become."

"I don't need any friends," I said despite feeling a peculiar pull to touch his hand. Touching people was a thing I limited to desperate occasions. And I wasn't desperate, was I? My brain was too sluggish to know.

"I don't know, Sketch Girl. Something about your little flower drawings makes me think you need somethin'," he said and nodded down at his hand. "Might as well be a friend."

What else could I do? I shook his hand. I was pretty sure he'd kick me off the bus if I didn't. At least he let my hand go right away.

"And you are?" he prompted, lifting his eyebrows.

"Lena," I muttered resentfully.

"Was that so hard? Lena?"

I just scowled.

"Okay, in about five minutes, it's wheels up, so to speak. You ever been to Steeltown before?" he asked.

"No," I lied, looking away even though he'd turned back to put on his seat belt. Something told me he might be good at spotting liars.

"Good. That means I can bore you with long stories about dead bodies of this tired little town."

The words "dead bodies" made me clench my bags against my chest and look around, braced for another appearance of my corpse dad.

"You okay?" Damon asked.

"Yeah, just... muscle spasm," I said and made a big show of turning my head back and forth.

"Uh-huh," he murmured, not believing me for a second and proving me right.

Funny. Something about a bus driver being able to spot my lies was... interesting.

And then he got more interesting.

"Did you know Steeltown was run by a crime family that still exists today?" he asked me.

I swore my jaw hit the floor, but it only hit the top of my backpack.

"It... what?" I asked weakly.

Had I just stumbled into the one person who could tell me everything I needed to know about finding Legs Olynyk? I pictured Damon taking me right there, on the bus of all things, and introducing me. Then there'd be casual conversation while Legs told me everything I wanted to know and even let me call Tommy Batman from his own cell phone.

If you need proof that people get stupid when they're overdosing on lack of sleep, that chain of thought says it all.

"That's right," Damon said, positively gleeful that my expression looked so rapt.

"Uh, what crime family?" I asked, gripping my bags.

"One that still runs it, so I won't name it. But more interesting is, those old-time mobsters were so proud of it, they renamed it Stealtown from Pleasant Valley. Steal, as in s-t-e-a-l. A council member convinced them to use steel in the name," Damon explained, checking his watch. "On account of the steel mill down on the waterfront. Since back then it was common knowledge the family ran things, that dude told them it might scare away commerce."

"Smart dude," I murmured.

"That mill's been closed, although there's still an office in the building. And ghosts," Damon said.

I couldn't help looking around at the word, relieved when the bus stayed free of dead ghost bodies.

"Been featured on some of those ghost hunter YouTube channels," Damon continued, swinging around to do whatever bus drivers did when they were getting ready to leave. "If you're one of them, don't go to the mill. It's old and falling apart."

"I'm not one of them," I mumbled.

"Wanna know another fun fact?" he asked, turning a lever which let a loud hiss escape from underneath the bus. He began to back out before swinging the bus forward into the long driveway and heading to the road. "The town is shaped like a gun."

"No," I said before I could stop myself.

I'd lived in this town for ten years, and while I was okay not knowing anything about the origin of the steel mill, how did I not know it was shaped like a gun?

"Yup," Damon said, shaking his head of dreads happily as he pulled onto the road and headed toward what was loosely considered downtown Steeltown. "An upside-down gun if you look at a map, but a gun. The coastline runs down like the handgrip, curving into the barrel. Arthur Avenue goes from the end of the barrel straight up the hill. They built a boardwalk thing into Rob's Harbor, and if you look at it on Google Maps, it looks like that thing that goes around a trigger."

"A trigger guard," I supplied and could have slapped a hand over my mouth when the piece of hidden knowledge leaped up in my brain and out of my mouth.

"Yeah, I guess," he said, casting a glance at me. "Anyway, we're gonna take Emmon to Main Street, then up Arthur to wherever you want to get off, Miss Trigger Guard."

I turned in my seat, wishing I could bury my face in my bags but not wanting to be a coward. I chanced a look out the window and waited to see if the shock would knock me unconscious onto the floor of the bus. Nope.

Damon followed Emmon Avenue to Main Street and took a left on it.

This was it. Time for the aneurysm to kill me. An ironic way to go because this was the street I was born on, had lived on for the first ten years of my life, and now would die on.

"Back in the day, Main Street, here, was where the rich folks hung out. That was back in the twenties, when they had cable cars. The tracks are still there, over on Arthur," Damon explained, tilting his head toward what I was already looking at. "Now it's just a pawnshop, the library, and seedy bars like that one,"

Halloran's Bar read the chipped painting on the front window.

"You all right?" he asked, frowning at me.

That's when I realized I was strangling the life out of my backpack.

"Uh, yeah. Just wondering if the drinks are cheap," I lied.

He frowned even harder at me. "You don't want to go there," he advised, looking me over broodingly.

"Why? Don't I look old enough to drink?" I joked in a strained voice. Anything to push away the memories that wanted to flood my tired brain.

"You don't need a driver's license to get in there—you need a Medicaid card. Nobody who goes there is under eighty," he said with a serious cackle.

"Huh," I replied, my eyes drawn back to the building. Not to the bar, but to the windows above it. Where the apartments were. One in particular on the second floor came back to me.

Damon lurched the bus forward and continued with his "tour."

"On the left is the library, another place you should steer clear of," he murmured, snapping my attention back to him. His gaze flickered to me, then away, and he hurried on to talk more history in a loud voice, as if he regretted mentioning the library at all.

Library. Something about the library—

"Now, this is Arthur Avenue, named for the man who bought out the mill owner in 1924...," he said, then stopped at the bus stop right before the intersection.

Two young women got on, one of them complaining about how some guy had ghosted her sister.

Damon watched in his wide rearview until the women sat down, then pulled the bus back into the street and took the left onto Arthur.

While he droned on about ferrous and nonferrous metals, I broke out in a sweat.

I thought I'd be relieved to be traveling away from childhood memories, but then I realized I was heading into a showdown of epic proportions. My aunt's house.

Thank God Damon made another stop. When two older ladies climbed on, I got up and motioned for them to take my seat. I waved bye in Damon's direction and hurried to the back of the bus, fighting a wave of nausea that bubbled in my stomach.

As I glanced out the back window before I sat down, a fleeting memory flashed. Me carrying a case—why was "music case" floating in my brain?—and holding my dad's hand. And a gun. Did he force me to take music lessons at gunpoint?

Geez, anything was possible to my tired mind. I rubbed my forehead with a shaking hand.

Suddenly the bus lurched to the right.

"Stay in your lane!" Damon roared from the front of the bus and leaned hard on the horn.

Damon waved a hand at the five of us and shouted back, "Sorry 'bout that, folks. Some fool in an SUV thinks he owns the road."

I sent a thank-you to whoever was driving the SUV. He'd jarred me out of my spiraling thoughts.

As the memories of Main Street and Halloran's faded behind me, so did some of my anxiety. It let me dip into the new panic of meeting my doom.

My Auntie Korinna.

Chapter Thirteen

Quinn

"**J**esus, fine! Sorry!" Quinn shouted over the horn of the bus, waving an apology at the bus driver.

He glanced back at Solo and the line of barf he'd just spewed out of his carrier, across the seat, and onto Quinn's jeans. "Buddy, you pick your moments, don't you?"

He grabbed a wad of napkins and swiped blindly at it, keeping his eyes focused on the road.

He turned right, then slowed when he saw the building his new landlord told him to look for. He eased into a parking space across from his future apartment.

The glass of the green door had "**Victory Apartments**" written on it in tiny, chipped letters. To the left was Halloran's Bar, to the right, Lucky Squirrel Collectibles. The door was so narrow, it almost didn't exist—something that suited him fine.

He pulled over and got out before walking around the car and unbuckling Solo's carrier.

Solo yowled at him, the sound prolonged and mournful.

"All right, I know. Chill out—we're here," he told him, grabbing the carrier and the box of memorabilia. His other stuff could wait.

Solo yowled again as Quinn locked his car and crossed the street, drawing a couple looks from people passing by.

A beefy man stepped out of Halloran's just as Quinn stepped up onto the curb. He looked Quinn up and down as he wiped his hands on a towel.

"You Quinn Magee?" he asked.

"Yup," Quinn agreed, nodding, since he couldn't shake the man's hand. "You're Floyd?"

"I'm him. I'll take you up—"

"Floyd," called a woman who'd cracked open the bar's door. "How long are you gonna be?"

"Ten minutes," Floyd said, pulling a ring of keys out of his pocket.

"It's almost noon," she said, a hint of a whine in her voice.

"Angela, Jesus! I'll be ten minutes!" Floyd shouted, using one of the keys to unlock the door. He looked at Quinn and murmured, "She's got one customer and she's overwhelmed. It's not like there's a lineup to get in, you know what I mean?"

Quinn mentally agreed, looking through the window at the empty bar.

The woman, her red hair in a crooked ponytail, threw up her hands and disappeared into the bar.

"Thursdays are half-priced bourbon shots at noon," Floyd explained, leading the way into the narrow tiled corridor. "You'd think she'd never poured whisky shots before. Anyway, there are the mailboxes. The key is on here."

Floyd shook the keys over his head as he led Quinn up the stairs to the next landing.

"There are four apartments—these two, and two on the next floor," Floyd explained, pointing to the doors marked 2A on the left and 2B on the right. "2B is owned but unoccupied, so you'll have peace. 3A above you works graveyards, single guy. Never had any complaints about him and noise, so you should be okay."

Floyd stopped at the door marked 2A and shook another key out, then pushed it into the lock.

"Do you know anybody who wants a room? 3B is available," Floyd said, though his tone had already made it clear he doubted Quinn knew anybody looking for an apartment.

"I don't know anybody in Steeltown," Quinn answered and walked into the apartment.

Straight ahead was the kitchen, a tiny island between him and the sink. To his left was a wide window, and to his right were two closed doors.

"This apartment looks out onto the street and is ten square feet bigger than the apartments that face the back. It's not too late to switch to 3B if you want to save a little on rent," Floyd offered and shrugged when Quinn shook his head.

Floyd jingled the key ring at him. "Lobby door, mailbox is the tiny one, and apartment door."

"Thanks," Quinn said, accepting the keys. They were heavy and old, which matched the apartment. The simple room with the green-on-green paint had a retro fifties style to it, which appealed to Quinn.

"Bedroom and shitter's to the right. Kitchen, obviously," Floyd said, pointing out the highlights of the small apartment. "All the rules are on the lease. Come down for a free drink on the house."

"Oh, yeah?" Quinn asked, his interest flaring for the first time that day. He and gin had gotten very close over the last few months.

"Don't get too excited," Floyd muttered and slapped him on the shoulder. What was it with guys and slapping people on the shoulder? "It's only Angela's drink concoction of the week."

"I never say no to free alcohol," Quinn said and walked to the kitchen to set the box down.

"You're my kind of tenant. Pay rent a day early and you'll be my favorite one," Floyd said with a grin, then headed for the door. "I'd better get down there before Angela quits. She does it every week."

Quinn watched as the man closed the door behind himself, then squeezed the carrier release and let Solo hop out. The cat crouched against the worn linoleum before gingerly walking toward the window.

"Welcome to our new life, buddy," he told him.

Solo ignored him, making his way to the sun shining through the window. He sat, yawned, then rolled back to lick the place where his balls used to be.

You celebrate our new life your way, and I'll celebrate it mine, he thought, heading for the door.

Living over a bar that had drink specials on a Thursday—he checked his watch—technically still morning just seemed like a good omen.

Chapter Fourteen

Thomas

Thomas slid the folder's edge under his thumbnail until he winced in pain. He stared out of his office at the small patch of green outside, the only life he could see.

"Mr. Palmer?" asked Brenda, his assistant. When he didn't answer she tapped on his door, saying again, "Sir?"

"Yup," he replied, swiveling the chair around to face her. "Staff briefing in five minutes. I'll be there."

The petite woman grimaced, her eyebrows crinkling together apologetically.

"The chief asked for everyone's expense reports," she said worriedly.

Brenda had been his co-conspirator in his scheme. She didn't know the depth of it, just that he was tracking his dad's killer in his off hours. She might have seen one or two questionable expenses, but a lunch here and there with her favorite cocktail—a Long Island iced tea—and she'd sworn a vow of secrecy for his "justice crusade," as she called it.

"That's fine," he commented, giving Brenda a tight smile as he lied. "All my expenses can be backed up by my cases."

"Okay," Brenda said, the crinkle in her eyebrows smoothing into a look of relief.

She returned to her desk, and he swiveled back to his window view. Not much of one, to be honest. But the last fifteen years had been spent working his way to an assignment with the organized crime division.

His eyes dropped to the framed certificate on the credenza under the window, the irony of it never fading. He'd gotten a degree in criminal justice, half of which his father's survivor benefit covered. The other half had come from the very man he'd just sent Galyna Kozek to meet.

Legs Olynyk had pretended he wanted his gift of tuition to be anonymous, but a reporter "found out." Thomas saw it as pity money donated to the kid of the slain cop. It had made the paper, although Thomas had refused to be photographed accepting the check.

He tossed the file folder on the credenza. Sour memories helped nothing.

He pulled out his phone and called the number he'd been trying on and off for the last hour. Finally, she answered.

"What?" his sister hissed, her voice sharp. Then he heard the muffled sound of her hand covering the phone while she talked to someone else for a few seconds.

He waited her out.

"What do you want, Tom, that you have to call every five minutes?" she asked.

"I'm checking in," he said, frustrated that this was news to her. "What have you heard?"

"Nothing."

"Are you at your office?"

"Yes."

"So? You had to have heard something."

"I haven't. Maybe she hitched a ride away from everything to do with your plan."

"No way. She should have made contact by now," he said, reaching for the folder again to keep his hands busy.

"In your perfect world she made contact and is a smudge stain in some back alley, but things rarely go according to anyone's plan," his sister said.

"Agent Palmer!" whispered Brenda from the doorway.

He frowned at her and wiggled the phone he held to his ear.

Brenda just grimaced and pressed her hands together, that apologetic look back on her face. "Chief wants everyone. Now."

He jutted his chin in acknowledgement but said to his sister, "Make a call. Help me out, here."

"I *am* helping you. I've *been* helping you. I don't think you understand just how *much* I've been helping you," she grunted, and he knew he'd better back off.

"Sir, I'm really sorry," Brenda said, pointing to her desk where her phone buzzed, looking afraid to answer it. "The chief asked me what case you had that required a flight to Seattle, and that's probably him calling to ask more questions."

His gut collapsed on itself, but he told her, "I'm coming right now." Then he shooed her with the file he held.

"Jesus, Tom, are you using agency resources—" his sister asked with a groan.

"I can't say, since it might implicate you," he replied, standing up and tapping the folder against his leg.

"You better think fast. Getting fired from the FBI isn't like getting fired from some fast-food place."

"You think I don't know that?" he muttered.

"Sometimes I don't know *what* you know."

"I've got it all under control. Just do me a favor. Dig a little harder for me, huh? In a day or two, this will all be over and we can both go back to our regularly scheduled programming," he joked, although at the moment, he didn't know what regular programming meant for him.

So much of his life had been steered toward these next few days. What was his regular program if it didn't include revenge?

"You're a minimum safe distance from all the ways this could blow up in our faces. I still have to live here," she said.

"It's better that I do this at arm's length, but don't worry. Nothing's going to blow up in anybody's face," he assured her.

He could hear her take a deep breath before she said, "All right, I'll dig on my side. But stop calling me. I'll call you if I find anything out."

He grunted into the phone as he gathered his open case files, stacking the Seattle folder on top.

"Tom," she prompted more loudly. "Are we clear on the 'don't call me' part of what I said?"

"Yup, yup. You'll call me when you find out she's contacted Olynyk."

"*If* she has," she corrected and gave a long sigh. "Now go do what you have to do to make sure you don't get fired. I don't need any of this to make it to *my* boss."

"Agreed," he said and ended the call. "Agreed," he muttered again in his empty office.

Chapter Fifteen

Lena

I got up and walked to the front of the bus, pulling the rope bell on my way.

"Hey, Flower Girl. You gonna give me one of those drawings before you go?" Damon asked, shocking me.

"No."

"Come on, Van Gogh, I'm just asking for that dandelion," Damon had said, checking his mirrors before pulling over.

"No."

A woman who looked like her first name was Nanna got up and stood behind me.

"I'm not opening this door until I get that dead dandelion," Damon said, folding his arms.

I contemplated the buttons and dials on his dashboard. None of the ones that looked like they opened a door were within reach.

"No," I repeated, giving him a stubborn look to cover the fact that I was a little bit flattered.

"For Pete's sake, just give it to him," Nanna complained in a perfect grandma voice. "I'm going to be late for book club."

"Now you just calm down, Ms. Blue Hair," Damon said jovially to the woman.

I glanced at her, wondering how offended she'd be, but she just shrugged and patted her hair. It was more a shade of violet than blue.

"Fine," I grouched and tore off the drawing he wanted. Then I added two more, just to be contrary. They weren't my best efforts. "But this is extortion. I could make a citizen's arrest."

"Citizen, nothing!" he replied, whatever that meant.

"Get her to sign them!" called out another lady a few seats back.

"Just open the door," I begged Damon.

He obliged, and I hopped down to the sidewalk.

"See you soon, Sketch Girl," he called, waving the small drawings triumphantly.

"Never sign anything for free," Nanna advised me, heading back down the hill.

I trudged up to my aunt's street, turning the corner as I thought about the rough plan I'd put together.

It wasn't much.

First, assuming my aunt answered my knock, I'd ask if I could stay for a couple of nights. Then.... Well, that's where the plan fell apart.

My imagination had her hugging me and crying about how sending me to New York was a terrible mistake. She would drown me in borscht and sprinkle me with her incredible garlic fritters, all why begging me to stay as long as I liked. Then she'd lead me to a magical bedroom covered in *Star Wars* memorabilia and *Call of Duty* posters, a giant TV, and a rack with every gaming console known to humankind.

Sigh. Heaven.

My practical side saw her opening the door and then slamming it in my face. After all, who sends away a ten-year-old orphan?

Instead of getting mugged in memory lane, I should be figuring out how to make contact with Olynyk without getting killed. My law-abiding aunt certainly wouldn't help me with that, so who else—

My trudging feet stopped, and I let my bags slide to the ground.

Vas! My goofy cousin Vas could help!

"Holy crap," I murmured, memories flooding back like I'd unlocked a new game level. I almost had to steady myself.

Dorky, skinny cousin Vas. The street in front of me shimmered in memory. There was the gigantic oak I'd shoved him against once. Not my proudest moment, since I'd shoved him from behind. He didn't get his hands out in time, so he'd face-planted into the trunk and ended up with a big black eye.

"Holy crap," I said again, this time with a chuckle. My dad had gotten told off by my aunt for that, but he'd never punished me for it.

"Always be ready to defend yourself," I remember him telling me.

"He only called me short," I'd said, still feeling guilty about the pushing him from behind part of it.

"Or he only punched you, or he only shot you," he reasoned. "It doesn't matter. Always react. Trust your gut."

I don't remember questioning the "he only shot you" part of his sentence, so I guess I was used to it.

Vas was a few years older than me, and a vague memory lurked about him hanging out with one of the Olynyk kids. If he still had those connections, maybe I could find out something, call the number in my pocket, and get out of town before dark.

Unless my fantasy came true. Then I'd do the huge Ukrainian backyard feast first, then ask Vas about—

Wait.

My feet slowed again, but this time I was ready for the memories.

Macaroni and cheese. And wieners. I looked down at my hands that I'd raised as if I were holding a basketball. The quivering round shape of an old casserole dish appeared. I could make out the noodles, orange sauce, and pink wiener chunks.

God, now I was being haunted by casseroles? I guess that was better than a dead guy.

I kept walking, ticking off the memories as they popped up.

To my left was the Dalchek's small greenhouse that Vas stole vegetables out of. Next was the house with the monstrous German shepherd. No insane barking, so maybe it was dead. Three doors further was Mrs. Breziak's house.

Tazia Breziak, or Mizbee as we all called her, looked part great-grandmother, part Ukrainian barbarian. She was the commander of the neighborhood bridge club my aunt belonged to. She and my aunt also alternated hosting the backyard potlucks.

Mizbee was neighborhood royalty. She got a lot of respect, even from my dad, who I had a sense thought everybody but my mom was a loser. I think her dad was Legs's boss, or...? That part of the memory stayed foggy, so I ignored it and focused on the new nausea starting in my stomach.

Auntie Korinna. She was intimidating in a different way than Mizbee, who looked like she could snap her fingers and break your back. Auntie Korinna was cold, disapproving. You were either wrong or very wrong with her, and I guess it bothered me because she was my mom's sister.

And there I was, Trauma Girl, returning to the family who sent her across a country to strangers. Would my aunt answer the door with a sawed-off shotgun or just freeze me with her laser eyes?

Wait. Maybe *I* was the dangerous one. If my dad was a hitman....

Some thought danced around, wanting to click into place but unable to find the right connection. Maybe it was good that it didn't.

When my aunt's house came into view, I recognized the flower bed and crooked sidewalk. This was the lawn I'd been dumped on when I was ten. There was the oak root I banged my knee on. Then Auntie Korinna, her compact body rushing down the front steps, her lined face staring down at me. My feet went cold as if reexperiencing the water from the grass soaking into my sneakers.

Auntie Korinna had never hidden her dislike of me, which I

guessed I weirdly respected. I didn't like fake emotions, so at least she was honest. She hated me the way you hate a mole that sprouts a fresh hair two days after you pluck it. And here I was, growing back almost fifteen years later.

I braced myself as I marched up to her front door.

Chapter Sixteen

Lena

I stood at Auntie Korinna's front door, forcing my shoulders to unclench. The green paint was the same, although more chipped around the edges. I leaned close and heard voices inside. They sounded mostly female.

I swallowed, wishing I had a bottle of water to wash away the acid in my mouth.

"Stop it," I muttered to myself. Opening the door to find me curled up in a sweaty ball would not persuade my aunt to let me stay with her.

Ne bud' durnym. The words of my corpse dad floated in my head. Don't be stupid.

I did not want to be reminded of that weird vision, but strangely, the words settled some of the swirling in my stomach.

I held my fist up, knuckles toward the door. It shook. I swallowed, then rolled my fist to the side so the flat of it thumped three times against the wood. Thumped hard enough to shake the doorknob. Yeah, that definitely sounded less timid.

The voices inside stilled, and I heard the familiar footsteps of Auntie Korinna's shoes. She had important company. She always wore her black, low-heeled shoes when someone who "mattered" was over.

"Yes," she answered as she opened the door.

I stared down at her black shoes, pleased to be right.

"Hi, Auntie Korinna," I greeted cheerfully as I looked up. Well, up was generous.

This? This five-foot-nothing woman was who I was 77 percent terrified of?

She was a couple of inches shorter than me, and I wasn't that tall. Her short, thick blonde hair had the brittle look of too many kitchen-sink dye jobs. Her beige top and pants were a strange complement to her hair, all of them coated in that fake sheen of Clairol and polyester.

Her mouth puckered in disapproval, resulting in the millions of tiny lines around it making a starburst. A vague memory of that weird halo of wrinkles was one reason I never smoked.

As if she could read my mind, she raised her hand and took a long pull from what looked like a kazoo. Then she blew a thick puff of strawberry-scented mist at me, her eyes glittering on the other side of the fog.

I was nervous, but I was still cocky enough to cough extravagantly and wave at the smoke.

"Geez," I choked out. "Vaping still kills, you know."

She didn't move, just stared at me with shrewd eyes. Their irises were brown like milk chocolate, but her opinion of my comment made them turn the color of frozen pond water. Then I noticed something I'd never seen in her before.

Outweighing the dyed hair and cold eyes was the tilt of her nose and the angle of her eyebrows. They were hints of my mother shining through her sister's sour face. Hints I remembered from a photo my dad kept in our old bathroom. The memory brought even more of my smart-assedness out.

"Surprise!" I said, giving her a flash of jazz hands and my sassiest grin.

This was what being nervous did to me. Made me act like a complete idiot.

Her face changed, and those cold eyes flashed several things at me. Surprise, uncertainty, then something like disgust.

"Why are you here, Galyna?" she grunted. Even after all these years, she clung to her Ukrainian accent like a knife under her pillow.

She looked behind herself, then stepped outside and closed the door to a slit, as if hiding a secret boyfriend.

"I had some holiday time coming to me, so—" I lied smoothly.

"*Why* are you here?" She spit the words out like they were a spider in her mouth.

"Oh, you mean my purpose?" I drawled out, and then inspiration hit me. "I'm talking to somebody about a job."

What do you know? Something close to the truth!

I dug into my pocket and pulled out the card Thomas had given me.

She huffed, but her gaze didn't leave mine even when I waved the card like a winning lottery ticket. She took another long draw on the vape device. This time, though, she angled her lips to the right before she exhaled.

"So, why are you *here*?"

Boy, she took being a person of few words to a whole new level.

"You mean on your doorstep?" I asked.

She didn't acknowledge the question.

"Aside from you and Vas being my only living relatives, I thought I'd pop by for a visit."

She just stared.

"A short visit. Really short. Maybe just a day or two?" I said, her silence making me think I had a chance.

I thought of several plausible lies for when she asked why I had a job interview in Steeltown. I could say I was on a secret assignment for the FBI, which was the truth if you ignored the whole felony part of it. But I was sure it would guarantee she slammed the door in my face. Even if she got past the outlandish sound of it, she distrusted the police as much as she hated my father's connection to crime.

She stared a moment longer, and I held my breath.

"Wait here," she finally muttered.

She disappeared into the house, and my body drooped, every muscle going slack.

Had I really given her crap for vaping? Or hit her with jazz hands? My missteps guaranteed my father's corpse would show up to mock me.

When the door jerked back open, I jumped back a foot, ducking in case she threw her vaping thing at me.

But it wasn't my aunt.

"Lena!" hissed my cousin, Vas, as he walked outside and closed the door behind himself. "Holy crap! My mom wasn't lying. You're here. Why are you back?"

"I—"

"She's freaking *out*," he whispered, frowning at me before pressing his ear against the door.

I tried to reply, but the skinny guy towering in front of me, wearing an Adidas tracksuit, shocked the words out of me.

Other than the wispy hairs attempting to pull it together as a moustache, he looked like a taller version of the Vas of my memory. I smiled that he was channeling my New York non-cousin, albeit in a West Coast style. At least it wasn't velour.

"Define freaking out," I finally asked.

"Yelling at me in Ukrainian. She only does that when she's freaking out."

My heart sank. I thought I'd be okay with seeing her and leaving, but it seemed like some sad kid inside of me wanted more.

"She's got the Wolf Pack in there," he continued, pressing even harder against the door.

"Wolf Pack?"

"The Kyiv Killers, the Slavic Syndicate. You know, the Finlay

Avenue Bridge Club," he whispered. "They're probably in there deciding whether to assassinate you or just run you out of town."

"What?" I demanded, joining him with my ear to the door. "I'd like to see them try."

A babble of granny voices muttered on the other side of the door, none of it intelligible. I tried to picture any of the starched neighborhood ladies marching me back to the bus stop. On the other hand, I didn't really know the extent of Auntie Korinna's connections. She'd sent me to New York Mike, after all.

I pressed my ear harder against the door, but it was still impossible.

"What were they talking about before I got here?" I asked.

"Something's going on with the Olynyks, and they're worried it will reach the neighborhood," Vas said, his face just a foot away from mine.

I tried not to be distracted by his wispy moustache hairs, which were right at my eye level.

"What do you think's going on with the Olynyks?" I asked. Maybe I could get what I needed and call Tommy's contact with it. Felony job: complete!

"According to Marko, there's been—"

"Marko? Marko Olynyk? You've talked to Marko?" I demanded, then tried to smooth the shock off my face. Hearing that name leveled up my memory.

Marko was Legs's son. For all I knew, Marko was his dad's hitman now. I had a foggy memory of a smoking teenager with bad tattoos, but even a ten-year-old knows sleazy when she spots it. "Does Auntie Korinna know you're involved with him? Or with his family?"

"I'm only peripherally involved, and are you *kidding*? Of course Mom doesn't know," he scoffed, fear in his eyes.

I filed that into the folder in my mind marked "Leverage." He may be a foot taller, but he wasn't a foot smarter. There was no "only peripherally involved" designation when it came to crime families.

"What did Marko tell you?" I prompted.

He kept listening at the door, not answering. I gave up eavesdropping, since I couldn't make out anything from the babbling going on inside. I couldn't even pin down an emotion from the tones.

"He's been talking about expanding his holdings, bringing in more—" Vas said, and then his pointy nose twitched like he'd just caught the scent of a predator. "Crap! You never saw me!"

He leaped over the railing and into a monstrous hydrangea—*Hydrangea macrophylla,* to be exact—the giant blue flower heads swallowing him with barely a movement. It was an impressive exit.

I thought about leaning over to see if he was okay, but a sharp voice snapped my head back to the door. Auntie Korinna peered at me through the crack.

"Go around the house," she ordered, and the door slammed in my face.

Chapter Seventeen

Lena

It took me a couple of seconds to realize my aunt wasn't running me out of town. Well, it was possible she was luring me behind her house for some other nefarious reason, but I had a tiny bud of feeling in my cold ten-year-old heart that made me think she wasn't.

I shoved that feeling down as I walked around the stuccoed mid-century bungalow. It wasn't cool to want something so bad that it would crush you if you didn't get it.

Other than remembering a bunch of old people looking down at the freaky kid who was the daughter of the bad seed in the family tree, I didn't have a lot of memories about Auntie Korinna's backyard. I for sure didn't remember a once-shiny lumbering hunk of metal in the back corner.

There, nestled into a ring of tall grass, was the bullet shape of a vintage Airstream trailer.

Vintage was being kind. So was calling it a trailer, now that I got a good look at it.

The weather in the Pacific Northwest had stripped away the trailer's luster, leaving weird, crusty residue running down the sides. Dotting the lines of the siding were rivets, many of which were missing. The window I could see was either covered with paper on the inside or was cloudy with God knew what crud.

The fwapping sound of a screen door followed by the snapping of flip-flops turned my attention. Auntie Korinna's compact body marched toward me, her fists clenched like she was about to throw some punches.

"Has this always been here?" I asked, gesturing to the silver hunk of tin in the small yard. It had to have been. It looked as permanent as her old wooden fence.

"You should go back," she said, confusing me. Had I misheard her back at the front door?

"Go back where? To the front door, or back to New York?" I asked, not liking the nervous feeling I had about what she was going to say.

"It's not safe to be in Steeltown," she said, crossing her arms and hiding those fists in her armpits.

I could have said, "No kidding, it's not safe for me to be in Steeltown." But I didn't. I waited, which if you knew me, you'd know this showed a lot of restraint.

She merely shook her head, made a wrinkled circle of disdain with her mouth, then strode across the lawn to the trailer.

I followed, stopping when she did. She put her hands on her hips and looked at me.

"I guess you can stay here," she said unhappily.

"Are you saying it's safe for me to stay in *this*?" I asked. "There's got to be a family of raccoons living in it. Or a homeless guy."

She didn't smile. Or disagree.

"You can stay two nights, no more," Auntie Korinna muttered, her stony gaze on me as she jerked her head at the trailer that may or may not have dead bodies stacked in it.

I followed her gaze to the door of the trailer, taking in the rusted hinges and sincerely doubting whether it would open.

I pursed my lips as if I was mulling over the offer. Honestly, it was two nights longer than I thought she'd give me.

"It doesn't look safe for human habitation," I suggested and heard her harrumph.

I glanced over and saw a matching harrumph expression on her face. Was she considering letting me stay in the house, or doubling down on the trailer?

"This or nothing," she muttered.

Crap. Doubling down.

"But I'm your only niece," I wheedled, glancing at the house and pointing at the tiny window under the eaves. "Can't you shove me in your attic like a normal evil auntie?"

Her back straightened, but finally, I saw the tiniest twinkle in her eye.

"It's because you're my sister's daughter that I'm letting you stay in this," she said, the flint still in her voice. "Show me you're not here to make trouble, and I'll consider different arrangements."

"Why would I come back to make trouble?" I asked, hiding my crossed fingers under my backpack's strap.

"You were *born* trouble," she snapped, the twinkle gone. "That man. Your mother's husband—"

"My *dad*," I said, my throat tightening. "And he's long dead, so what's it to you?"

Auntie Korinna was the only link I had to my mother, and I was her only link to her sister. If I was willing to take a chance to know her, why couldn't she put the past behind her and do the same?

"Your father is nothing to me," she agreed, her voice dropping into her low register.

I looked back at the trailer, blinking and confused. I didn't want to care what she thought about me, but I did.

Tell her you're a felon and find out what she really *thinks of you,* goaded an annoying voice in my head.

"So," my aunt muttered, sounding all businesslike. "What kind of job are you here for?"

I thought about not answering, but that wouldn't help me at all.

"Something like the one I had back in New York," I replied. I counted the rivets that lined one of the dull metal panels on the trailer. It helped keep my voice uncaring.

"At a bank?" she asked.

I couldn't hide my surprise. She knew where I worked?

"Uncle Mike kept me up-to-date on a few things—" she explained, her eyes shifting away.

"I know he's not my uncle. You don't have to pretend," I said.

She grunted and waved her hand in a way I would have thought was embarrassment, except I wasn't so sure Auntie Korinna felt actual emotions.

"Sometimes family isn't blood related," she muttered. "Anyway, that doesn't matter. When is your interview? I assume you have one?"

"Uh," I stammered. I hadn't developed my lie that far. "I'm not sure. I have to check."

"And you're wearing that?"

I looked down at the suit I'd worn for almost two days straight. "Yeah."

"Huh," she grunted, then turned and marched toward the house. "No friends visiting you in the trailer."

"Seriously?" I called after her. I could tell by the way she said friends she meant men.

She muttered something under her breath and waved a hand in the air, likely asking the gods to explain how she'd ended up with a niece like me.

After she'd climbed up the slanted steps to the back door, she stared me down, one hand on the screen door.

"And stay away from the library," she warned.

The library. It was a comment out of left field when Damon mentioned it, and yet... my memory clanged again. Like there was a dark history at the library that had nothing to do with the number of books in its reference section.

"Uh, okay," I said, since she looked like she wouldn't go inside until I answered.

Her eyes flickered over my rumpled suit again. She sighed and looked like there was no hope left in the world for me.

"Show me you can be a normal person and we'll see what to do about you," she murmured, shaking her head like I was a tragedy.

"Normal?" I asked. "And do what about me?" I asked, but she'd already disappeared, slamming the screen door behind her.

I had so many questions.

The most important one, though, as I looked back at the cut lock —the only thing keeping the door closed—was what kind of animal was about to jump out at me?

This was silly. I was a New Yorker at heart, if not by birth, but in my days there, I'd never actually seen a rat. However, I didn't want to let down the team by being afraid of wildlife.

I plucked the lock from its hasp and jerked the door open.

All the breath left my lungs.

There, nestled between two stacks of bundled, yellowed newspapers, sat my corpse dad.

Chapter Eighteen

Lena

I blinked. Then blinked again.

"Pakhne secheyu bilky," he muttered at me, looking around in disgust.

"Pakhne secheyu bilky," I repeated like an idiot. I knew some Ukrainian, but not that.

"It smells like squirrel *and* raccoon piss," translated a voice right behind me, making me back against a wall so hard, I lost my breath.

Vas stood there with his hands jammed into his pockets, as if he'd dropped out of the sky into the backyard. His stealth mode was truly impressive.

"What are you doing here?" I babbled.

"Checking out the carnage. Mom takes no prisoners when she's in a mood. You look like you survived, though. What did she say to you?" he asked.

"She didn't kick me off the property," I replied.

I swallowed, looking from corpse Dad to Vas, the two of them facing each other.

My father remained where he was, his paperlike expression austere. If he was worried that Vas would have something to say about his dead uncle being on his property, he didn't show it.

Vas stepped closer and poked his head inside the trailer, looking left, up, then to the right. He stepped back with a sour look on his face, and I held my breath.

"It smells more like something died in there right *after* it pissed all over the place," he muttered.

I glanced back inside. Corpse Dad smirked at me.

"He's not wrong about the dead part," Dad allowed in a raspy huff.

My gaze shot back to Vas, who definitely didn't look like he'd heard a disembodied voice.

Corpse Dad looked so real. Sounded so real. But if Vas didn't see him, did that mean I was going insane? I didn't feel less sane than usual, just tired. Did insane people even *know* they're insane?

"Mom's got you staying in this?" he asked, laughing as he patted the side of the trailer fondly. "The Jack Shack."

I squinted at him.

"You know," he murmured, then moved his hand in a tugging gesture near his waist.

"Don't make me gag," I said, then made gagging noises anyway.

"I would gag, too, if I had a throat," my father said, looking warily at the cushion he sat on.

"All the same, at least she's letting you stay on the property," Vas continued, leaning against the metal side of the trailer. "You're our bila vorona."

White crow. An ironic Ukrainian expression for being a black sheep.

"I can live with that," I murmured.

"So why are you back?" Vas asked, looking at me with interest. "The granny clan thinks it has something to do with Olynyk."

I could only hope I kept the surprise out of my expression.

"Why would they think that?" I asked.

"Because all they do is gossip about Legs and the family and how to get them out of Steeltown," Vas replied.

I squinted at Vas, remembering his connection to Marko.

"What's your angle in all of this?" I asked him, trying to butter him up with simple conversation.

"Good question," corpse Dad grunted.

"Why do you think I have an angle?" Vas asked, an excellent deflection.

"You treated me like crap when we were little. Why are you hanging around now?"

"Why not? You're the most interesting thing to happen in months," he explained, then grabbed the edge of the doorway and hauled himself past me into the trailer.

I grimaced, bracing myself for I didn't know what, but corpse Dad had disappeared.

Vas whacked the cushion where he'd been sitting, and a cloud of dust floated up. He shoved the two stacks of newspapers out of the way, and they sent another cloud into the air.

"Back there is where—" Vas started.

"Stop. I don't want to hear you reminisce about your Jack Shack days. I want to know how your mom doesn't know you're a spy for Marko and his dad." I leveled the accusation at him with a dollop of respect and a garnish of admiration. Most guys loved being complimented. But the shock on his face told me something else.

"I'm not a spy," he protested, and his pupils dilated in fear, which confirmed that he wasn't lying. "I just hang around with Marko from time to time. He's the kind of guy that if he sees you and wants company, you do what he says."

Vas sat on the cushion, leaning back as he looked around.

I stepped up into the tiny trailer hand set my backpack and bag on the floor. I looked around for where my dad might have reappeared. Nothing. I was about to reply to Vas when a "Yeow!" screeched from the floor of the trailer.

I jerked against the doorway, and Vas screeched, jumping to his feet.

"What the hell!" he yelled.

A raggedy white-and-gold cat pounced out of nowhere onto the pile of newspapers Vas had shoved over. The cat arched its back and lowered its head at us, showing a tuft of dark bronze fur that stood straight up.

It was the lost cat, the one that looked like Bruce Willis.

As I stared at it, it hopped to the back of a worn cushion and out a broken window.

"Christ on a cracker," Vas breathed, scanning the trailer, his body tense in case another animal jumped out.

I flinched when a movement caught my eye. Corpse Dad had reappeared, hunched at the back of the trailer. He looked disgusted.

"I hate cats," he muttered.

I looked at Vas, who still scanned the trailer. His eyes moved right over my dad, but when they did, Vas shivered.

"This place is creepy," he muttered and shuddered.

"You're not kidding," I agreed.

"Why are you here, Lena?" Vas asked, his voice serious.

"For a job," I said.

"That's what Mom said. But what *kind* of job?" he asked, and he examined me nervously.

That's when it sank in.

"Not the kind my dad used to do," I replied, and the way his expression changed confirmed what I had thought. "Seriously, you think I came here to kill somebody?"

He shrugged in self-defense.

"It's no secret that your dad trained you to be an assassin," he replied. "Or that my mom sent you away instead of taking you in. It's possible you... have a score to settle."

Now I shuddered.

So it was true. I was a trained assassin. Normally, I'd think that was pretty cool, but his implication freaked me out.

"I don't have any problem with Auntie Korinna," I assured him. "Or with you, or with anyone else in this town."

I ignored the grunt that came from the vicinity of corpse Dad.

"That's good," Vas said but still looked nervous.

"How do you know my dad trained me?" I asked.

"*Pfft*, like he knows anything," my father huffed.

"Are you kidding?" Vas said with a disbelieving laugh. "The two of you spent almost every weekend up at Copper Ridge. Mom argued with your dad about it all the time. He laughed at her and called her ridiculous. He said you two just went up there to hike. But one time I skipped school and went up there myself. I found bullet casings and a log that was shot to hell."

I glanced over at my dad, who looked away, waving a hand at Vas in disgust.

"Those could have been anyone's casings," my dad said dismissively, but I saw a twitch of annoyance in his ragged lips.

"I don't remember any of that," I said, frowning from my dad to Vas. "I don't even remember him being an assassin, exactly. Although I guess I knew he was involved in something... less than legal."

Vas chuckled dryly.

"Your dad being Legs Olynyk's assassin-for-hire was the worst-kept secret in town. But only our family knew he was training you," Vas explained. "I don't know if that's why Legs killed him, though."

My breath stopped. I sensed my dad step closer. Then closer again. He kept coming until he stood right beside me, making my arm feel like it was touching an ice cube despite the trailer being a sauna.

"What did you say?" corpse Dad asked him, bending and poking a finger against Vas's chest. Only it went right through him.

Sweat popped out on Vas's brow, and he rubbed at it with a shaking hand.

"I've got to get out of here," he choked and pushed past me to jump out of the trailer. He kept going until he stood in the middle of the yard, pulling in deep breaths. After about ten of them, he finally laughed. "I don't know how you're going to stay in there with that dead animal smell."

I might have wondered the same thing, but as I sensed my dead dad stand somewhere behind me, a weird pride welled up. Pride or stubbornness. Which one didn't matter. I felt strong.

"I'll make it work," I told him. And damn if I wouldn't.

Vas, however, looked doubtful. "Well, if your job doesn't work out, maybe my girlfriend can find you—"

"You have a girlfriend?" I couldn't keep the words from bursting out of me. "Sorry, I just… didn't think… never mind."

Vas, though, looked at me as if he got this question a lot.

"That I could get a girl? Well, I did. I've got a job too," he said with a mix of pride and resentment. "You know what Mom always says. About a job and a wife…?"

"I don't know," I said.

"A job and a wife make a good life," he recited, looking at me expectantly.

"I never remember her saying that, but to be fair, she didn't talk to me a lot," I allowed.

"True," Vas agreed with no hint of sympathy. "Anyway, no job and no girlfriend means no place to live for Vas. Mom would kick me out otherwise."

"Don't you *want* to move out?" I asked, trying to remember how much older he was than me. He had to be biting on thirty.

He looked at me like moving out was the stupidest idea ever.

"I was living on my own when I was sixteen," I told him, remembering how Mike had let me move into a studio apartment higher up in his building. At the time I thought it was because I was mature, but it must have been for other reasons.

"In New York," he said, as if that made a difference and didn't all New Yorkers move out before they finished high school.

"Yeah, in *New York*," I repeated, as in, it was a lot more dangerous to live on your own there than in Steeltown.

Vas just blinked at me in an "I don't get it" way.

"It's lost on him," my dad muttered behind me. "He's porozhnya holova."

Empty-headed, my dad called him. Well, maybe.

"Does Auntie Korinna make you pay rent?" I asked.

"No," he said proudly.

I smiled at him, though. I needed somebody on my side.

"That's something," I told him, punching the air with my fist. "Way to go."

He stood up straighter, and it made me feel a little bad that I hadn't been sincere.

"Thanks," he said and started walking backward toward the house. "Since you're going to be here for at least tonight, we should hang out."

"Yeah," I said, hearing tiredness make the word slur. "Maybe after I get some sleep?"

He chuckled. "Good luck sleeping in that thing, but okay. Maybe later tonight? Or in the morning?"

I nodded, then thought about his connection to the Olynyks. "Will you be seeing Marko?"

"Marko," he murmured, all the humor draining from his expression. He might sneak up on people, but he sure didn't have a poker face. "It's more like whether Marko will decide to see me. If he knows you're in town...." His words trailed off and he looked away, uncomfortable.

"I don't know why he'd know that," I replied.

"News has a way of getting around" was all he said. He pressed his lips together, then walked away, disappearing into the back of the house.

I looked back to where my dad still stood.

"You're still here," I said.

He looked down his thin, dead nose at me.

"Of course I'm still here," he replied.

"Shouldn't you be at peace now that Vas told us who killed you?" I asked, walking through him to the bed. I didn't gag or feel sick, but the air was freezing and smelled like dirt.

"Why would that matter, knowing who killed me?"

"It's how it works in the movies. The dead need to find out why they can't move on."

"This isn't a movie. And it's no surprise that Legs had me killed. It's the way.... What are you doing?" he asked.

I had unbundled one stack of newspapers to arrange them in a layer on the thin floral mattress. My body felt like it weighed twenty pounds more than usual, and my interest in talking to my corpse dad was fading fast.

"I said, what are you doing?" he demanded, materializing beside me.

"This is the closest I can come to sterilizing the bed so I can sleep," I moaned, reaching through his cold ghost body to slam the trailer door closed. I grabbed my bag and tossed it onto the newspapers.

"*Tsk*, sleep," he scoffed. "We have work to do."

"Look," I muttered, crawling onto my crinkling bed and trying to get the image of the stained mattress out of my brain. "If you're going to haunt me awake and asleep, can you do it quietly? Just for a couple of hours?"

"What is this laziness?" my father asked from somewhere above me.

I cracked an eyelid to see him beside me, the lower half of his body disappearing into the mattress, the upper half still looking very real. And comical with his bony hands on his hips.

"Sleeping," I said, but a muzzled sound came out that sounded more like, "Zlppin."

I heard one more "*Tsk*" of disgust, and then it was lights out.

Chapter Nineteen

Quinn wasn't sure checking in at his new job with a few drinks under his belt was the best idea, but he liked the confidence the booze gave him. He was sure he could keep it together enough for a quick meet and greet with his new chief.

Even now, looking both ways before crossing the street, he was acting completely sober. As long as he didn't slur, he'd be fine.

He liked that his job was just a few blocks away from his apartment. A quiet town with quiet people and a desk job typing up reports about backyard vandalism or stolen mail.... He couldn't have chosen a more perfect situation. He would ride that desk for thirty years until he checked out with a big fat pension.

He was a few feet away from the door when it burst open, and two muttering men walked outside.

The older, heavier one wore some version of a tracksuit, while the younger one wore a sharp-looking suit.

"Loser chief. What's the point of talking to him?" grumbled the heavier one.

"He owes his job to you," replied the younger one, who Quinn guessed was his son.

They both had heavy-lidded, dark eyes. Women might call them dreamy, aside from the fact that they looked cold.

"Maybe he won't have it for long," replied the father, unzipping his jacket and reaching inside a sleeve. He withdrew a small white square and threw it to the ground. His son opened a packet and held a new white square out. The man grabbed it and rummaged inside his jacket to apply some sort of patch, re-zipping when he was done.

"There's a trash can right there," Quinn suggested, pointing to the large metal can right beside where the two men stood.

He was curious how they'd take his interruption. Hell, Quinn was curious why he'd done it. Getting on anybody's radar wasn't in his game plan. Must be the gin.

The older man ignored him. The son, though, stared at Quinn as he took something else out of his pocket. There was a crinkle, and then he tossed a candy in his mouth and the plastic wrapper on the ground, close to the white patch.

"Chief will talk to someone in licensing and fix it," the suited man told his father but maintained the dead stare he'd fixed on Quinn. "And if he doesn't, I'll have a private conversation with him."

"Fine," the old man said with a wave, then muttered something that sounded Russian and walked away.

The younger man hesitated, then slowly followed his father.

"It's just polite to throw garbage into a garbage can," Quinn called. He took a step closer and looked down at the garbage, but he didn't pick it up.

He wasn't sure why he was making a point of this other than the fact that something about these men made his eye twitch. He also didn't like bullies, and they had that sullen look about them that said bullying was their main profession.

The older man coughed, and Quinn saw that they'd stopped at

the crosswalk that had a steady orange hand. He muttered something to his son and shrugged toward Quinn.

The son turned back and strolled toward him. He paused a few feet away, the garbage on the ground between them. After another second, the man bent, picked up the garbage, and walked to the can. He wadded it up, gave Quinn another look, then opened his hand to release it over the opening.

Quinn smiled at him. "Thanks," he told him.

The son walked over, stopping close enough to allow Quinn to smell the sweat under his heavy cologne. He leaned even closer, as if sharing a secret, and murmured in a hard, accented voice, "Nema problem."

Quinn lifted his chin in a half nod.

The suit took a step backward, then lifted his arm and pointed at him with his thumb out, then twisted his wrist to mimic a gun pointing at him sideways. He pulled his finger trigger, then laughed smugly, swinging around and returning to his father.

Ah, the local gangster welcoming me to town, Quinn thought. *How nice.* Something he would never tell his sister.

The light changed, and the two men crossed the street.

Quinn continued to watch them, pushing his cop intuition aside. As long as they didn't make any trouble for him, he didn't care who lived in the town.

He walked into the air-conditioned lobby of the Steeltown Police Department, his head only slightly buzzing. They wouldn't be issuing him a firearm until Monday, his first official day. He made a mental note to definitely not drink on Sunday. Or at least to stop by noon. Two o'clock at the latest.

"Can I help you?" asked the woman—Officer Danbury, according to her badge. She sat at the counter behind the glass.

"I'm here to see Chief Carter," he said, curious about the cagey look that came over the officer's expression.

"Do you have an appointment?"

"I have a new job here, if that's what you mean," Quinn said, leaning an arm on the counter. He wouldn't argue if she turned him away. Sucking up to his new boss would pave the way for later when he planned to slack off and put in the minimal effort. "I'm Quinn Magee. He knows about me."

Now she frowned at him.

"One moment," she said and picked up the phone, turning away as she mumbled into the mouthpiece. After a few seconds, she hung up, and the door beside the window buzzed.

"Come through," she said and stood to walk out the back door of her small cubicle.

He followed her stiff back through a scattering of desks, most of them empty. He liked the small, shabby look of the place, especially the lack of towering stacks of paperwork on the desks. It was a welcome change from the hectic energy in Seattle.

When he'd first joined the force, he'd loved the hectic pace of the office. He'd felt like he played an important role in the busy city, but after everything that had happened, the office had become claustrophobic.

This office, though, with its lack of clutter and quiet phones, calmed his heart rate. He hadn't even realized it had doubled the moment he'd walked into the tiny lobby.

"Chief?" asked the officer, gesturing to Quinn but standing in the doorway. "I've got Quinn Magee?"

"Right, Officer Magee," the man inside said and set aside a stack of papers before he waved him inside. "Or should I say Detective Magee?"

Quinn smiled at the woman, but her expression remained skeptical as she stepped aside for him.

"You're a few days early," the chief said, standing up and holding out a hand. "If you want to start today, you'll have to share a desk."

Quinn shook it and stepped back before saying, "Nope, just stopped in to introduce myself."

The chief nodded, his expression friendly and showing no sign he'd smelled anything unusual on his breath for a Thursday afternoon.

"Sit," the man invited, pointing to a worn chair and sitting down himself. "How long have you been in town?"

"Just today," he said.

"Ah," Chief Carter said, moving some folders around on his desk. "Well, we're a small force in a small town dealing with minor problems."

Quinn noticed a flash of contempt pinch around the man's eyes and thought of the two men he'd met outside. Minor problems might be relative.

"That's good to hear," he replied.

"Yeah, well, anything big and we call a guy down in Everett to come in and take over the case. Although I guess with you here, you'll handle the big stuff, such as it is."

Chief Carter laced his fingers together and held Quinn with a steady gaze. Or was it a glare?

"You know, we have a few people here who hoped we'd create your position without having another force create it for us," the chief said.

"Is that so?"

"And we've got some smart officers who've been putting in their time and hoping for a promotion," the chief continued.

"That doesn't sound surprising," he said. Now he saw anger in the chief's gaze, no doubt about it.

"I know you don't officially start until Monday, but you should make sure you bring your credentials with you," Chief Carter advised.

"Luckily I have them right here," Quinn said and pulled the letter out of his pocket. "I probably should have started by giving you this."

He handed the envelope to the chief, who took it, grimaced, then laid it on the desk unopened.

"There it is," the chief said, flicking the embossed stationery in the top left corner of the envelope. "I assume this contains an order for me to clear a substantial portion of my already-small budget to fit you in."

"I'm assuming the same," he replied.

"I hope you're used to working with a partner," the chief said with another grimace.

"Oh, I don't need a partner. I'm used to—"

But the chief's grimace deepened as he looked over Quinn's shoulder.

"Is this him?" asked an angry voice behind him.

"Yeah...," groaned the chief, rubbing a hand over his face. "Come in, Baxter. Quinn, this is Officer Brooke Baxter."

Brooke Baxter marched around and stood in front of Quinn, her hands on her hips and her eyes sweeping him from his worn running shoes to his short-sleeved shirt. She squinted and leaned closer, peering into his face, which was impressive, seeing as how she obviously had a massive stick stuck up her butt.

He broke her gaze by standing up and holding out his hand.

"Quinn Magee. It's nice to meet you," he said.

She leaned even closer and gave his hand an angry shake. Her eyes told him she smelled the cheap gin on his breath that nobody else had.

"Has this guy even processed a crime scene?" she demanded of the chief, releasing his hand like it was slime.

"Um, no, never. Do you get a lot of those up here?" Quinn asked cheerfully.

The woman's lips compressed, and he smiled at her annoyance.

He reached over to the envelope on the chief's desk. "Maybe you're the one who should read this. I performed an important act for the city of Seattle and was granted a transfer to a department of my choosing. I chose this one."

Brooke's eyes narrowed as she snatched the envelope and tapped it against her palm.

"What important act?" she asked.

"The specifics are confidential, but it involved neutralizing a criminal and keeping a certain mayor's son out of my police report," Quinn said, folding his arms.

"Chief," Brooke complained, turning to look at the older man.

The chief just lifted his hands and shrugged. "It's out of my hands. Update him on the case files and on the new goings on with the Olynyks. And give him a set of keys," the chief said and pushed himself away from the desk. "I'm taking my Chevelle up to Lynden for a car show, so... work it out, you two. Preferably before Monday."

"Look," Brooke said, slapping the letter down on the only file-covered desk in the office. She leaned on two tall stacks and gave him a warning look.

When she didn't complete her thought, he smiled at her. "Look at what?" he drawled, pulling out a chair on the other side of her desk. He dropped into it, enjoying her hostility.

He didn't care about this job beyond making sure he didn't get fired. He looked up at her scowl, and something the chief said finally clicked.

"Ahhh, I get it," he murmured, nodding.

"Get what?" she demanded, straightening.

Wow, she really made it easy for him to push her buttons.

"You're the one."

"What 'one'?"

"The one who wanted my job before it was created," he explained.

She let out a hiss and dropped into her own chair. She picked up the envelope and tapped it on a pile of file folders, glaring at him.

He wanted to laugh. She'd led a sheltered life if she thought a look could intimidate him.

"I'm not here to ruin your life," he said, but Brooke was already shaking the envelope at him.

"You already have, whether or not you meant to."

"I'll tell you what, partner," he said, enunciating the last word sarcastically. "I'm assuming you're the partner Carter told me I'd have?"

She grunted.

"Well, partner, I'll let you keep doing all the detective work. I bet you've been working cases yourself before the chief pulled in your Everett guy," he said, and the way she sat up in her chair told him he was right. "My intent is to do the least amount of work possible and retire. When that happens, I'll put in a good word for you. You'll be a shoo-in to take over the job. Deal?"

He smiled kindly, enjoying the way her jaw clenched.

The situation was getting even better. He wouldn't even have to work, just show up to punch the clock on time. He'd either die of boredom or pickle his liver and grab the parachute of long-term disability.

She just stared at him, tapping the envelope slower and slower until she stopped. Then she pointed it at him.

"Will whatever's in this envelope tell me whose butt you had to kiss to get here?" she asked, enunciating the word "butt" mockingly. "Because I don't think I believe the mayor would feel he owed someone like you a favor."

"It's possible a senator's son was also kept out of my report," he agreed. "I'm not sure. I didn't actually read the letter."

She shook her head but finally set the envelope aside. She folded her hands and looked prim.

"Officially, most of the investigations are property claims and assault," she said. "There was an officer shot on duty, which was cleared up quickly. Years ago another officer was killed, and that case is still open despite it being obvious who was behind it."

He thought of the two goons he'd passed outside, but he kept his mouth shut.

"Unofficially, I've been watching the Olynyk family. They're involved in—"

"Wait," he said, holding up his hands to stop her. "Are we talking a specific work case?"

"Uh... yeah. Isn't that why you're here?" she asked.

"Nope. I was here for formalities. And I guess to meet you, which was unexpected. A good unexpected, though," he replied, and he wasn't lying. She was going to make his job so much easier.

"If you're here, though, why don't we—" she tried, but he waved his hand again.

"Well, I think *you* should definitely carry on," he said, getting up from his chair. "You've got that very important quality for advancing in any police department I've ever been in."

Her eyes narrowed, but he could see the need to know fighting in her eyes. He waited until it won.

"What's that?" she asked.

"You're an overachiever," he said and chuckled when the interest in her expression soured. "Like right now. I can tell you're going to overachieve on all those files on your desk before I officially start work on Monday."

"Jerk," she muttered under her breath, but he was already walking away.

When the late afternoon sun hit his face, he smiled. It was an odd feeling when the worst thing you ever did turned out so well. That made him crave another drink.

He headed back to Halloran's and what he was sure would become his favorite barstool.

Chapter Twenty

Lena

The combined odor of garbage and sweaty feet woke me up, but I was nervous about what new entity might have decided to visit, so I waited for another sign before I opened my eyes.

That sign was a purr.

I rolled to my side, and the smell moved away. I felt a blob plopping beside my stomach. Opening my eyes, I peered into the annoyed face of feline Bruce Willis.

"Hey," I greeted in a croaky voice, the hot air of the trailer not helping.

I reached out a finger and gave his chin a scratch, smiling when he let me.

The cat had a black tuft near its eyebrow, and its greasy fur looked like he'd been through hell. Exactly like Bruce Willis in *Die Hard*.

"What's the statute of limitations on missing cats?" I asked him.

He blinked.

"If I name you, I get to keep you. How do you feel about that?"

His purring revved up like a garbage truck, which was a good enough answer for me.

"I christen you Bruce Willis, the tough but lovable detective who'll save me from high-rise terrorists. And hopefully small-town mobsters."

Bruce Willis cocked his head sideways so I could scratch his ear. If I died from heat exhaustion, the cat would probably eat my face, but that was okay, since he was family now.

"That animal probably has rabies," muttered a gravelly voice from the front of the trailer.

Ahh, so the haunting continued. So much for a solid nap fixing my psychosis.

"You're still hanging around, huh?" I asked.

"Yes," he said, walking into view to stand by the door.

He stood with his arms folded and glared at my new-to-me fur baby. Bruce Willis let out a low growl and inched closer against me.

"What would you know about animals? I was never allowed to have a pet," I said.

"Your mother was allergic," he said, his sunken eyes taking on a melancholy glint.

Bruce Willis's body relaxed slightly, but he didn't take his cat eyes off my dad. If I was having a psychotic break, at least the cat was having it with me.

"I'm not allergic," I said, but I held that new piece of information close. *My mother was allergic to cats.* I waited for another memory of her to come to me, and it did, but it didn't make sense. It was an image of blue-and-white squares, like a tablecloth.

"Pets are things you care about, and in my business, caring is dangerous," he said in a huff.

It sounded like the start of a lecture.

"Let me guess. Being emotionless and uncaring made you a successful hitman right until it killed you. Got it," I said, laying on the sarcasm like a thick slice of Velveeta.

Instead of going off on the thousand things I didn't understand about his profession, his shoulders folded in.

"I cared about one thing," he murmured, his sunken eyes staring into space. "I cared about your mother."

I stopped scratching Bruce Willis's chin, and he grumped at me in a cat complaint. I realized the corpse in front of me had a whole life's worth of memories about my mother.

Mom, my brain whispered. I didn't speak in case it snapped him out of whatever memories he seemed to be lost in.

"Adeline. Addy," he murmured and let out a rusty sigh. "Korinna tried to talk her out of marrying me, but your mother knew it was the best thing."

A hundred questions flooded my mind, but I played it cool, going back to scratching Bruce Willis's chin.

"The potlucks were Addy's idea," he mused, then gave a dry chuckle. "To give you a sense of your heritage. She also made me buy the apartment instead of renting it. Ah, Addy. There was nothing I wouldn't do for her."

I wanted to ask if training me to kill people had been my mom's idea, but he sighed and turned transparent around his edges. It was the perfect lesson for his rule about caring. It made you transparent, insubstantial, weak. And I was not a weak, melancholy person. I was, however, curious.

I cautiously pushed myself up into a sitting position, worried the crunching of the newspaper would jar him out of his reverie, but he just sighed more deeply.

"What else do you remember about Mom?" I ventured to ask, my voice low. I leaned against the trailer wall, and a disgruntled Bruce Willis crept onto my lap.

"She liked to twirl. She would turn up the radio and twirl in the kitchen, making her skirt flare out. When you were born, she'd hold you and spin, and you would both laugh," he mused, his tone making it clear he didn't understand that kind of whimsy but that he was okay with it.

More questions bubbled up in my brain. What kind of music did she like? Did I get my love of drawing from her? Do I have other family I don't know about?

A whisper of air came through the broken window, cooling my sweaty neck. Corpse Dad must have felt it, too, because he straightened his shoulders and his expression hardened.

"If she were here, she would tell you not to trust anyone, not even family," he said.

"So not even you?" I challenged.

He glared at me, then stepped forward and punched the air with a bony finger.

"What you don't know is kraplya v mori," he shouted.

"I don't know what that means!" I shouted back.

"It means what you know is a drop in the ocean. Close to nothing!" he yelled back.

"And whose fault is that? You died, and I got shipped across the country to live with complete strangers!"

He threw his hands up and turned away. Then he walked to the far end of the trailer and back before stopping to stare down at me.

Bruce Willis tensed but otherwise kept up his steam-engine purring. I kept up with scratching his grimy fur, feeling better with the cat between me and corpse Dad. The only afterlife rules I knew came from *Doom Eternal,* and that had more to do with demons. I could only hope yelling at my dad wouldn't unlock some extra creepy spirit level.

"I don't like... this," he muttered, waving a hand between us vaguely.

"I already know you don't like the cat," I replied.

"Not that. Well, yes, I hate animals," he agreed. "I mean, I don't like this arguing. You never used to talk to me like that, Galyna."

I blew out a breath.

"I don't have a ton of memories of *anything* I used to do," I retorted, and he flung his hands out in exasperation.

"You can't blame me for you not remembering. I was killed, remember?" he argued.

I looked down at the lump of likely flea-ridden fur on my lap. Then around at the filthy trailer of the only living family I had—the matriarch who hated me. And I was talking to a ghost.

I shot him an accusatory look, but he was already shaking his head at me.

"We might have lived over a bar, but it was nothing like this," he muttered, disgust on his face as he looked around. "Korinna hated me, but I wouldn't have thought she'd feel the same way about you after all these years."

"Maybe she agrees with you about not caring about things, even family," I suggested.

I followed his gaze around the trailer, and a weight heavier than Bruce Willis settled on me.

It didn't get more screwed up than this, and that didn't even include the felony hanging over my head.

"Crap," I said, remembering what had forced me back to Steeltown in the first place. "I need a plan," I muttered at Bruce Willis. He had no comment.

"Yes," my father agreed, slapping his ghostly hands together soundlessly. "I was thinking about this while you were sleeping, and I know exactly what you need to do."

"What's that?"

"Kill Legs."

Chapter Twenty-One

Lena

I stared at him as the muddy heat of the trailer swirled around me.

"You want me to kill Legs," I repeated.

"Yes," my father replied.

"That's got to be the stupidest thing I ever heard," I muttered, shaking my head.

Corpse Dad jerked his head back in shock.

"It's the *smartest* thing you've ever heard. It solves both our problems."

"It solves nothing!" I yelled, startling Bruce Willis to his feet. "Shh, I'm not mad at you."

"Getting revenge on my killer will let me move on," my dad argued.

"Last night you didn't know *why* I'd brought you back, and now you know the exact solution to your ghostliness?" I challenged.

"Well," he said with a shrug. "Like you said. Knowing my killer didn't do it, so it must be avenging my death."

"Avenging your death," I repeated, more than a little disgusted. "You're a ghost able to come and go as you please. *I'm* the one who could go to jail if I don't get the FBI some information. You're making this all about you."

"Yes, it *is* about me," he said, relieved I was seeing it his way. "Why else am I here?"

"Maybe this is your chance to act like a real father. To advise me on how I get out of this mess?"

"Exactly!" he said, staring at me as if he couldn't understand why I didn't get it. "And I'm advising you, as a father, to kill Legs."

I wanted to smack my head.

"Committing another felony is not good advice."

He threw his hands out, waving me off as if to say I didn't know good advice when I heard it.

"You know, I thought maybe you were a weird part of my brain that wanted closure with Auntie Korinna. But now I think you're testing me to see if you can mess me up. I would never come up with an idea that was so dumb."

He looked offended. "Explain how it's dumb," he said, his words stilted.

"I don't even have a weapon—" I cut myself off with a groan. Was I really trying to justify myself to something from my imagination?

I looked up at whatever was peeling off the ceiling, trying to get back to my good old analytical mind. My eyes followed the curved ceiling to the dark plywood of the walls. It was smaller and smellier and crappier than my New York apartment, and yet there was something promising about it.

Was it because no matter how much my aunt didn't like me, she'd let me get this close? Did I just need to prove myself worthy of getting an upgrade to that attic room in her house? Maybe this trailer was my crucible where my life compressed around me until I turned into a brilliant, crime-busting diamond. Or would it just compress enough that I turned into a lump of felonious coal?

As Bruce Willis purred like an engine on my legs, I realized I'd need to get out from under the felony.

"Tell me what you know about Legs," I said to corpse Dad.

He was looking away, his expression still butthurt.

"If you tell me about Legs, I promise I'll let you plan his killing." Yes, I was bluffing a corpse, but from the lightening of his cold expression, it was working.

"Do you have to talk to me with that cat on you?" my father complained, then squinted at Bruce Willis. "He looks like he has mange."

"How do you know what mange looks like?" I asked, although I stopped petting him.

My dad poked his finger at the cat and said, "Psssst!"

Bruce Willis hissed and dug his claws into my legs for leverage to jump through the broken window.

"Geez!" I complained, rubbing the top of my thigh.

"Problem solved, although if that cat scratched you, you could have tetanus," he said, sounding overly satisfied.

"Not helpful," I replied but knew I would check the scratch out later. "Why does Bruce Willis see you, but Vas couldn't?"

"He doesn't see me, he senses me. Senses my hate." He spit the words in the window's direction.

"You should work on that," I said.

"Work on what?"

"Hating. I wouldn't be surprised if that's the real reason you can't find peace. You hated too much in life," I reasoned.

"I hate cats, yes. But I don't hate people."

"You killed a lot of people," I reminded him.

"You can't be an assassin if you hate people. You need to be emotionless," he explained.

Despite the muggy air in the trailer, a cool trickle slid down my spine. Those words were familiar. I waited for a rush of memories, but nothing came.

"So where can I find Legs?" I asked.

"Yes. Legs," my father said, smacking his hands together and smiling. "He works at the library."

"He... what?"

"He has a room at the library. That's where he works," my father explained, then rolled his eyes. "The Steeltown Library, just down the street from—"

"Yeah. The library. I heard you, but I don't get how a crime boss works at the library," I said, but both Damon's and Auntie Korinna's advice to stay away from the library made sense.

"Behind the children's section," my dad continued, holding his hands out as if that was helpful.

"Wait, behind the children's section?" That seemed so evil. And yet... maybe running a crime empire from a library was genius?

"Yes, that's what I said," he told me, glancing at the ceiling. He must have been rolling his eyes, only they were so black, I couldn't tell. "It was a reading room, but he made it into an office. He runs the business from there."

"Huh," I said, nodding. "I guess I'm going to the library."

"Yes. You'll confront Legs and—"

"No confronting. I'm just going to talk to him. We'll see what happens after that," I explained.

He looked disgruntled, then stoic. It made me wary.

"You're not allowed to show up there either," I reprimanded, pointing at him sternly, like he was a misbehaving teenager. "You'll be a distraction."

"It might help. Maybe he'll be able to see me like that cat, and you'll be able to slit his throat—"

"No! There'll be no slitting of anything," I warned him.

He shrugged in acceptance. "I never trained you in knife work, so it's just as well," he allowed. He stared at me. "What's your useless plan that doesn't include killing him?"

"I was thinking I'd start by saying I was your daughter. That should get his attention," I stated.

"No," he murmured, waving his hand like I was a fly. "He'll just shoot you. Or get Marko to shoot you."

"Right, Marko," I mused. Of course, Legs's son would be a hurdle. "I think Vas might be in his good books, so maybe I should say I'm Vas's cousin...?"

I trailed the words like I was trolling for his approval. Which was dumb because he'd probably just want me to kill Marko too.

"*Pfft*," my dad hissed. "Marko doesn't have friends. He's mean and incompetent. A dangerous combination."

"So what should I say to him?" I asked.

Part of me couldn't believe I was taking advice from a hired killer, corpse or not. Another part marveled that I was reconnecting with my dead dad. That part of me, the reconnecting part, slapped a hand to its forehead at the idea I was listening to a hallucination in a run-down trailer.

"I don't want you to say anything," he replied, stubbornly folding his arms. "If you can actually get close to him, you should just kill him."

"This is the last time I'm saying this. Nobody's getting killed." This was what I got for chatting with a dead killer. "Why don't *you* kill him? Just pretend he's a cat."

Instead of scoffing, he rubbed his chin thoughtfully.

"I would, but I can't affect anything. Even this bed," he said, then glided into it, his legs disappearing from his thighs down. "It goes right through me."

"Maybe it's like in the movie *Ghost*, where Patrick Swayze channels his emotions—"

"Enough with the movies," he groaned, holding his hands against his head as if to block out the shame of what had become of me. And he didn't even know I spent most nights playing video games yet. "You're mostly a killer," he continued. "I can't remember it all, but you were ready to take over my contract on the day I got killed."

I froze.

"What are you saying? That *I* was supposed to kill somebody?"

"That was the plan."

"Did Legs know?" I asked, another chill sliding down my spine. Was *I* the hitman, and I'd blocked it out of my memory? Was I the *Manchurian Candidate*, about to be activated?

How about you focus on something real, like just avoiding prison? my felony-fearing self piped up.

Good point.

"Of course he didn't know it," he scolded. "Do you think I'm an idiot?"

"Well, it's a fair question," I joked, but he ignored me.

"It was going to be your first hit," he continued, his black eyes even blacker as he relived the moment. "It was a beautiful setup for you too. The mark would be down the street, no more than a hundred yards—"

"Wait just a minute," I said, holding my hand out as flashes of memory rolled through me.

A saxophone case, except... no saxophone in it. Holding a bony hand—his—as I crossed a street. The street that Damon's bus had driven up. Arthur Avenue.

"Holy crap, did I kill somebody?" I demanded and jumped up, accidentally sliding into his body.

My skin tingled as his ghostliness combed every hair on my body into rigid alert.

"Don't be so dramatic," he complained. "I don't know exactly what happened the day I died, but so what if you killed somebody? I've killed... several people."

An image of a saxophone case quivered in my mind. The bone-colored handle and blue velvet interior, but lying snugly inside....

The vision disappeared.

"No," I said, dropping back onto the newspaper-covered mattress.

But I was relieved the memory slipped. I didn't want to know what I had or hadn't done or what was or wasn't in that saxophone case.

"What do you mean, no?" my dad demanded. "Just three weeks before the day I died, I killed—"

"I need a plan," I said loudly enough to drown out his death count.

"You need a gun," he corrected, his accent sharp as a knife.

"I just need to get in front of Legs and somehow find out who he's talking to," I said.

"Marko guards access to Legs," he replied.

"And Legs is in the library," I murmured. "I mean, anyone can walk into the library, right?"

"Sure. You look... knyzhkovyy enough," my father murmured.

I turned that word over in my mind. "Book? I look like a book?"

"Yes. You read so much, you're a book," he said.

"Thanks," I said, genuinely flattered.

"It's not a compliment," he said, looking me over and grimacing when he got to my surplus army boots. "You need to look sexy to get past Marko."

I plucked at my sweaty T-shirt. He was right. Even if I had something borderline feminine in my bag, I was not what I'd describe as the sexy type. Flirting was not the role-playing I was good at.

"I could get into the library and lie low. I just need a minute to tell Legs I'm your daughter. There's no way he wouldn't at least talk to me, right?" I proposed.

My dad's lips compressed, and he shook his head.

"I think it's an 80 percent chance he has Marko shoot you," he said, then let out a short, sharp breath. "Are you thinking of offering to be Legs's hit... woman?"

"Actually, my plan was to ask for a job. Any kind of job. He'd probably give me something out of respect for you," I suggested. "Once I'm inside—"

"Respect? He killed me, Galyna! That he did it quickly is all the respect you can get from a man like that," he argued.

"But up until then, he respected you, right?"

He stared at me, not wanting to admit it. Aw, was corpse Dad trying to keep me safe?

"Yes. Until he killed me, he respected me. Asked me for advice on many things," he admitted.

"And you gave him good advice, right? I mean, better advice than you gave me?"

He gave me a withering look, an especially hideous expression when it came from a withering dead person.

"I answered questions truthfully," he clarified. "I'm always truthful."

"Did you do anything on your last day that might have angered him?"

"No," he said, then shrugged again. "Well, he didn't know I was bringing you along to kill the mark."

"Do you think he found out?"

"I don't know. Possibly. It was the first hit I was making in Steel-town. Do you remember that lesson? Don't kill—"

"Where you eat," I finished, then smiled at him. "Hey, I remembered something."

"Huh," he grunted, unimpressed. "Here's another lesson. Don't walk into a cave with an angry bear in it."

I was about to tell him I would never wander up to any cave when my stomach growled. How long had it been since I'd eaten anything?

"Sounds like bear in your stomach," my dad said, looking me over critically. "Maybe Korinna has some syrniki you could steal."

Ooooooh, syrniki! A vision of lightly fried thick breakfast pancakes popped into my head, and my stomach growled even louder. Wandering into Auntie Korinna's for food sounded a lot like the cave scenario my dad mentioned.

My starving imagination took over, and I saw myself hanging from her gutter to grab a handful of biscuits through an open window, my backpack counterbalancing.... Why was my imagination always inserting my computer into—

And that's when a brilliant idea popped into my head.

Chapter Twenty-Two

Thomas

Thomas eased himself onto his couch and rested the flat bottom of the martini glass on his thigh.

It hadn't been a good day, but it had been a good-enough day. Good enough for the apple martini that nobody knew was his favorite celebratory drink. Good enough not to change out of his expensive suit and into FBI sweats.

Good enough to take the box out of his closet.

He sank against the cushions and propped his foot on the coffee table, pushing his toe against the side of the box. He exerted just enough pressure to square the box perfectly along the table's edge.

"Here's to fast-talking," he murmured to the spartan living room. He raised the heavy martini glass to the box, then took a sip. He eyed the murky green drink, then drained half of it, relaxing back as he imagined his body absorbing every molecule of the vodka.

It had been a long meeting, with his boss having saved all his frustration to rain on Thomas as the last topic.

It started with Duncan reading out a list of his expenses in New

York. His flight, three nights in a hotel, and the requisition for a driver and IT personnel. He'd finished with the plane ticket for Jane Doe.

"All this to follow a lead on some cold case out of Seattle?" Duncan finished, his voice taut. It was the tone his boss used right before he tore you a new asshole.

The time had come for Thomas to knit a few half-truths into a believable story.

"I found a link between the New York Danchuk family and a cold case north of Seattle. A witness came to light, and there was only a small window of opportunity to send her west to give a statement," he'd explained. "You've always said we should follow—"

"I'm aware of things I've said in the past, Palmer. What's the connection between this witness and Danchuk?"

"The witness is the daughter of one of Olynyk's former hitmen. Ilya Kozek. Kozek was killed, and the case has been open ever since," he explained, hoping his boss would think it was plausible. "The witness moved to New York, into the heart of Danchuk's territory. My gut said that wasn't a coincidence."

"So?" Duncan grunted, tossing the list of expenses on the table.

"So... I thought the Seattle office might want to talk to her," he lied.

It was a weak reason. All Duncan had to do was bring in Lena's age at the time and he'd be screwed. A ten-year-old recounting her version of events around her father's death was ludicrous.

He sipped his martini as he remembered how he'd had to snivel for forgiveness the way Duncan liked. Duncan had ended the meeting but not before suspending Thomas's requisition privileges. The ultimate humiliation in front of the office staff, only his boss didn't realize that he didn't need it. Lena was in Steeltown, maybe even already lying in that alley his sister mentioned. Mission accomplished.

Now, draining the martini and pouring the last one from the mixer, he stared at the box. He was ready to allow himself a small celebration.

He still had a job, much as he hated his asshole boss. And the last link to his father's murder was snipped.

"To closure," he said, taking a healthy sip before flicking off the box's lid.

Inside were the belongings from his father's police locker and desk.

He'd sorted through it once, his attention always captured by the one thing he stared at now. The green cotton hat in the plastic evidence bag.

It was labeled "green fedora," but he'd looked it up online and discovered it was actually a trilby. Frank Sinatra had worn both, and while that was mildly interesting, it hadn't given him any clues about why his father had worn it that day. His dad never wore hats, let alone classic ones from the fifties.

When his mom had gotten the box of his belongings, she'd opted to keep his journal and anything that had his handwriting. Bella had kept an unsent birthday card he'd written a note on for her. He'd been killed two weeks before her birthday, and she'd cherished the fact that buying her a card hadn't been a last-minute purchase on the way home on her birthday.

Thomas had taken the rest of the box, but the only thing he was interested in was the hat.

He'd seen his dad with it that day, adjusting it on his head as he'd stood outside Ice Cream Junction. He remembered how his dad had tugged on the short brim. Down, then up, then down again, trying to find the right fit.

Thomas wished the details of that day had faded. Or that the trauma of seeing his dad shot in front of him would at least fade into a soft blur. Instead, the detail of it got sharper every day.

The red bloom that had soaked the upper chest of his dad's shirt, forcing him into a hunch. The distant report of the gun sounded in Thomas's left ear, then a half heartbeat later in his right. The way his dad fell to his knees, then to his side. For such a large man, his collapse had been graceful. Like something choreographed in a movie.

Thomas had frozen on the sidewalk like everyone else, his heart beating out of his chest. Then he ran. Everyone did. He was certain none of the other people had felt the knife stab of guilt, though. It still stabbed him years later.

Thomas had been ditching school that day. He'd been on a mission, although running into his dad hadn't been part of the plan.

He drained the last of the appletini and reached for the corner of the evidence bag. He lifted it just until he could see the black stain that soaked the underside of the brim. It had made an oval shape, with two tracks of stitching dashing through it in either direction.

He felt the heavy thudding of his heart, the anxiety from that day settling over him. Today was supposed to be different. To *feel* different. All his planning had come together, but the guilt of that day was still there, buried in his cells, just waiting for the sight of the hat to trigger it.

Maybe he should burn the hat. Now that he'd fulfilled his goal, he no longer needed this painful reminder.

His phone bleated, making his arm jerk back and release the bag. He jammed the lid onto the box and fumbled for his phone.

"Palmer. It's Duncan. Get packed," his boss ordered.

"Packed for what?" he replied, hoping his words weren't slurring.

"Seattle. I checked on that cold case. Turns out you sending a witness over was news to them. Turns out," Duncan drawled, the gloating in his voice a palpable thing, "they don't have the interest or warm bodies to interrogate someone for a cold case that's *fifteen years old*."

"Uh," he mumbled, the martini churning in his stomach as his mind raced to find a suitable lie.

"Since you're so familiar with the case, I volunteered you to help," Duncan said.

This wasn't how it was supposed to go. The situation he'd set up was supposed to unravel miles away. An inconsequential woman to anybody else, snipped like a dangling thread.

"Sir, I think—"

"I don't care what you think, you entitled son of a bitch," Duncan growled. "I talked to the lead in Seattle *and* I talked to the agents working the Danchuk case. Nobody's even heard of you, let alone talked to you about open cases."

His mouth opened, then closed. He was caught, and no clever lie would get him uncaught.

"My guess, you little pissant, is that you thought I wouldn't check. Well, I did. Then I dug a little deeper and found out about your daddy."

Thomas held his breath.

"My guess is, you used agency resources for personal reasons, and that's a fireable offense," Duncan said, which made Thomas hold his breath. "It wouldn't take much for me to make it a *criminal* offense."

He went from visualizing himself working in a call center to sitting in a jail cell.

"I understand, sir," he said.

"But since I have to back up your lies or else explain to my supervisor how I allowed one of my staff to go vigilante, I'm assigning you to Seattle. You're going to work on this cold case and make a significant contribution. If you don't go, you're out of the bureau for refusing your supervisor. If you *do* go, I'll make up a reason to kick you out of the bureau for failure to meet performance standards. And once you're out, you'll be out of any level of law enforcement. The notes I'll put in your file will ensure it. Understand?" Duncan demanded.

"Yes, sir," he said.

"Plane leaves in an hour," Duncan said, then hung up.

Thomas swallowed, looking back at the green trilby.

"Yes, sir," he said to the dead phone.

Chapter Twenty-Three

Lena

"What are you doing?" my dad asked as I flipped on the tap on the grungy sink.

A fairly clean stream poured out, and I let a little puddle in my hand. I slid it under my T-shirt and into one armpit.

"This is the closest to washing I can get," I replied, splashing and rubbing the water into my sweaty pit. I repeated it on the other side, then stretched my T-shirt around to dry the area. I dug in my bag and pulled out my deodorant and my Radiohead T-shirt.

"Either turn around or close your eyes," I told him.

"Why?" he asked, looking at me warily.

"Because I'm going to change into something less smelly, and ghost or not, you don't need to find out I don't wear a bra," I replied, but he'd already turned around.

"Maybe this would make more sense if you told me of this brilliant idea you have," he reasoned.

I quickly switched tops. At least the thinner Radiohead T-shirt would be cooler. I caked on some deodorant, then pulled my jacket back on. I had another jacket, but it was army green and heavier than the black one.

"I'm still working it out, but it involves getting the information I need with nobody getting killed," I replied.

"You should at least bring a gun with you. For when your brilliant plan fails," he said, his corpse-like face twisting with sarcasm.

"I don't have a gun to bring," I said, swinging the backpack over my shoulder. "And there will be no failure."

I thought about what I was about to do and looked at the bag. It was likely I wouldn't be welcomed back if my aunt found out about my plan. But something about her seeing me leave with all my worldly possessions didn't sit well either.

I left the bag but swung it onto the mattress under the broken window. If my aunt forbade me to return, I could sneak behind the trailer and grab it.

"Let's get this mission going," I said and pushed open the trailer's door.

I jumped down and closed it before turning and walking, literally, right into corpse Dad.

"I told you, you can't come," I said with a sigh.

"You shouldn't talk to me. It makes you look unstable," he replied, waving at me like I was a fly buzzing around his head.

I rolled my eyes and tried to walk through him. He kept backing up to stay in front of me, and I fixed my eyes on the ground.

"I wouldn't talk to you if you didn't keep showing up," I said, sounding sulky.

"Why wouldn't I show up? This is my house," griped Auntie Korinna.

My head jerked up to see her standing in the open back door.

"Oh. Hi. Um, yeah," I stuttered, trying to find a believable reason for talking to myself. Luckily, she had other things on her mind.

"Are you going for your interview?" she asked, shoving the screen door open and glaring at my clothes.

"Yes!" I said, thankful for the perfect excuse to be going into town.

"Isn't it late for an interview?" she asked, looking at her watch.

I pulled out my phone to check the time. It was almost four o'clock.

"Not really," I bluffed. I looked up to see her looking me over.

"You're going in that?" she asked, already shaking her head. "And without eating?"

"These are my work clothes," I said, the disdain on her face poking my pride just a little. "Everyone in my line of work wears this."

That might have been true, but as I rarely socialized with anyone but my gaming buddies, I wasn't speaking from experience.

She grunted.

"Also, you smelled bad earlier. I didn't want to tell you and hurt your feelings," she said briskly, then made a tsking sound through clenched teeth. "Come in for a shower and a bowl of okroshka. And maybe I have something better than... that"—she waved her hand at me—"for you to wear." Then she disappeared into the house.

"Oh, no, this isn't good," my father groaned, and I glanced over to see him cover his mouth with a long-fingered hand.

I covered my mouth and cough-muttered, "How can a shower be bad? I smell. And I haven't had okroshka soup in ages."

"The shower is fine. The soup is fine. It's the tracksuit she's going to put you in that is bad. The pants will be three inches short," he muttered. "It's the opposite of sexy. Look at her!"

He jutted his chin out at Auntie Korinna. But at the offer of a shower and soup, my opinion of her outfit had softened.

"Stop it," I whispered. "She's dressing me to look professional, not sexy. And I need something more to eat than a crushed granola bar."

He tsked at me, rolled his eyes, and disappeared.

"Well?" my aunt called out, returning to the doorway. She held the screen door open.

I nodded and bolted inside.

You didn't know how amazing the world was until you'd showered off thirty-odd hours of caught-in-a-felony, kicked-out-of-your-apartment, returned-to-possible-death sweat.

It's pretty freaking amazing.

It was also kind of nice to be inside a home. Not an apartment bathroom with my sad handful of toiletries, or the sterile staff bathroom at the bank, but an actual people-live-here bathroom.

Auntie Korinna's bathroom was dated but well-loved. The tile work was fifty years old, but the cozy blue and white sparkled. The faucet had those porcelain handles in the shape of plus signs with H and C on them. A toothbrush holder was tiled right into the wall beside a sink that sat on spindly metal legs, the steel piping exposed underneath.

But the towels. The towels were like luxurious fur coats, so thick and soft and large, I could have rolled around on the floor in the one I'd wrapped around myself. I looked down at the hexagonal tiled floor and was thinking about it when a thump on the door startled me.

"What's taking so long?" Auntie Korinna grumbled.

"I'm just drying off," I grumbled back. She didn't need to know how much I liked her bathroom. Or her towels, her house, and the bowl of okroshka I'd gobbled down before hitting the shower.

"I found something for you to wear," she said, then banged on the door again.

"I don't need—" I said, ending in a yelp when the door clicked open.

The towel wrapped around me twice, but I still clutched it like it was a bulletproof vest and Auntie Korinna was packing heat. Trusting my corpse dad to turn his back was one thing. My scornful aunt was another.

"*Cha*, you'd think I was planting a pig on you," she muttered through the crack, my Auntie Korinna staying in the hall.

I smiled at the old expression.

"I didn't think you were playing a trick on me. You just surprised me," I replied, breathing easier when only her hand thrust through the opening.

She held out a hanger, and on it dangled a slip of blue-and-white checked material. It was narrow, even for my skinny body, and looked unlike any of the dark pants or band T-shirts I'd packed in my bag.

"I don't think that's job interview appropriate," I objected, everything in me rebelling at touching what had to be a dress.

"Dresses are always appropriate for interviews," she declared and shook the hanger. "It's not a bomb. Take it and try it on."

When the door opened and her arm reached further into the room, I grabbed the hanger.

"Fine. But it won't fit," I said.

"It will fit. You have your mother's build," she said, her hand disappearing.

"Was this... hers?" I asked, but I knew the answer before she replied, "Yes."

I touched the cotton fabric of the skirt, then the stretchy gathered material across the bodice. Shoulder ties kept the dress on the hanger. I held it in front of me and saw it reached to just below my knees.

"Don't think, Galyna, just put it on," my aunt muttered, and the way her voice faded, I knew she'd walked away.

I held the material up, then brought it close enough to smell. It smelled like... fabric.

"Huh," I heard myself laugh, then laughed again. What had I expected? To be transported into more memories of my mom?

But that was exactly what I'd been thinking. This dress could have been the one from my memory. The pattern looked familiar, as did the feel of the fabric, but overall, it was less than dramatic. Maybe if I put it on, something would come back.

"Here goes nothing," I said to my reflection in the mirror and dropped the towel. Without looking, I slipped the dress off the hanger and over my head. I tugged it down, my less than average rack making barely an impression in the ruched bodice. The cotton had an unexpected flow, though, swirling around my knees as I twisted.

Looking up at my reflection, I had to admit I liked the juxtaposition of my spiky, dark hair and the feminine dress. It was an odd mix, and being odd was definitely my jam.

"An improvement," my aunt murmured from the now open door.

"Hey!" I complained, crossing my arms in front of me.

"*Gah*, the dress isn't see-through."

"Still. I thought you left."

"I did. To get these," she said and walked fully into the bathroom with her hand out. "Earrings."

"No thanks," I said, immediately raising my hands to the simple silver studs that I considered my signature and only piece of jewelry.

"But your mother loved these," she said, and I glanced into her palm at the pair of delicate silver earrings shaped and painted like pansies.

"They're nice, but they're not me," I insisted.

"Whether or not you wear them, they're yours," she insisted right back. "Take them."

"Why don't you keep them?" I said and clamped my earlobes until the posts of my earrings stabbed into my thumbs.

"They're not mine to keep."

"She was your sister."

"You're her daughter," she said, and now she looked stubborn.

She tsked in that way I recognized and grabbed one of my wrists. She pried my palm open and dropped the earrings into it.

I squeezed my hand closed over them as she bent to pick up my smelly clothes.

"I'll wash these, but you need to comb that messy hair. I'll get Vas to drive you to your interview. Where is it?"

I clutched the earrings in my hand and swallowed several times before I replied, "I don't need a ride."

"You'd rather take the bus?" she asked, looking at me like I was nuts.

"Yeah. I like the bus," I assured her.

She seemed like she had more questions about the interview, so I looked around distractedly before saying, "Do you have a comb I can use?"

While she disappeared into her bedroom, I grabbed my backpack and boots and snuck down the stairs at light speed. I liked being in the house, but something about it and my aunt's behavior felt... unsafe wasn't the word, but it was close. I wasn't in any physical danger, but I sensed my heart might be in the crushing zone.

I ran outside into the muggy August afternoon and hid behind the oak tree. I pulled my boots on, making sure I kept the tree between me and the house.

I didn't question running away without saying goodbye. I also thought my aunt would find out about what I intended to do and might set fire to my clothes or even the bag I'd left in the trailer. Or maybe the entire trailer.

I glanced back at the house, and when I was satisfied she wasn't looking out a window for me, I hurried to the sidewalk and down the street, jamming the earrings into the deep pocket of the dress.

Chapter Twenty-Four

Lena

"Hey there, Dead Flower Girl, you're back for more!" called Damon when the bus screeched to a stop.

Despite not wanting to be, I was glad to see him. I flipped my notebook closed as I got up from the bench. My attempt at a dead replacement dandelion was abysmal, anyway.

"Hi," I said and reached into my backpack for the fare.

"You look like you're trying to pick up a guy at a church picnic," he mused until his gaze fastened on my boots. "But aren't sure how to do it."

"As my bus driver, I don't think it's any of your business who I'm trying to pick up," I said, not hating the idea of having an almost friend. I wondered if he gamed and what JP and Brick would think of him.

"Those boots made it my business," he said with a serious wink. "My mama would have words with you about that 'fit or getting some on your first day in a new town."

144

I smiled. Why not go along with his assumption? It was an adequate cover for why I was going into town.

"Should I wait till my second day?" I asked as I sat in the seat I had before.

"In this town? You should wait forever," he said, gearing down the bus as it approached a red light. "Where are you heading?"

I didn't think I should say the library, since that seemed to be a "known place." So I said the only other place I knew. "Halloran's."

"Halloran's!" he laughed, his voice sounding like a hooting owl. "Halloran's? Girl, I told you. That place is a cemetery. You better have some voodoo in that dress because if you're looking to get laid, you'll need to raise the dead at Halloran's," he said, his expression telling me he was second-guessing my sanity. "What were you working on?"

I flipped open the notepad with one hand and tipped it down for him to see.

"Oh, another dandelion, looks like. You got any roses in that book? That's my mama's favorite."

As he pulled to a stop at the light, he turned in his seat and waved my sketchbook over. He flipped through the pages.

"You've got a lot of tiny roses in your tiny book," he said, checking that the light was still red. "You didn't finish this one. What's wrong with it?" he asked, holding it up.

"*Rosa* hybrid is just... meh," I said with a shrug. There was something dark about drawing the unwanted, and I liked dark.

He tore the page off and handed my notepad back.

"Since you don't like it and I do, I'mma add it to my collection," he said, satisfied. He faced forward and pulled out the other drawings I'd given him, then clipped the newest one to it. "You got a gift, girl. Hm-mm"

"Yeah," I said, putting the notepad into my backpack.

"Really," he insisted and turned back to look at me. "One day, if you try drawing something living? Like a person? I'll hire you. My mama's birthday's coming up, and she'd love a picture of me, even a tiny one on your tiny book."

"Whoa, I think I should start with a live flower first," I murmured, and he leaned his head back and boomed laughter at the ceiling of the bus.

The light changed, and he put the bus in gear, his tied-back dreadlocks swinging.

"Start with a live flower," he repeated as he rolled the bus through the intersection. "Are you saying I'd have to be dead before you tried to draw me for my mama?"

"Now that's a thought," I said, pretending to think the idea over.

"That's a thought," Damon echoed with a chuckle, turning the wide wheel to guide the bus into the middle lane.

I looked down the road, swallowing as block after block took me closer to the library. Maybe grabbing a drink at Halloran's to bolster my courage wasn't such a bad idea.

"How far away is Halloran's?" I asked.

"Sit back. You got a few minutes yet, Miss I-Draw-Dead-People," he replied, laughing again.

Damon spent the rest of the ride telling me a hundred jokes about "dating" any of the old guys at the bar, and I laughed along with him.

"Just remember," Damon said as the bus rumbled onto the main drag. "If you hear clinking, it's not the ice in the guy's drink. It's his dentures."

"Hah," I said with a mock laugh. "Good one."

"Halloran's coming up. *If* any guy can get it 'up' at Halloran's," he said, then boomed his dreadlock-shaking laugh.

"You crossed the 'get it up' joke limit ten jokes ago," I said.

"You know, I heard something about old guys and canes—" he said, looking when I stood up.

"Yeah. I get it. Old guys can't get erections," I said. I could only take so much. "Can you stop up there?"

"Ah, don't want anybody to see Miss Fancy Dress going into an old geezer's place, huh?" he guessed.

I scanned the storefronts as he pulled up to the stop, spotting a pawnshop.

"No, I need to go in there to find a charger for my aunt's old phone," I lied.

He pulled over at the next stop, this one being one of the few that had a bench. Probably to help the late-nighters after Halloran's closed down.

I clomped down the stairs, not used to feeling air swirl under the skirt. I honestly thought I'd spent my entire existence in pants.

"Just so you know, my last run is at 12:21," he said, shaking his head as he watched me fidget with the dress.

"That's a long shift," I commented, not liking the speculative look in his eye. It smelled suspiciously like concern.

"It's a double, and I take all the extra shifts I can get. I was joking about you staying out for the last bus. There's been a lot of strange folks in town lately, and—"

"Are they senior citizens? Cuz if they are, look out!" I joked and made an awkward gesture of I didn't know what with my hand. Geez, how could I hold my own with an FBI agent but not a small-town bus driver?

"Sketch Girl, that's just sad," he said, thankfully returning to his joking self. "Anyway, maybe I'll see you on your way back home."

"If you're lucky. If not, that means I *got* lucky," I said with a wink. Compared to his jokes, that one was pretty clever.

"All right, all right," Damon said, his mouth twisting as he considered my wit. "A tiny joke, but a joke. Just like your drawings."

"Tiny but skilled," I said, patting the notepad in the outside pocket of my backpack.

Damon angled his head at me, giving a nod of respect which

made something bloom in my chest. Then he looked me up and down, the twinkle back in his eyes.

"Be careful when you get to Halloran's," he said, chuckling. "Those vintage army boots might trigger some flashbacks."

He closed the door before I could think of a witty comeback and pulled the bus into the lazy traffic of Steeltown.

Chapter Twenty-Five

The pawnshop door made a noise that was closer to a cowbell than a door chime.

The place had the musty smell of other people's belongings and left-behind sadness. I didn't bother looking around, though. I just needed to wait until Damon's bus had turned the corner.

"Can I help you?" asked an old but eager voice from the back of the store.

There was an odd clicking sound, and Damon's comment about dentures came back to me. I shuddered and decided to put the drink off until after I'd accomplished my mission.

"Nope," I replied and leaned halfway out of the store.

I peeked around the door. Halloran's was to my right, but my actual destination—the library—was to the left. I watched until Damon's bus was out of sight, then headed out.

I tugged the dress down, still not liking the way the air moved underneath the skirt. I also didn't like how flimsy the shoulder ties were or the way it showed the world how flat my chest was. But it was my mom's, and, well... it felt a bit like a talisman I shouldn't go into battle without.

I reviewed my brilliant plan.

I didn't need to get into the library—I just had to get close enough to pick up their Wi-Fi signal. Technically, it should be easy. Realistically, in my dress and not-matching army boots, I would look odd as hell.

The library was a converted house set back from the street between two other heritage homes. One had become the Steeltown Museum and Archives, and the other looked like it was still the private residence I remembered it being.

Auntie Korinna's warning hummed in the back of my mind. I didn't like people telling me what I could and couldn't do, but I didn't overly mind her words. And technically, I *was* staying away from the library.

Anyway, the museum had a small **CLOSED** sign on their front door, which was a relief. Nobody would question me about what I was doing. Another bonus was the laurel bushes near the entrance and the overgrown hedge that was the boundary between the museum and the library. I could go up the sidewalk, pretending I didn't know the museum was closed, then slip behind the laurels to the hedge.

I looked around as I headed to the museum's walkway. I glimpsed the pawnshop manager behind me, standing on the sidewalk with a sad expression. Then he waved. I frowned but waved back, assuming that's what small-town people did. I didn't want to stand out any more than I already did. Thankfully, he went back into his shop.

A car pulled up to park on the other side of the street, and then two people got out. I slowed my pace, pretending to be interested in "seeing the sights" of Steeltown.

Oh, look! I made my body movements say. *A museum. How interesting. Maybe I'll visit.*

I added an excited bounce to my step as I walked up the concrete walkway, positive anybody watching me was buying my act. I followed the sidewalk to the stairs, but just before climbing them, I slipped into the space behind the laurel bush to the right.

For the record, laurel bushes are awful. When they grow untrained, they're okay. But they had trimmed and shaped these into a flat wall, making the branches sharp points that scraped as I shoved myself through them.

Prunus laurocerasus, I hate thee.

I couldn't back out now, though, otherwise the people on the street would think I was a deranged garden gnome in a dress. Definitely memorable. So I gritted my teeth and jammed myself harder into the tight weave of branches.

After climbing through the center where they were the thickest, the branches thinned where they met the cedar hedge of the library. *Thuja plicata* "virescens."

The Western Red Cedar of the pyramid variety. Compared to the laurel, their branches were positively soft. I crouched down near the trunk of the nearest tree.

I shrugged my backpack off and pulled out my laptop, then flipped the lid open. I tethered to my phone and found eight networks, one helpfully labeled **Steeltown Pub Lib**. There were also several generically named networks. Perfect. I opened my scanning software and let it get to work.

One thing I'd learned from my final college project, and had proven by my snooping, was that businesses set up protected networks but rarely spent the time properly securing them. They usually felt that securing the network the business would use was all that was needed and ignored their routers.

Wrong. Oh, so wrong.

JP, Brick, and I had written a spider program. You just type in a network name, and the program crawls the digital path and identifies all the computers on the network.

After storing the addresses of all the computers sending and receiving data, the spider program listens and records their secret digital handshakes. It then uses the handshakes to redirect the dataflow through to my other program, which collects it for me to decipher later.

The only downside is that it needs a significant amount of data to ensure it has enough data to capture something useful—in this case, names in Legs's email. From what I could see on the status bar, Thursday evening at the public library meant a slow Internet connection. The data flowed only one percentage point at a time.

In my crouched position, my knees ached. I didn't want to sit on the dress and get it dirty, so I leaned an arm against the cedar's trunk. The shift in weight sent a shower of dead cedar fronds all over me, then into my mouth when I grunted, "Crap."

As I spit out the dead scales of the branches, I lost my balance. The surrounding trees shook, and by the time I realized I wasn't causing it, an enormous hand wrapped around my arm.

It dragged me out of the hedge and threw me onto the grass. I sprawled inelegantly, grimacing as I pictured the grass leaving green skid marks on the only dress I owned.

I glared up at the yellow stucco of the library, the blue sky, and a mean but somehow sexy face scowling down at me.

"Who the hell are you?" he growled, brushing at the cedar detritus clinging to his sleeves. He tugged down his jacket, and I could tell by the cut that it was not cheap.

My radar pinged a warning.

"I'm... just... lost?" I stalled, not having a single believable reason for being in the hedge.

I looked back, relieved that my laptop and bag were still hidden somewhere in the cedar hedge. My gaze shot back to his face before he noticed I was looking for something. I rolled to my side to stand up, but he grabbed me again and jerked me to my feet.

"Oh, thanks," I said, trying to act like someone new in town who was definitely not trying to hack into the library's computer network. Wait, wouldn't someone new in town be angry at being pushed around? "Actually, take your hands off me!"

Instead of responding, he hitched my arm higher, which resulted in me swinging into his cologne zone. I had to say, he smelled great. But he looked deadly angry, and... well, just plain deadly.

If Tommy looked like Christian Bale as Batman, this guy looked like a Slavic, early-days Marlon Brando, if you can follow that.

"You say you're lost, but you were in the trees," he mumbled, jutting his jaw. "What are you, a landscaper? Grooming the hedge?"

"That would be an arborist, and—"

A thought cut my words off. He had the slightest accent that reminded me of my dad. And those droopy eyelids. Something about them rang a bell of doom. I broke out in sweat under the ruching of the dress.

"A *what?*" he demanded, his expression making it clear he was trying to work out whether arborist was an insult.

"Nothing," I murmured, flexing my arm to see if he'd let me go. He didn't.

Those heavy eyes stared at me, and I caught a flare of his nostrils and a twitch at the corner of his mouth. His emotional train was pulling away from Annoyed Station and heading to Pissed-Off Town.

"Do you know who I am?" he gritted and gave me a little shake to emphasize the seriousness of the question before shoving me away.

I stumbled backward against the stucco wall of the library. He brushed down his jacket again, then tugged on the shirt underneath. The collar jerked down, and I noticed a tattoo that wrapped around his neck. That's when the pieces clicked into place.

"You're Ukrainian," I blurted, nodding pointedly to the tattoo. But he was more than just Ukrainian.

He ugly-smiled and opened his collar to unveil the markings that encircled his neck. They resembled the patterns on a traditional vyshyvanka shirt.

I'd learned about the symbols used in embroidery as a kid and how they represented values that mattered to Ukrainian people. Stars, poppies, and crosses all represented warding off evil. Those had been inked around this guy's neck but had been needled upside down, as if he was inviting evil in. A little cliché, but I doubted he saw it that way. Even the grapes, the symbol for family happiness, were upside down.

"I can tell you think little of your family," I said, pointing to the cluster.

"You know who my family is?" he asked, but his eyes said he already knew the answer.

What a smug ass, but he was right. I knew exactly who this had to be and therefore who his family was.

"The Olynyks. You're Marko Olynyk," I said, my feet inching me closer to him but only because it brought me closer to the front of the library. Closer to where people were, hopefully. It was way too secluded back here.

When Marko stepped closer to me, though, a memory flooded back, making me light-headed.

Little-kid me lying on top of a crushed carton of eggs. Little-kid Marko standing over me, at least five years older but just as mean looking.

"Galyna Kozek," he'd sneered, then spit at the growing puddle of raw egg under me. A little mist of it hit my face. "More like Galyna Ooze-ek."

It had been the first and last time my dad had let me run an errand on my own to the store, which was only a few blocks away from our apartment. Only one block away from where I cowered now.

"That's right," present-day Marko said, grasping my wrist to shove me toward the front of the building. "I thought you were a rat on the camera." He pointed up at a dated but apparently functional security camera. "Only to find out I know you as well. You're Galyna Kozek. Now why would little Galyna Kozek come back after all these years?"

My upper lip broke out in sweat, and I swiped at it.

He knew *me*? Well, remembered me. How was that possible?

Why would he remember a kid he bullied once when he'd probably bullied every kid in town every day of his life?

I tried to look calm, but I wasn't sure that I was pulling it off.

"Well, as interesting as that question is," I muttered, hating how far away the front of the library still was but refusing to hurry. I was scared, but I was damned if I'd let him know it. "I should get going. I'm in town for a job interview, so—"

"Really?" he mocked, his thinned lips curving down into a leer of contempt. "I know everything that goes on in this town, and I don't know anybody looking for someone like you."

"Someone like me?" I said, mildly offended. "How would you know anything about me?"

"You're Ilya Kozek's daughter. Daughter of my father's hitman. *And* you're a killer. The killer of a hitman," he said and laughed.

The words made little sense to me. Was it some kind of joke that I wasn't getting? Normally I was good at getting somebody's terrible puns and could fake laugh along. This time, though, it went right over my head.

"A hitman's daughter, yes. But I handle network security. On computers," I clarified as his words still spun around in my head like angry bees trying to get into the hive.

"Yeah. Right," he muttered. "Don't play dumb. You're not good at it. I'll refresh your memory. I helped you get out of Steeltown when you were, oh, so high."

He held his hand out, palm down at the level of his waist, then bent forward to emphasize his next words.

"Right after you killed your father," he said.

Chapter Twenty-Six

Lena

I was ten. No, ten and a little bit, holding my dad's hand as we crossed the street in Steeltown. I looked down to see cobblestones, then the tracks of the old cable car that hadn't run in decades.

I remember being surprised the job was walking distance from our apartment, and judging by the way my dad gripped my hand, he was stressed about this whole thing.

My Star Wars backpack bounced on my back, and in my other hand was the white handle of the saxophone case, weighted with the weapon my father had methodically taught me to fire, clean, and care for like the pet I wasn't allowed to have.

If my dad was nervous, I was excited. This was what the years of target practice had prepared me for. It was going to be easy, he said. A big man in a green hat, he said. Even easier than shooting a can off a log, he said.

"Who is he?" I'd asked the day before, on the bus back from Copper Ridge.

"You never get a name. You only get a description and a place."

We crossed the street and walked down the sidewalk. My dad's steps were purposeful. Mine skipped and scurried to keep up.

"Where are we going? Is this where the green-hat man lives?" I asked.

"You never get that close to a mark," he replied, gripping my hand tighter. "Here we are."

He guided me into a doorway and yanked the glass door open. It was one of those skinny doors in between businesses. The secret kind like ours around the corner and down the street. The kind that led to apartments on the other floors, where people lived tiny lives that nobody knew about.

My dad was tense, which was different from his usual stillness.

"What's wrong?" I asked.

Bad idea. My dad wasn't somebody who wanted to have feelings, let alone talk about them. But he'd always said to not let feelings interfere with work, and I thought maybe he was doing that.

"Nothing's the matter. Just remember what I taught you," he ordered.

We climbed up the dark stairs, our footsteps hissing against worn linoleum. At the top, he led me toward the window that faced the street.

"Just get close enough to see the bus bench, but stay out of sight," he said, waving me up to the window. He shrugged one shoulder and pulled at his jacket. I knew he'd brought his own gun, but he'd told me it was just for backup.

I did as he told me, feeling my way along the wall until I could see outside. I only got close enough that I could see our favorite ice cream shop. There weren't many people outside, seeing as how it was a weekday morning.

"I see it. I see the bench," I said, then crouched down to flip open the closures on the saxophone case before he told me to.

Inside was my AK pistol. The pieces of it fit into perfectly shaped, velvet inserts.

The next moments ticked by like flash cards.

Clicking the gun together. Finding a comfortable pose against the wall. My dad sighting through the gun over my shoulder.

"See him?" Dad murmured just as green-hat man strolled into my sights.

Everything shut down in my brain except for that green hat. Then I followed the rules. Wait for him to stop. Breathe out, long in-breath, out again. Longer in-breath—

"Finger on the trigger?" he asked, and I slid my finger down from the barrel to curl around the trigger.

"Yes," I whispered on my out-breath, then stopped breathing altogether like he'd taught me.

I squeezed, and there was a blast so loud, it loosened all my muscles and jerked my head away from the gunsight.

I dropped to the floor, a heavier weight on top of me.

Something hot poured onto my neck, and I shifted, pushing at the weight until it rolled.

It was my father, a light spray of red on his cheek and his gray-blue eyes staring, his pupils big, black dots.

Then a wave of cologne surrounded me, and I blinked—

—and saw the dull-black eyes of Marko close enough to my face that I thought his long lashes might brush against me.

My heart drummed inside my chest, and I breathed as shallowly as I could.

"That's right, I saved your skinny ass. My father would've killed you without blinking if he knew you'd shot his number-one man," Marko hissed, and a sliver of my mind—the sliver that wasn't completely freaking out—registered the sour smell of his breath in direct opposition to the sexy cologne.

"Saved my ass?" I questioned, trying to hide my shaking hands in the dress's skirt. Amazingly, I found two deep pockets. I jammed my jittering fingers out of sight. "How did you do that... exactly?"

"I saw you two go into the building and followed you. I got there just in time to see you push your father's body off."

My radar pinged.

"You're saying I shot my father? On purpose?" I asked, scrunching my face into genuine curiosity. When he rolled his eyes, I took more steps toward the safety of the front of the library.

"How the hell should I know? I only dealt with the problem you created," he grunted. "Which means you owe me."

The ping was louder this time. He was lying.

"Owe you for what?" I asked, wanting him to talk long enough to let me figure out what the truth might be.

"I took you to your aunt's house and told her to hide you. Guess what she said? That she wanted nothing to do with you."

Well, that part sounded plausible.

I kept my expression bland as my brain crawled back into the memory, looking for more details.

I remember being shoved toward my gun case, and I guess disassembling it? Someone moved behind me, then jerked me to my feet. I was barely able to grab the saxophone case.

I stumbled down that stairwell as someone guided me with a grip on my backpack. I remember being scared, not just by being shoved down the stairs by a bully, but of what we'd left behind.

My dad. Lying on the floor and eyes glazing over. But now it made sense why I'd erased most of those ten years from my memory.

A heaviness came over me at the thought that I'd killed my dad. It hadn't been intentional, no matter what Marko suggested. My gun must have misfired, although shouldn't that bullet have hit me?

Another memory pushed into my mind. The smell of leather and gunpowder and a hand grabbing my cheeks and squeezing.

"Say nothing," a voice had warned that belonged to the man looking down at me now, the words merging into whatever he was saying to me right at that moment.

"...she thought sending you away was a good idea. She was probably right," he murmured. "Coming back here, though. That was a mistake."

His hand shot out, and he cupped my jaw and neck, pulling me closer to that sweetly sour breath.

"I think you're right," I mumbled, and my stomach cringed at the dead look in his eyes.

His thumb was rough, and it rubbed at the part of my jaw under my ear. The look in his eyes changed, and I pushed against his chest with both hands.

"Very right, so I'll just be going—" I grunted, the words squeezed off when he tightened the hold he had on my neck.

His expression twisted into something ugly, and my gut twisted right along with it.

"Marko!" shouted a voice.

It loosened his hand, which let my feet hit the ground. My legs wanted to crumple in relief, but I forced them to step back. I ended up against the hedge in the corner, the front of the library to my right.

While I kept an eye on Marko, a large, ugly man approached. I spared him a glance to see him staring at me like I was a bug.

"Jesus Christ, Marko, quit screwing around," he said, his jowls bouncing as he spoke.

Marko's face returned to its normal smugness, like a werewolf shrinking back into its semi-human self.

"I'm not screwing around," Marko denied, straightening his jacket, and strode past the big man. "Just dealing with a pest who showed up on security."

"Who is she?"

"Nobody important who's leaving town," Marko said, giving me one last evil look. "Isn't that right?"

"Absolutely," I agreed, my voice shaky.

Marko punched the man in the shoulder and walked past him.

"It's a big day, Stefano. It sounds like Dad's ready to announce," he said.

"He's asked for you, so—" The last of the giant's words disappeared as they walked up the steps and into the library.

I let out a breath and found myself plopped on the ground. My legs had finally given out.

Chapter Twenty-Seven

Lena

In a scientific first, my brain had split in two.

The practical half took over my body. I brushed myself off and checked for grass stains, then marched down the library path to the street. Then it doubled me back to the museum hedge to retrieve my computer. A quick grab and I was back on the museum's sidewalk. Hopefully Marko was too occupied to be watching the security camera.

The other part of my brain was freaking out.

Anybody else would do exactly what I told Marko I would. Go back to my aunt's, grab my stuff, and get the hell out of Steeltown. Since I was on the same coast as JP and Brick, either of them would offer me an off-the-grid couch where I could plan the rest of my life, which would now happen on the run from the FBI.

See why I was freaking out?

But freaking out wasn't me, so I gave myself two minutes to get my crap together before I deployed Plan B.

Plan B was simple. Down about twelve drinks, then pick up a random guy for a hookup.

Don't judge me. I'd just found out that, in some kind of weird fluke, I'd killed my father. Also, I probably didn't have enough information on my laptop to get the FBI off my back, and I just knew my aunt would find out everything and torch my belongings. See? I'd earned an evening of oblivion.

I hitched the backpack over my shoulder. My practical brain tried to channel that empty-headed tourist persona for the benefit of anyone looking at a rumpled girl in a sundress who was picking cedar fronds out of her hair. The freaking-out part of my brain could already taste the shot of Fireball I was itching to down.

"Were you up at the library?" asked a creaky old voice from the doorway of thc pawnshop.

"The museum. But it's closed," I replied, sounding like a robot.

"Right, the museum. They open at nine tomorrow. There's nothing good for you at the library," he said and hitched his mouth to the side as he stared, first at my face, then took in my whole appearance.

"Nothing good," I echoed, and he jutted his chin out. Compared to Marko, his appreciative look at my scratched legs was a welcome change.

"Take care, now," he said and backed into the pawnshop like a hermit crab into his shell. He turned the lock with a *thunk* and disappeared.

Geez, I was in an old Western movie right before the villains rode into town.

Wait, did that mean I was the villain?

I jogged across the street to Halloran's Bar, expanding the idea of a dozen shots to polishing off the bottle.

A couple of facts materialized about this place as if they'd always been in my memory and just needed the thick, aged lettering above the plate-glass window to activate them.

Halloran's was a dive bar my dad had used like an office—probably because we lived right above it. Short commute.

From the outside looking in, the business had an Irish pub look to it. The outside had about a thousand coats of dark green paint, while the inside was narrow and dark with a wall of booze behind the bar on the right and a few chairs and tables scattered along the left.

Walking through the front door was the closest thing to time travel that I'd ever experienced.

The musty Eau d'Attic smell, complete with microscopic asbestos particles swirling in the air, surrounded me in the lung-killing cocoon of childhood memories. The flooring was the same checkerboard with the smear of decades of dirty feet still making an endearing trail from the front door to the back where the bathrooms were.

The decorations, though, warmed my heart. It might have looked like an Irish pub, but it was in homage to *The Shining*—exactly how it flashed into my memory bank.

Back when I was a kid, a woman named Lucy owned the place and worked at the bar. Round-faced and mean, she tolerated me because I was Ilya Kozek's daughter. When she saw I could keep quiet and not mess around, she even let me sample her latest drink concoctions in tiny shot glasses. Was that illegal? Absolutely. But as a hitman's daughter, I was already pretty fringe.

I squinted through the dim light to the bathroom doors at the back. The horror show was still there.

Lucy had rigged the restroom doors to look like elevator doors with a plexiglass case on the front into which fake blood would cascade every few minutes, draining from a tube back to the top. Classic scene from *The Shining*. The walls also had a ton of framed photos just like in the movie, and the drink specials always had some connection with it.

Hence, the Danny-tini that was being promoted on a whiteboard on the wall. Named for the psychic kid in the story, a hand-drawn martini glass held an eyeball on a toothpick. It made me smile.

Now, should a ten-year-old have watched that movie? No. I remembered my dad telling me, though, that it was the perfect exercise in managing fear.

I looked to the left where a few old men sat, guarding pint glasses.

The table where my dad did "business" was empty, and for once I wished his corpse would show up. The idea of having a few drinks with my dad and getting his advice on the current situation seemed like a nice one.

"Bathrooms are for patrons only," said the red-haired woman behind the bar. She had pink and blue plastic bracelets on one wrist and a purple scrunchy holding her ponytail together. Not Lucy but someone I could see Lucy approving of. "If you're drinking, I'll need some ID."

I dug out my driver's license and held it out for her to inspect.

"New York. Wow. Why are you in this dump?" asked the woman. Angela, according to her name tag. Then she tilted her head and smirked at me. "I meant Halloran's, but I guess I could mean Steeltown too."

"Uh... I need a drink to answer your first question. A shot of Fireball. And I'm in town for a job interview, to answer the second," I replied, going with the lie out of habit.

I looked at the worn, blood-red stool. It had flecks of glitter and was the prettiest thing I remembered from my childhood. I eased onto it and parked my feet on the supports. I was no longer the little kid who'd had to reach up to the bar to climb up onto the slippery seat and wait for my dad to conduct his business. No, I was the woman whose hands shook as she rested them on the counter.

"Job interview? You mean at the bank?" Angela asked, grabbing a full bottle of Fireball off the glass shelf and pouring a shot.

"Yeah," I lied, glad she was making it easy for me. "At the bank."

I downed the harsh liquid and smiled as she poured me a second one. I sipped at it, enjoying the way it scraped down my throat. It was almost as good as a slap across the face.

"You must be pretty connected to things around Steeltown if you know about it," I said, happy for the distraction of inane conversation. I took a second sip, which turned into downing the shot. I nodded for a third one as I set the glass down on the counter.

She eyed me, then poured another shot. "Are you celebrating or something?"

"I don't know yet," I replied. I took her wary expression to heart and slowed down on the drinking. "Seriously, though. Does news like that get around town so easily?"

"Naw, one of the trustees is a regular," she answered and jerked her head toward an old man sitting at a table. "Although I don't think he's much of a trustee." She put air quotes around the word. "He's always blabbing about who got turned down for a loan or who's behind on their mortgage. Stuff he probably shouldn't be blabbing about."

Angela rolled her eyes. But I bet she loved getting all the inside information. I'd even bet she fed the old guy drinks to keep him talking. It's what I would have done.

I dug my wallet out of my backpack and pulled out a twenty. When I laid it on the counter, she put the bottle of Fireball on top of it.

"That'll get you two more shots," she said, then leaned against the bar and looked me over. "So, you're new to Steeltown," she said.

"Newish," I agreed, the Fireball loosening me up.

Angela leaned closer as if to tell me a secret. "You didn't come in here looking to get laid, did ya? Cuz the pickings are slim," she murmured through clenched teeth and shook a thumb toward the men by the wall.

I looked back at the decrepit trustee and the two other guys who shared a table near the back. They looked well into their nineties. Damon hadn't been kidding.

"If I was, I'd need another bottle of Fireball," I replied, and she brayed a sharp laugh.

"No kidding," she agreed. "So you want a job at the bank, do you, Miss Newish? You must know a lot about computers, then."

She folded her arms on the bar as if settling in for my answer.

I downed the shot and poured another.

Now that some of my memories had loosened, something my father had drilled into me came back—the danger of talking. You never talk. Not about work or friends or life. Not to a friend, not to yourself, not even in your sleep. Keeping your mouth shut had a currency.

But knowledge was a currency, too, an exchange of information. Maybe Angela had access to more than bank gossip. I still needed to find something to get Tommy off my back, and it needed to be something more than Marko's bad breath or the short amount of data I'd skimmed on my laptop.

Or how you're to blame for your dad's death, a voice in my mind taunted me. I sipped some more Fireball.

I thought about all the things I could tell her, sifting through them like change in my pocket.

"I know a bit. Network security and stuff like that," I offered, having no idea what kind of computer skills the job needed.

She nodded, though, pulling her head back in respect. Whatever I knew about computers, it was more than she did.

"Do you run this place?" I asked, wondering what happened to Lucy. I doubted Angela owned it, but the compliment that she could cost me nothing.

"Like I want that headache. No. Floyd does. Owner-operator. He's in the back, making sure we got enough cheap bourbon for our regulars," she answered, then hooked her thumb toward the geezers. "All three of 'em."

I laughed, and she smiled. I was getting somewhere. I wondered how much she knew about Legs and whatever was going on in town. Marko had said something about an announcement. Maybe she'd heard something.

The back door swung open with a bang, and a big man in a grimy apron stumbled out, carrying a box.

"Here's all the bourbon we got," he announced, lifting the gate to the bar with the back of one arm.

"Like we'll need much," she murmured and winked at me.

And just like that, I had another friend. Dammit, I was going soft.

"I've got my Fireball. I'm good," I said, pouring my last shot. Eyeing it, I wondered if I could make it last.

"We might have to order a few more, the way you're going through that one," she said and tugged the twenty out from under the bottle.

"No, I think I'm done for now," I said, enjoying the warm wave of the alcohol shimmy over me from my head to my toes.

When a man walked out from the bathroom at the back, I knew I was most of the way to being drunk. He looked at least thirty years younger than anyone in the place.

I sipped at my last Fireball as I examined his clean-cut yet worn look. He looked like a narc, but also a geek, and also a soft-in-the-middle dude who maybe spent too much time in dive bars. Those were the loudest pings on my radar, but in my rapidly deepening Fireball euphoria, I couldn't sort out which ones were dangerous. All I could focus on was his smooth skin. He was the least-wrinkled dude in the place.

"Who's that guy?" I asked Angela, only it came out, "Hoo-zagguh?"

Uh-oh.

I'd rounded the corner on Fireball euphoria and was wading into booze stupor.

I tried to focus on Angela's lips as she replied. Thank God they moved in slow motion. Or maybe I was moving in slow motion. Either way, they said, "Oh-thaz-kwin."

What... did that even mean? And why did I care? I nodded knowingly at her, and she made a weird face that looked apologetic.

"Tie-muh gemmee-zum," I slurred and winked at her.

"Whatever you say, Fireball Queen," she replied and slid a glass of water in front of me. "Maybe sip this before you make any big moves."

Since the bar had suddenly tilted at an angle, I thought she might have a point.

Chapter Twenty-Eight

Quinn

"Another one?" Floyd asked as he waved Quinn's empty glass at him.

Quinn slid onto the padded barstool and eyed the bartender. Floyd was a professional. Waiting until Quinn got back from the john before coaxing him into another drink was smart business.

"Uh, I guess," Quinn said. The Danny-Whatever-It-Was-Called was a disgusting drink, but it had a base of gin and was cheap, and those were his only rules about drinking. "What's in it again? Besides the gin?"

"Let's see, apple cider, apple brandy... Shit," Floyd muttered, eyeballing the premixed pitcher of the murky concoction. "Angela, what's in this Danny-tini again?"

His words stopped Angela in midlaugh, and she turned to answer.

"One part apple juice, apple brandy, apple cider, sour apple liqueur, and two parts gin," Angela answered, leaning back against the bar and fluttering her eyelashes at Quinn.

At the opposite end of the bar, hidden behind Angela until this moment, sat someone new. A woman. Or... maybe a girl? She looked young, which was confirmed by the orange bottle of Fireball whisky in front of her. In his experience, Fireball was the drink of choice for college kids.

The woman-girl's dark eyes drilled into him like he'd done something wrong and she was about to give him hell for it. Then Floyd turned back to him, blocking both women from sight.

"There you go," Floyd said with a shrug. "A crap-ton of apple junk and some gin."

"Any chance I can get another one on the house?" he asked.

"No. One free drink for new tenants, one free drink cuz you're a cop, and *that* one," he said, gesturing to the glass he'd just put in the washer unit, "was your last free Bartender's Choice drink so I could put a dent in that apple-junk mix. Jesus, you're the only guy comes in here with a decent-paying job, and you're trying to bankrupt me!"

Floyd smirked, a thick toothpick with a green tassel tucked in the corner of his mouth.

Quinn couldn't argue. Floyd had been pretty liberal with the booze and chatter since he'd walked in the door. He could even see the cozy stool becoming a second home after the worn couch upstairs.

"Then just give me a double shot of gin," Quinn said. "I'll let your regulars help you polish off your drink special."

Floyd looked at him, then at the old geezers around the room nursing glasses of cheap draft.

"Heh!" Floyd barked. "Yeah, right." His loud laugh drew a few nervous glances from the old-timers.

Floyd slammed a glass with two ounces of gin in front of him, then folded his arms and looked studious.

"Not that I give a damn, but you don't have a lot of belongings with you," Floyd said, his mouth working that toothpick.

"Nope."

"I never met a guy had a cat," Floyd commented, stroking his stubby goatee.

Quinn lifted the glass at him, then sipped half of it.

"Well, now you have," he said.

"You said that you asked to be transferred here. To Steeltown. Have you seen much of the town yet?" Floyd asked.

"Just the main drag and the upper street. Pete's Lounge looked interesting," he said, remembering his walk around the block as he did reconnaissance on the other drinking establishments.

Floyd's expression screwed into a disgusted frown.

"That's one of Olynyk's places. Avoid it unless you're a vigilante kind of cop. You show up regularly over there, they're gonna lean on you. Like your boss," Floyd murmured, then looked uncomfortable. "That's off the record, by the way."

"No problem. Off the record is kind of my motto," Quinn assured him, thinking of the two men he'd run into earlier. They definitely believed they had the chief's ear.

"Anyway, I'm an 'enjoy a drink in a quiet place' kind of cop," Quinn replied. "Especially when they're free."

"Well, don't get used to the discounts," Floyd grunted.

"I'm paying for this one," he complained, then knocked the rest of the gin back before tapping the glass with two fingers, ordering another double. "And the next."

Being a cop sometimes made life easier with people like Floyd. People who appreciated hard work and finishing a day with a glass of something stronger than coffee. Did it mean Quinn would have to keep an unofficial eye out for his bar even though he wasn't a beat cop and his new partner would bitch about it? Probably.

But looking around the room, he couldn't imagine the old grandads could knock over a chair, let alone another patron. There wouldn't be any trouble unless that asshole in a suit followed him in here to make trouble.

"Damn right you are," Floyd groused but gave what Quinn thought was a version of a smile.

After pouring him another, Floyd grabbed a cloth and reached for a clean glass as it inched out of the washer.

As the bartender moved, Quinn caught sight of the woman at the other end of the bar again. She was still staring at him. When he frowned, she drank what looked to be water and set the glass beside the orange whisky bottle, not breaking eye contact.

"Jesus," he muttered, looking down into his fresh drink.

"Yes, my son?" Floyd intoned with a chuckle, then straightened as he glanced down at Quinn's glass. "Don't give me that bullshit line about finding a bug in your drink."

"Who's the woman in the dress over there?" he asked, not looking up. "Is she even legal to be in here?"

Floyd glanced back, continuing to dry the glass in his hand.

"No idea. We check everybody, though. Even those old bastards. If she's drinking, she's legal," he replied. He flashed her a quick second glance, then laughed at him. "Jesus is right. She's drilling you with a look. Better watch out."

"Watch out for what?" Quinn asked, downing the gin, then tapping the glass on the counter again.

"She's got that desperate look. And she's looking at you, so—" Floyd grinned, filling Quinn's glass with another healthy pour of gin.

"So what?"

"She's probably looking to score. If she's clean, you should go for it. New guy in a new town, new job.... You could have yourself a celebration."

"*This* is my celebration," he said, holding up his glass and taking a good drink.

He hadn't gotten laid in ages. He also hadn't started a new job in ages. Or moved to a new town since moving away from home after high school. He should probably go upstairs to his personal bottle of gin and unpack his last box of DVDs, but something about the quiet bar and the early evening light had a lazy feel to it.

"Uh-oh, incoming," Floyd mumbled and shifted away like any good wingman would.

Only Quinn didn't want a wingman.

He watched the girl round the far corner of the bar. He sat up straighter, but she weaved her way to one of the old guys. An ancient guy. But the full view of her as she walked from behind the bar distracted him.

Her short dark hair and heavy boots were at odds with the crisp lines of the summery dress. The ragged backpack she dragged had seen better days, and as she lugged it onto her shoulder, he recognized a button pinned to the back.

"Amiright?" she yelled at the old man with a hearty chuckle and slapped his thin arm. He raised his almost-empty beer glass to her with a murky smile, and she turned to walk to Quinn on steadier legs, making the skin behind his ears sweat.

As she got closer, he saw he was wrong about her age. It was the choice of whisky and enormous eyes that made her seem young. His years on the force had made him pretty good at guessing age. Now, looking at the lines around her eyes and near her mouth, he would peg her being at least twenty-five.

"Hey," the woman murmured, pulling out the stool beside him and sliding onto it. She jammed the blue-and-white checked skirt modestly between her knees, exposing skinny kneecaps. It had him second-guessing her age.

The way she said the one word—"Hey"'—caught him off guard as well. It had a deep, velvety quality to it completely at odds with her appearance. It made it impossible for him not to reply "Hey" back to her.

Quinn glanced at Floyd, but he only lifted his hands with raised eyebrows and pivoted to talk to Angela.

"You look weird," she commented in that satiny husk, not a single word sounding buzzed. She leaned forward to lock her eyes onto his buttoned-down collar, propping her head on her hand in a companionable way that women never did with him. "How come?"

Despite Floyd's advice, he didn't want to get mixed up with a woman. He'd tried that once, and it had ended in arguments about his job, his drinking, and his cat. He could handle the first two, but nobody bad-talked Solo. He'd broken up with her, and she'd laughed all the way to the door.

Now, looking this woman over, he imagined she'd be even more critical of a guy with a cat. Talking to her would just encourage her. But the longer she looked at him, some mysterious intent glowing in her eyes, the more he kind of wanted to encourage her.

She just called you weird, his gin-soaked brain reminded him as it fumbled for a witty put-down. *That's a red flag.*

She, however, kept talking.

"Are you a narc? You look goofy, like a narc," she said, adjusting herself on her elbow and now squinting at him.

"I'm not a narc," he answered, both offended and impressed with her guess. He thought he gave off a dad vibe. "Why do you want to know? Are you a drug dealer?"

The corner of her mouth deepened in a hint of humor or scorn. The dim lighting at the back of the bar made it difficult to tell which. Then her mouth blossomed into a full, down-at-the-corners type of smile that, he had to admit, surprised him. It made those lines around her eyes crinkle, and it felt like he'd scored a point in some secret game.

"Not a drug dealer," she promised, the words sliding through that funny smile with a hint of a slur.

"What do you do, then?" he asked, annoyed that he wanted to know.

"I'm a bank robber," she confessed huskily, her smile disappearing.

"Oh, yeah?" he asked.

She twisted on the stool, those skinny knees facing him, and readjusted the way her cheek rested in her hand yet again.

"When somebody's doing bad things to other people, I hack into their bank account, and voilá! Financial justice," she said, the fingers she held against her cheek rippling when she said voilá.

"Financial justice... how?" he asked.

"It's complicated, but recently I set a trap to make it look like they committed a felony. I worked at a bank, so it was easy to do," she explained. Then frowned at him. "Don't worry, it's nothing they don't deserve."

He held back a laugh. There was no way this... kid even worked in a bank, let alone could alter algorithms, but he had to admit—he was entertained. And maybe a little drunk. Or more than a little. But he was convinced she was, too, which balanced out this whole strange conversation.

"I don't know if that's *exactly* robbery," he murmured, distracted when that smile crinkled her eyes again.

"Nope," she agreed, popping the *p* and giving him a full dose of her upside-down smile. "But it's definitely a felony."

"True," he agreed, curious as her eyes darted around the bar. He looked around, too, but nothing had changed in the last few seconds. "Are you expecting someone?"

"Not exactly," she replied, her eyes settling back on him. She looked him over again, and it seemed to calm her down. Her next statement caught him off guard.

"I can tell you're a *Star Wars* fan."

"You... what?" he asked, astonished and scrambling to hide it. He wasn't just a fan—he was a massive fan. Not the nutjob kind who dressed up as a Sith Lord and slept overnight on a sidewalk for a premiere. Okay, he'd toyed with the idea, but he hadn't acted on it. But how could she know?

"Calm down. I didn't hack your computer or anything. Everyone's a *Star Wars* fan to some extent," she said and kicked at the backpack she'd put on the floor, the button with the Jedi symbol glinting.

"I noticed that," he said.

"Of course you did," she said smugly. "But I figured you might be more of a fan than one of those guys," she continued, hiking her thumb toward the old-timers on the other side of the bar.

"Your clothes don't make *you* look like a fan," he said, eyeing her dress. It looked a little like what Dorothy wore in *The Wizard of Oz*.

"Oh, believe me. I am," she assured him, her face slackening into a serious expression.

"I think you'll have to prove it," he said, draining the last of his gin.

Floyd stole over and refilled it. The second he set it back down, the woman snaked out a hand and grabbed it, downed half of it, then replaced it in front of him.

She wiped an arm across her mouth and jutted her chin out.

"Try me," she invited, squaring herself to face him and resting her fists on her thighs. Something about the way she sat with her legs open made him nervous.

"Um, okay," he said, clearing his throat. He channeled all his attention into scanning for a question. "What is the battle armor used by Boba Fett?"

"Oh, please, it's Mandalorian. Everybody with a TV knows that. Give me a hard one," she challenged, leaning forward, fists splayed open so her fingers caged those skinny knees.

He looked up at her eyes, so dark they almost looked all pupil. A golden ray of sun lit the wavy lines of her irises. They glittered like shards of hematite, as if she were a demonic foundling out to transfix him.

Whoa, where had that thought come from? And why was it so... enticing?

Okay, she wants a question? She's getting one.

He turned to face her, careful not to let his knees touch hers.

"What was the name of Yoda's home?" he demanded.

"Dagobah," she shot back.

"Who built C-3PO?"

"Anakin."

"What's the name of the animal that lives in the garbage compactor of the Death Star?"

"Which one?"

"Which animal?" he asked, triumphant.

"No, which Death Star?"

Dammit.

"The original," he replied.

"Dianoga," she answered, straightening her arms and taking a deep breath as she leaned back. "Good question, though."

Chapter Twenty-Nine

Quinn

He wasn't entirely sure when he decided he'd let her drag his drunk self out the door.

It might have been when she argued the ridiculous position that Ewoks were cannibals, or that, while labeled whisky, Fireball Cinnamon Whisky cannot legally be called whisky. Since he was a gin drinker, he had no fixed opinion about that, but it made him smile to hear her passionate argument.

It might have been a strange fascination with the way she drank his last gin, her wrist flicking the glass back in a determined movement. More likely, it was just the gin.

"I'll run you a tab," Floyd promised, giving his booming "Heh-heh" laugh as the woman pried him away from the bar.

"All right, big guy," she told him, letting him lean on her. Her body had a wiry strength. "I'll help you upstairs, but don't think you're getting into my panties."

Her voice echoed all around, and he was pretty sure some oldies still drinking beer cackled as he stumble-walked beside her.

He made it outside the bar, then did a sharp turn to the narrow door that marked the entrance to the apartments.

"Where are you going?" she asked, confusing him by tugging him away from his own door.

"To my place."

"You... live *here*?" she asked, all humor drained from her expression.

"I do. Just moved in today. I'm not *so* drunk I don't remember where my apartment is," he said, proud that the words didn't slur too much.

He dug into his front pocket, trying to remember where his keys were. It threw him off-balance, and he lunged at the door, bracing himself against the frame. A moony face loomed blearily in the glass, and he got ready to challenge the stranger before he realized it was his own reflection.

Damn, he *did* look like a narc. A sad, drunk narc hanging out with a woman who was proving she could hold her liquor better than he could.

The woman's reflection joined his, and then he felt something rummage in his pockets.

"Hey," he complained. "No groping on a first date."

"Just... don't talk, okay?" she muttered, tense all of a sudden.

Was she put off by where he lived? He'd have thought living over a bar would be a plus in her book.

Once inside, he grasped at the railings, trying to haul himself up the stairs. After stumbling on the first two, he felt her bony hands pushing between his shoulder blades.

Jesus, she was strong. He could almost let go of the railings and let her propel him up the stairs on her own. He didn't know why, but the thought of her strength connected straight to his groin, and if she wanted to have sex, he would definitely oblige her.

He stumbled onto the second-floor landing and grabbed the knob on the post to swing himself toward his door.

"I'm right there," he said, pointing at his doorknob and stumbling toward it. He expected her to be right behind him, but she wasn't. When he looked back, he saw her at the top of the stairs, flipping his keys around on the keyring as she stared at the other door.

"Hello-ooo," he called, waving. "I'm over here."

She looked down at his keys, then shuffled her big black boots over to where he stood.

"Whoever owns that place doesn't live there, so nobody will hear whatever we get up to," he promised, leaning against the doorjamb.

She reached past him and unlocked his door.

"Good," she muttered and pressed her lips together as she grabbed his sleeve and shoved him into the apartment.

She handed him his keys, then slammed the door shut behind her. She hooked her thumbs under the straps of the backpack on her shoulders and stared at him with a hard look, as if deciding whether she would stay.

He should want her to go, shouldn't he? Tell her thank you. It was nice. See you around?

"Kitchen and living room," he said instead, arms out as he circled in one spot. He staggered when he became instantly dizzy.

He stumbled toward the open bedroom door, hopping awkwardly when Solo shot past him. The cat made a beeline for the woman, who now stood over his box of unpacked DVDs. When Solo meow-yelled at her to pick him up, she did. Solo promptly nuzzled her neck.

What the—? Solo didn't even nuzzle *him*.

"Stop that. You're derailing Solo's guard cat training," he admonished as he tried to assume a sexy stance by the bedroom.

"You know you have two *The Force Awakens*?" she asked, pointing into the box.

"One's a collector's edition," he defended.

Her comical glance told him she'd just confirmed his geekiness.

"Get out of my movies. That's a personal thing, and this hookup isn't."

She snorted at that. "This isn't a hookup. I'd have more luck hooking up with your cat. At least he isn't too drunk to perform."

"I am *not* too drunk to perform," he argued. He thought she might be right, but he wasn't going to let this Ewok-hating girl prove him wrong.

He headed into his room, casually waving his arm for her to follow if she wanted. She wore that downward smile again. Hell. What was it about that smile?

"All right, get undressed, Jedi," she said, still carrying Solo as she strolled into the bedroom.

"I can't exactly get into it if you're going to be fondling my cat," he said. As if on cue, Solo meowed and jumped out of her arms.

"Fine," she said, slipping off her backpack and stepping closer.

He looked down at her, at the elastic top of her dress that hugged her skinny body. The skirt flared out, and the soft fabric drew him closer. He put his hands on her waist where the fabric hid a petite but distinctly hourglass shape.

"You're tiny," he murmured, sliding his hands down to the curves of her hips. On the bony side, but there all the same. He almost commented on it, but she immediately moved closer and started fiddling at his waist.

A second later, cold air rushed around his junk. He looked down to see she'd depantsed him, her head tilted disappointedly as she stared at said junk.

"I would say the same about you," she said, shaking her head.

He closed his eyes, willing the blood to rush to the focus of her attention. When he opened them, the room swirled. It was working! At least... the blood had left his head. He assumed it was en route to his crotch.

When the room finally stopped tilting, he was flat on the bed with her straddling him, her dress scrunched up on her thighs and one of the spaghetti straps off her shoulder.

"I don't think this is going to work," she murmured, her face sympathetic.

She sighed, and her lips parted, revealing a crooked front tooth. It looked tilted, slightly overlapping the one beside it near the bottom. She patted his chest, and when she leaned to one side to climb off, he grasped her waist again.

"Wait, I think I'm sobering up," he said.

She settled back, looking at him doubtfully.

"What's your name?" he asked. It was a stupid question. A too-personal question. But he hadn't picked anyone up in a bar in a few years. "Sorry. That's probably breaking a rule, isn't it?"

She studied him, then shifted her hips, pressing herself down against what he hoped was a growing erection.

"Probably," she agreed, her eyes drifting shut as she moved her hips faster.

"And I guess I shouldn't ask—"

"How about... don't talk unless it's dirty talk," she muttered.

She was right. Talking would just interrupt her grinding his dick to life.

Seeing her moving on him shot some adrenaline into his system.

"Okay," he said.

As he prodded his brain to think up some dirty phrases, he slid his hands under her skirt to her hips, not sure how far he could go. She seemed to have a plan, and the last thing he wanted was to interrupt wherever her plan was going.

But he'd been drinking so—

"That feels hot," he murmured, hoping his voice sounded sexy.

"What?" she asked and frowned. Her hips adjusted their rhythm.

"Uh, you're sexy," he mumbled. "You're a dirty girl, aren't you?"

Her hips slowed.

"Maybe no dirty talk," she suggested.

He held his breath and waited for her to climb off, but she leaned over and pulled something out of her backpack on the floor. She was fast, tearing a package open, reaching under her dress, then rolling a condom on him in record time.

He squeezed his eyes closed, determined not to do anything else that would ruin the moment. And by the moment, he meant sex. They were having sex. Well, he was having sex, which hadn't happened in quite a while. She was directing the sex, and he could only pray she was enjoying it as much as he was.

Her movements against him alternated between fast and fluid. Sometimes her hands were on his chest; sometimes she leaned back and rested them on his thighs. He heard her breath huff in and out in quick pants. Then she moaned and froze, and he froze, too, watching her above him.

Her face was a grimaced mix of anguish and melancholy.

She stayed suspended like that for he didn't know how long, and instead of going limp, he got harder. There was something about the harsh lines of her otherwise smooth face lit blue by the glow of the alarm clock.

The melancholy in her expression changed to anger. No, rage. Enraged by an orgasm. He didn't know if that was cool or frightening.

In a blink, her face smoothed into blandness.

"Okay, your turn," she whispered, then lowered herself again, slick and warm and pulsing.

She didn't have to move much, though.

Because it had been quite a while for him, or because she liked his cat, or maybe because he admired women who could mix Fireball and gin, he orgasmed in a rush.

Chapter Thirty

Lena

I knew right away I wasn't in New York. I didn't have to open my eyes to realize that.

I was lying on an inflatable mattress, which was about five hundred levels worse than my old mattress. I had a moment of regret that I'd left it behind.

However, it was a few hundred levels better than that ass-thin mattress in Auntie Korinna's trailer.

Another difference was the blanket tucked under my chin. It was soft and had a fresh smell, which was nice. My stuff never smelled as good as whatever this guy used.

This guy.

This guy?

Crap.

One second I was floating in the April-fresh scent of a stranger's sheets, and the next I was Spiderman jumping to stand in the middle of said stranger's dark bedroom, wrangling my brain out of its Fireball-induced fresh-linen fantasies.

The room was dark, but I could tell it was empty. The only problem would be getting out of this guy's apartment without running into him. My head was muzzy, but I knew I'd have to go through the main room, probably past the guy, to get to the front door.

How did I know this? Because this apartment mirrored the apartment beside it. The apartment where I grew up. Down the street from the library. Which was around the corner from the stairway where... where...

"Nope," I muttered, when memories threatened to push in and take over. I would not get lost rehashing Marko's accusation bomb in some strange guy's bedroom. So much for sex alleviating anything.

I scanned the dim interior out of some ingrained habit. I saw the mattress with the tangle of sheets I'd jumped out of. Empty walls, very little furniture. Then, on the other side of the mattress, I saw the blue glow of a *Star Wars* clock on a cardboard box. Specifically, a Death Star clock. It looked like someone had taken a vinyl record and melted it for a craft project.

I wanted to groan. I'd guessed the guy in the bar to be in his thirties, but then again, I'd had my Fireball goggles on. He wasn't some old-looking teenager, was he?

A shuffling sound drew my attention to the door. Was that... muttering?

I looked around, grabbed my backpack, and checked all the zippers. Thankfully, every one was closed. With excruciating slowness, I slid it over my shoulders, then mouthed, "Crap," when I realized I was bootless.

This made me feel more exposed than being fully naked. I scanned the room again and spotted my boots tucked neatly against the wall. The laces had been looped in a circle on each boot.

The guy must have done that. Was that psycho or sweet? I couldn't tell.

I scurried to the boots and pulled them on. A metal clanging and a groan from outside made my fingers freeze as I tied my laces. Then a click and a golden light shone through the partially open door.

As I tied the second lace, the door creaked, and the golden ring around it widened. I froze, hoping some kind of physics would make me blend invisibly into the wall.

Instead of flinging open to reveal Benjamin Button standing there, the door widened just enough to let in a mewling, scraggly cat.

Solo.

I may have regrets if this guy turned out to be a teenager, but this furry guy was something I definitely counted as a plus.

He padded over and looked up at me, letting out a demanding meow that sounded like a rusty hinge.

Damn cats. They're so "Screw you," and then somehow they burrow right under your skin.

I picked Solo up and let him butt his purring head against my jaw. Or I might have butted my jaw against his head, I wasn't sure. All I knew was, his fur smelled like sweaty socks, and he looked like he might claw me at any second.

Yeah, cats were definitely my people.

"Dammit," complained a muffled voice through the door, followed quickly by, "Okay, that's okay."

Solo pushed away, his back claws digging into my arm as he jumped and ran behind the cardboard box. The Death Star bobbled, then stilled.

I tightened my backpack and stepped into the wedge of light coming through the door.

Star Wars Guy stood about twenty feet and to the right, mostly facing away from me as he worked on something beside the stove. He wore a worn terry-cloth robe in powder blue.

"Haha!" he laughed, tossing something onto the counter, "No shells!"

The front door stood an impossibly far distance away to my left. I was a genius at pump and dump, but I usually left while the guys were asleep. This guy wasn't just awake, he was doing something in the kitchen. Very abnormal for a hookup guy.

I consulted my phone. Crap, it was midnight!

"Hey!" he called, and my eyes shot from my phone to his crooked smile. He waved a flipper at me. "Just about to make some pancakes."

I stared, not sure if I'd heard right.

"The first batch had shells, but these will be better," he explained, picking up a bowl and mixing vigorously.

I walked over to the island warily. It got me fractionally closer to the door.

Examining his face, I was relieved to see he was indeed over thirty. A sad, maybe-alcoholic thirty, but then, what did I care? I wasn't planning on seeing him again. In fact, maybe I'd finish my business with the FBI and leave town. I didn't expect Auntie Korinna to think kindly on my spy mission, still positive she'd somehow find out.

"It's kind of late for pancakes, isn't it?" I asked, looking at the pan that was now smoking.

"Ah, it's ready," he said, following my gaze.

He picked up a bottle with a spout, unscrewed the top, then blobbed some batter in. Some of it gooped over the side, which he scraped up and in, then refastened the top.

"You're about to see art," he promised over his shoulder, then waved the bottle over the smoking pan.

The word "art" had me stepping beside him, skeptical. This rough-looking dude in a fluffy robe did not strike me as someone well-acquainted with art.

He carefully drew an unrecognizable shape, grunted, then squeezed out another one.

"What are those?" I asked, tilting my head to look at the sad shapes from a different angle.

"Pancakes," he replied, glancing at me.

"No, I mean... are you trying to make some kind of... shape?" I asked.

"They're hearts," he said like it was the most obvious thing in the world.

"Uh, no they're not," I replied. "They're blobs, and now one of them is trying to combust."

I pointed at the smoking glob, and he said, "Damn."

He grabbed a flipper off the counter, slid it under the thing, and flipped it over. Smoke tickled my nose.

"Isn't it late for pancakes?" I repeated.

"It's never too late for pancakes. Although it's a *lot* too late for these," he said sadly, opening a lower cupboard and flipping both blackened cakes into the garbage.

He lowered the heat and started whistling, which was way too cozy for me.

"Look, I don't need you making me breakfast," I said, backing away a little.

"I'm not. When the booze doesn't help me sleep, sometimes cooking does," he said, dropping a spoonful of butter into the pan and squirting more batter into it. He sighed a long "Ahhh, nice" while he looked at the crooked heart shapes he'd made.

I looked him over as several questions ran through my mind. Despite wanting to leave earlier, I had to admit, something about the guy intrigued me. Maybe because he seemed so weird.

"Why don't you sleep?" I blurted, surprised that *this* was the question I'd asked.

"It's a long story," he said, hovering the flipper over the pan.

I knew from his body language and tone that it was a dark story too. It actually made me like him just a little.

"What shape are you going for this time?" I asked, coming closer to peer into the pan.

"Are you serious?" he asked, disappointed.

"Maybe... blood splatter at a crime scene? Or a sort of melted face?" I was only kind of joking.

He turned to stare at me, his eyes widening in a way that made his forehead wrinkle.

"Still hearts. The rounded top and the pointy bottom.... They're hearts," he insisted.

I snorted. "Those aren't anything-shaped pancakes," I said.

"Oh, would you like to draw something, Ms. Da Vinci?" he asked, holding the bottle out to me.

Oh hell, it was on. I checked the time on the stove and slipped my backpack off. I absolutely loved how he smirked with pancake-making smugness.

"What do you want me to draw?" I challenged him, pointing at the sadness in his pan and waving at him to get rid of it.

He flipped the raw globs onto a plate, clearing my canvas.

"Surprise me," he invited, handing me the bottle.

He adjusted the burner and plopped more butter into the pan. He folded his arms as he leaned against the counter, his fluffy robe open to reveal a T-shirt underneath.

"Okay," I said, smirking back at him and relishing the moment.

I closed my eyes to see what ideas would come to me. I tried to picture a *Lavandula latifolia*, a lavender species with spiky oval petals. I'd flattened and drawn one earlier that year that I'd picked in the small park near my New York apartment. Reproducing that would be an impressive feat.

Instead, another image came to me. An image that challenged and frightened me but didn't surprise me. Not considering my current proximity to my childhood living quarters.

The feel of the bottle I held took on the shape of something harder, narrower. A handle attached to my old saxophone case. The knowledge of what lay inside knitted its way up my arm and into my brain.

When I opened my eyes and looked down at the glistening black pan, it was like looking at a blueprint.

I went to work.

A chill enveloped me, drawing out goose bumps and a weird energy that shook every pore so hard, it made everything but my hand and arm go still. My vision ratcheted down until all I saw was the stream of batter squeezing out of the bottle.

That sounds kind of woo-woo, but drawing was the one thing that got me out of my body when things in my mind got too hectic. I didn't draw so much as I released the vision in my mind onto the page and with it the bad energy of the day. Often it was so satisfying, it would have made me cry if I were a crying person.

"You look pretty sure of yourself," the guy mumbled, momentarily pulling me back from the creative mist I was wrapped in.

"Huh," I grunted, then shut him out again.

I could see my subject three-dimensionally in my mind. It was like augmented reality with my subject superimposed on my vision, and all I had to do was follow the lines with the pen.

As if the remnants of Fireball in my system had fine-tuned my mind-eye coordination, my hand instinctively knew which part of the metal stuck out on the sides. I painted the layers like a 3D printer spewing out its product.

As I got closer to finishing, squiggling a batter line over the whole thing, I could tell the guy in the fluffy robe wasn't impressed. He shifted and sighed a few times, one time leaning too close that I had to shove him back.

"All right, all right, Jesus," he complained, then resumed his slouch against the counter.

A minute later I was done.

"Nice glob," he muttered.

I punched the empty bottle against his chest, making him grunt. I turned the heat off and reached for the flipper, holding it out to him.

"Flip it," I ordered him when he took it from me.

He slid the flipper under the pancake, loosening it, then flicking his wrist.

It flipped, and I folded my arms as he feasted his eyes on my artwork.

It was pretty beautiful, if I said so myself. And the longer I looked at it, the more it raised goose bumps on my arms. It was damned accurate too.

"Christ, how did you do that?" he asked, sliding the pan to a cold burner.

In it lay the gun my father had trained me to use. To kill with, although I ended up—

Nope, not going to go there—even though the creative side of my brain had.

"It's a skill. I don't know where I got it from," I said, which was the truth and more than I should admit to a complete stranger. A hookup. A guy I would never see again whom I should walk away from even as I was thinking this.

But he was still staring at the pan, and the awe on his face was something that made me want to stick around for just a few more seconds. Until he murmured the next words.

"That's an AK pistol," he said reverently.

An alarm went off in my brain.

"Do you own an AK?" I asked, backing away from the stove and grabbing my backpack.

Always trust your gut, I reminded myself.

I cast through my mind for what had set my intuition off and stepped closer to the door when I found it.

He'd said, "That's an AK pistol," not "That's a gun." Like any normal not-a-cop guy would say.

I reexamined everything about him.

Short haircut, sparse apartment, and a permanent-feeling place at the bar downstairs. I didn't know a lot of cops, but Mike had clued me in on a lot of their habits over the years. I hadn't thought to check on his cardboard box beside the table for a gun belt, but it could have been behind the Death Star clock.

"My father had an AK," he answered, his eyebrows sliding together. "Had a few guns, really."

I shuffled until I bumped into the door.

I'd just had sex with an alcoholic, pancake-making, probable cop. Cops always had cop fathers and cop secrets. There was something that kept him up late making pancakes.

"Look... I gotta go," I said, reaching behind me for the doorknob.

"Sure, just—"

I jerked the knob, and something banged by my ear, making panic leap into my throat.

I was trapped. All the oxygen left my lungs. I was trapped in a cop's apartment. Why had I even gone to the bar instead of leaving town after Marko threatened me? Why had I even come to Steeltown—

"The chain's on. If you just close the door," said the guy from way over in the kitchen, pointing a furry blue arm at me. A cop who was no closer to detaining me than he was making an accurate heart-shaped pancake.

I closed my eyes, embarrassed. I never panicked, dammit.

"Like this," he murmured, suddenly in front of me. He pointed at the chain.

I could smell that linen freshness, and it turned my embarrassment into anger. "Yeah, I got it," I muttered, slamming the door closed.

Before I could get to the chain, his hairy forearm was already there, almost brushing my hand. His thick fingers gripped the end of the chain and slid it free.

Breathe, breathe, breathe, I commanded myself. But dammit, he smelled good. A little like *Lavandula latifolia.*

A few seconds passed, and then he said, "It'll probably help if you're not blocking the door." The sarcasm in his voice brought me right out of my lavender daydreams.

"Maybe if you didn't crowd me," I said scornfully, and he stepped back.

The door opened, and the sad hallway loomed just a foot away. I walked into it, not feeling any safer.

"Do you always panic at the idea of a midnight breakfast?" he mused, but his eyes looked different. They didn't have the drunken, gropey sheen from earlier. They were hard and doubtful as he looked me over the way Tommy had when he'd recited the actions that had gotten me a felony.

"I'm not a breakfast kind of person, so... yeah," I replied.

"Maybe I'll see you around," he said. The words sounded like what someone would say if they wanted to see you again, but his expression said he thought he'd probably see me around in jail.

"Doubtful," I responded, inching toward the stairs. A weird energy pulsed from my old apartment, and I deliberately didn't make eye contact with it.

"Shouldn't you tell me your name? I mean, when I frame your pancake, I'd like to put the artist's name on it," he reasoned.

"Frame my pancake," I chuckled as I stood at the top of the stairs. At the bottom was safety, though I'd have to run to make Damon's last bus.

I looked up and saw that his expression had changed. Softened. It almost looked like admiration.

I thought about my pancake. As dumb as it sounded, I was proud of it. It was the first thing I'd ever drawn that wasn't a dead flower. What harm would there be in telling him my name?

"I'm Lena," I said, gripping the backpack's straps.

"Lena," he said, as if analyzing to see if it fit me. Or memorizing it. "I'm Quinn."

I didn't acknowledge him, just scurried—there's no other way to describe it—down the stairs. He called something down to me, but I was already out the front door and into the muggy air of the early morning, sucking in every breath as if it would cleanse the last few hours from my consciousness.

I didn't stop, just slammed one boot in front of the other as I frantically looked for the bus stop. Of course, I didn't realize the importance of the direction I was running until it was too late.

Chapter Thirty-One

Lena

Running in army boots was hard, and I'd already done too much of everything in them that day, which made my feet sore. I woke up without them, though. Huh. Had that guy, Quinn, taken them off? How weird, especially since I'd still been dressed. You'd think he would have—

"Hey!" shouted a familiar voice, shocking me into a statue.

Marko. He stood outside the entrance to the dark library.

Damn, the bus stop was right across from the library. You'd think a library would be empty at midnight, but I guess crime never slept.

I started backing up, praying that Damon's bus wasn't too far behind me on its last run.

"Where are you going, little Lena?" he yelled, striding down the steps to the street.

I spun and started jogging back toward Halloran's and the other bus stop.

"Povertaysya syudy do bisa!" he shouted, which turned my jog into a run.

I think he'd screamed a version of "Get back here," probably with a few swear words thrown in, but there was no way in hell I was going to stop and face Kid Gangster to ask him to translate.

In a split second, I decided there was no way in hell I was going to stay in this town. I'd run all the way to the bus depot if my panicked brain could remember where it was.

Who was I to think I could outsmart an FBI agent? Even worse, why hadn't I figured out that I'd blocked out all memories of my father for a spectacular reason? Like because I'd killed him? That was one hell of a reason not to remember and another justification for getting the hell out of Steeltown.

I could feel my blood pressure amping up as running let the air breeze around my bare legs.

I was a felon on an impossible mission that I was failing at. I was being chased by a Ukrainian gangster and had just hooked up with someone I was pretty sure was a cop. But what was most confusing of all was that I was wearing my dead mother's dress.

Yup, leaving town was my new objective.

JP and Brick would help me out with cash and a new identity. I could connect with other gamers and scrape some money together by playing online gaming tournaments. I'd lived in a crappy apartment before. I could do it again.

Normally, having a solid plan would calm me, but my heart rate didn't settle down from full throttle until I saw Damon's bus pull around the far corner of Main Street.

I flailed my arms and hoped like hell Marko had slowed down. That he wasn't pulling out a gun to kill me along with my new friend.

The bus pulled over, hissing to a stop as the doors opened.

"Girl, what?" Damon scoffed as I jumped up the stairs and cowered my sweaty self out of sight behind his seat. "Whatchoo—oh, no. You really hooked up with some old dude! And now you're running to hide your shame. Wait... you didn't give the guy a heart attack, did you?"

He leaned around the barrier behind his seat, looking at me with horror.

"What?" I panted, panicked that he wasn't pulling away.

"Oh, you trying to deny it. Well, that's just—what?" he asked, when my vigorous head shaking got him to stop talking.

"There," I said, pointing around him and down the street. I could hear Marko's murmurings and footsteps approaching, although at a slower pace than I expected.

His eyes followed where I pointed, and then he settled back into his seat with a low, "Oh, hell no."

The doors closed with a pneumatic hiss, and the bus lurched forward, the engine roaring as he floored it.

I peeked around Damon to see Marko, now with two of his goony friends, standing in the middle of Main Street, maybe fifty feet away. I was impressed with how far I'd run even though my lungs were wheezing in agony.

Thank God for Damon, who cranked the bus's engine higher to a screaming speed. I ducked down and looked out the window as the three men jumped out of Damon's way.

Damon shot past the last stop, only slowing to turn onto Arthur. The bus was almost on two wheels around that corner.

"Dammit, that was my stop back there!" a man complained as he hauled his short, round body out of the seat near the back.

I crouched down and scuttled past the man to the back of the bus and peered over the back seats. My heartbeat picked up when Damon pulled over at the next stop. I mentally willed the old man to hurry off the bus and for Damon to pull away before Marko and his clowns rounded the corner.

The doors hissed open, and Damon said, "Calm down, Charlie. It's only a couple of blocks past your stop."

The doors shut the second the man's foot hit the sidewalk, and Damon jerked the bus forward and up the hill toward Finlay Avenue and safety. Well, temporary safety until I could get out of town.

The lights flickered off, with only the strip of ads over the windows lighting the aisle.

"Sketch Girl," Damon called out. "C'mon up here."

I plodded up and dropped into the seat I usually took, pretty sure I'd made giant sweat marks on the dress under my armpits.

Damon guided the bus through stop signs and traffic lights, stopping at every bus stop even though there was nobody to get on or off. When he pulled up to the stop before my aunt's road, he flipped a switch over his visor. The route sign above him read, "ecivreS fo tuO."

"Why do I see trouble written all over you?" Damon demanded as he turned in his seat to glare at me with folded arms.

"You don't know the half of it," I mumbled, which wasn't entirely true. He didn't even know the quarter of it.

"And now you've pulled me into your trouble," he continued, pursing his lips. He glared up at the ceiling as if there might be some good advice up there.

"I don't think anybody will connect me to you," I offered, only for him to shake his head at me.

"I think Marko Olynyk will remember the bus driver that almost ran him and his goon-squad friends over," he said in a heavy voice.

"I don't.... I mean, probably not?" I finished, sounding lame even to myself. "Anyway, I'm leaving town, so none of this should affect you at all."

"Leaving town, huh? You think it's that easy?"

"Yeah," I said, frowning for the first time. Why wouldn't it be that easy? Only Tommy knew why I was really here. Well, my corpse dad, too, but since he hadn't shown up in hours, maybe he'd moved on. Gone into the light, so to speak. Not heaven, but maybe someplace not as bad as hell—

"Hey!" Damon shouted, snapping his fingers in front of me. "I said, half of Steeltown knows Ilya Kozek's daughter is back. And not the good half, if you follow me."

"How... how does anybody know who I am?"

"How can someone who seems smart be so dumb? The Olynyks run Steeltown. They own the police chief, and between that family and the cops, they make it their business to know when somebody new comes into town," he finished, then planted his hands on his knees and leaned forward. "What's your plan for leaving town?"

"Well," I said, sensing he was ready to help me with my escape. "Get back on the airport bus, then fly out on the first plane?"

"The earliest bus to the airport is at 5:00 a.m. I'm on my way to the garage on the other side of town. You got a way to get to the depot?" he asked.

"Uh, walk?" I suggested. "Unless you have a car and can—"

"I'm helping my mom tomorrow," he said, shaking his head at me. "Can't this family of yours take you there? Whoever lives up on this road?"

"Maybe," I said, wondering how I'd explain to my aunt that I hadn't just gone to the library, I'd hacked into it and gotten on Marko's bad side. Although she had gotten me out of town before.

"Give me your phone," he said, holding out his hand.

I unlocked it and passed it to him, then watched as he tapped the screen.

"Do you think it's smart to put your phone number in there? Especially if Marko catches up with me?" I asked, accepting my phone back, along with his sarcastic expression.

"At least you're admitting you're on the Olynyks' hit list," he murmured, not quite making eye contact.

I swallowed. The "hit list" remark "hit" a little close to the truth.

"Get on that bus out of town. Call me when you land wherever you're going. If you need money—" Damon said, but I cut him off.

"I'm fine for money," I said. Tommy had likely frozen my US accounts. I hadn't checked them yet, so I wasn't sure. But I didn't think he'd find my PostFinance account in Switzerland.

"Get going, then. I don't want to be late getting this baby back to the garage," he said, patting the steering wheel, then shooing me off the bus.

I stood on the sidewalk and watched him pull away. Instead of a wave, he flashed his taillights as the bus lumbered toward the ridge.

As I walked down my aunt's street, I couldn't blame Damon for not looking me in the eye. After all, I'd been the reason Marko chased after his bus. No doubt he'd be getting a visit from Mr. Stinky Breath soon.

I tightened the straps of my backpack. I wanted to be tough and just be grateful that Damon had gotten me out of trouble. But this strange feeling hovered over me. A bad feeling. Like maybe I hadn't been a good friend by dragging Damon into my mess.

Damn. It sucked to care about people.

Chapter Thirty-Two

Lena

Somewhere between the bus stop and my first sight of my aunt's house, the events of the day sank in. By the time I got near the oak tree, my legs were shaking so badly, I had to stop walking before I fell down. And then I fell down anyway.

Among other things was the fact that I'd shot my dad.

Me. *I'd* ended the life of the only family I had. Auntie Korinna and Vas didn't really count. They'd disowned me and only associated with me now because.... Well, I wasn't sure why. For my aunt, out of respect for her sister, maybe? Or guilt? Vas because I was an interesting diversion?

The grass was damp, probably from the humidity that still hung in the warm air. My body was so tired. Just a few minutes of rest, and then I'd haul my ass up and grab my bag from the trailer. I hoped my dad wouldn't be there. He thought he needed revenge. Well, his revenge would be me living a horrible life on the run from the FBI and now the Olynyks. Seeing as he was a figment of my imagination, it was always possible he'd hang around and taunt me. He was annoying, but it was sort of nice to have him nearby.

I looked down at the dress that had been through so much excitement. I'd probably have to get out of it even though I didn't want to. It was too identifiable.

As I ran a hand over the smooth fabric, lights flashed behind me. My instincts had me scrambling into the shadow of the tree.

I pulled the skirt of the dress tight around me as I shuffled to keep the tree between me and the car as it drove down the street. Crap, it was pulling into Auntie Korinna's driveway.

I snuck a look and saw my aunt's pale, round face staring out of the passenger window. She peered right at me like she had a sixth sense regarding my whereabouts.

The car bounced along the gravel ruts as it pulled up to the house.

"Lena!" hissed Vas after he'd jumped out of the car, his eyes frantic. "What are you doing here?"

A few hours ago, I would have had a smart-ass comeback for him. After all, I was staying in their trailer. Now, though, after everything that had happened, the innocent query felt tinged with danger.

"Where should I be?" I asked.

Vas ran a hand over his buzz cut, then leaned on the car as if about to give me a talking-to. My aunt shoved her door open with a creak and climbed out.

"In the house," she ordered Vas over her shoulder, the words a staccato command. He didn't argue, just closed the door and disappeared into the house.

"What did I tell you?" she demanded, a mix of regret and anger in her voice. She walked in a swaying gait to the front door, glancing back and waving at me to follow her.

"I...." The word trailed off in a sigh as I got to my feet. She'd told me a lot of things, but it was probably safer to treat it as a rhetorical statement and not answer.

"I said not to bring trouble here," she said, and this time I heard a threat in her voice. She flung the screen door open with a bang, and I knew she expected me to stay put.

I did, despite imagining her finding some weapon to come back and beat me with for bringing trouble to her doorstep. Part of me thought I deserved it, but I stayed at the bottom of the stairs to give her a lot of club-swinging room. I'd be screwed if throwing knives were my aunt's weapon of choice.

A minute ticked by before she returned, her round figure appearing in the doorway. I finally noticed her clothes, which were a wide left turn from her regular outfit.

She wore a dark jacket with a flowered blouse underneath and matching slacks below. A pantsuit, but a formal one. That forced my eyes down. She had her good shoes on.

All dressed up on a Thursday night? No, a Friday morning. A very early Friday morning. And out somewhere in her car with Vas as her driver.

"What were you and Vas—" I said before I could stop myself.

"Here," she grunted and swung a case into view. A familiar case.

The shape of it made my scalp crawl, and I could already feel the thick handle tingle in my palm.

It was a music case. A saxophone case.

I climbed the stairs, pulled by the gravity of it. By the antimatter that lived inside it. I had no evidence that it was still in there other than the way the weight of it stretched my aunt's arm taut.

I stared at the scuffed top. The silver latches had been dulled by time. I saw a familiar gouge in the plastic handle, a rough scratch that I'd always run my thumb over. Looking at it now was almost like looking at my fingerprint.

"When you were dropped off after... after all that happened, I thought I'd better hang on to this," Auntie Korinna explained, and I could picture her face tightening as her mouth pinched out the words.

"Sure," I agreed but wasn't really listening.

Like I had X-ray vision, I could see the components of my AK pistol inside. I pictured the dull gleam of the black metal, its straight-edged shapes tucked into the precise cutouts.

A memory popped up. My father trimming the thick foam and gluing it into the case. Then carefully tucking deep blue velvet into each compartment and wrapping it around the foam.

"You have to go," my aunt said, her bitter tone shattering the memory.

My eyes slid up to hers as if the gaze was a physical thing being pulled through the thick air.

She shifted, and I heard a scrape. Looking down, I watched her nudge the case against my foot.

"You have to *go*," Auntie Korinna repeated. I heard the urgency in her voice, more worry than a threat, but I couldn't take my eyes off the case.

Everything was in slow motion. The moment, my mixed emotions, and her words. It all smothered me like a heavy blanket. I was being sent away all over again.

I watched my hand reach down and grasp the handle, my thumb finding that crooked scratch. It was like touching a live wire.

The tiredness fled, and my ambivalent emotions hardened. I knew as solidly as the recoil of my gun that leaving Steeltown was the last thing I was going to do.

"I'll get my stuff," I said, my voice full of certainty that hadn't been there just a moment ago.

I looked up to stare into my aunt's eyes.

The worry there turned to surprise, then to hardness. I think she nodded slightly, which made no sense. Not then.

"I don't think you could go there now. There's too much going on. But you should know that your old apartment is yours," my aunt said and gripped her hands together in front of her rounded belly. "One day you could... go there. The keys are in the case."

I should have been surprised, but I wasn't. Of course my father would have done that. Of course I had a convenient place to go.

Although after my hookup earlier, maybe not so convenient. Ah, well. You couldn't have everything.

"There's something else in the case. Something that belonged to your mother," she said in that tight voice.

I thought she might go on, but she didn't.

I nodded. She nodded back, and her rigid shoulders relaxed. I didn't know what was in the case, but her posture gave her the look of a person who'd just unloaded something more dangerous than my AK.

I wasn't sure how long I stared at the sax case I'd set on the trailer's mattress. It could have been a minute or an hour.

Bruce Willis jumped through the missing window slats and broke me out of my daze.

"M-r-r-o-w-w-l-l," he whined, aggressively snuggling against the black plastic case while fixing me with his smirking stare.

I scratched his goofy tuft of forehead fur, then scooped him up.

"Hey, boy," I said, then dropped him when he twisted angrily in my arms.

I heard a noise behind me, and in a flash, I'd jumped up on the bed, clutching the saxophone case against my chest.

"Whoa," murmured Vas, a strip of his face visible in the partially opened door. "We good?"

I relaxed, but I didn't let go of the case.

"Sure," I said.

He climbed in and looked around, then backed out onto the top step when he saw a hissing Bruce Willis near his feet.

"That thing's going to give you rabies one day," Vas warned.

"I'd say it's a fifty-fifty chance," I agreed, dropping into a cross-legged position and setting the case across my knees.

I wouldn't explain my reaction. *Any surprise is dangerous*, my dad told me. And I remembered him drilling it into me to always react accordingly. Hopefully, more of his advice would come back to me now that I was staying in Steeltown. I was going to need it.

"What's in the case?" Vas asked, jamming his hands into his pockets.

"You don't know?"

"I'd guess some kind of instrument, but I didn't know you played," Vas explained. He shifted his feet, and when it caused his arm to brush against the wall, he grimaced and wiped at his sleeve.

"It's a saxophone case," I said, sliding my palm over the scratched and gouged case. "I used to play."

It was one of those lies by omission, but it was also true. I'd "played" what was in the case. Once at a major performance, I thought derisively, with much worse consequences than hitting a wrong note.

My dad had not been in the trailer to welcome me, so I assumed finding the truth had let him move on. Now I had to move on too.

"Where were you and Auntie K just now?" I asked.

"She had a meeting with the Blue Hair Mafia."

"Where?"

"At the community center," he replied. Nothing in his expression or body changed, and I assumed he was telling me the truth.

"Were you there the whole time?" I asked.

"No. I just drop her off and pick her up. Why?"

I thought about where the community center was, on Lusk Street, one block up and almost behind the library. I didn't know why I thought the mafia meeting and whatever was up Marko's ass were related—I just knew they were.

"What were they meeting about?"

"The same thing they always meet about. How to get drugs out of the high school or at least how to prove the Olynyks are behind it. What do you care?" he demanded, looking sulky now. "Ma says you're leaving town."

"I'm leaving the trailer," I corrected and patted the mattress beside me. Like magic, Bruce Willis hopped up and butted his head against my hand. "Any chance you could find something to carry my cat in?"

"You're taking that fleabag?" he asked with a huff of a laugh. "I don't know if they'll let you on the bus with that."

I smiled when Bruce Willis crawled into the small space between the sax case and my crotch. When he clawed me, I laughed even though it hurt like hell.

"Who said anything about a bus?" I asked.

Chapter Thirty-Three

Quinn

Quinn wrapped a tea towel around the cast iron handle and slid it onto the back burner. He had few things in his life that he took special care of, but his skillet was one of them. It had become a good friend most nights.

He draped the towel over his shoulder and threw the last singed bit of his heart pancake into his mouth. The gun pancake—an AK pistol—he'd set on a separate paper plate.

He poured himself a second coffee as he studied the pancake.

The detail was impressive. He hadn't been lying when he talked about framing it.

"Lena," he mused, remembering how reluctant she'd been to tell him her name. Then he remembered how fast she'd wanted to get out of his apartment once she'd told him.

He leaned on the counter, covering up the words "World's Best Brother" on his coffee mug with his hand. He examined the raised lines of the barrel, noting the open style of the stock and precise dimensions of the parts relative to one another.

She hadn't just drawn some gun. She'd replicated something she knew well. It was too exact to be anything else. What his brain puzzled over was how a scruffy young woman with thrift-store boots and a grass-stained dress owned such an unusual weapon. An AK47 was one thing, but an AK pistol wasn't your average shooting-range gun. It was a kill-at-a-distance weapon.

He straightened and took a swallow of the strong coffee. He wandered over to the box beside his collection of DVDs and shoved aside the miscellaneous kitchen implements until he found an almost-empty roll of plastic wrap. He tore off a strip and headed back to the pancake.

He wrapped the pancake AK twice, then folded the edges underneath. He placed it in his empty fridge, then picked up his mug again to take another drink.

He didn't want to be this intrigued by the Fireball-drinking woman. He also didn't like the tingling at the back of his neck, like something back there had fallen asleep and was just waking up. He'd promised himself he'd get a job he didn't care about in a town that was barely on any map and just drink himself into retirement.

"Lena," he murmured again, staring at the pancake inside his fridge. He didn't know if the tingle meant the woman had done something wrong or was about to. Or that he shouldn't be having random sex with someone in the same town he lived in. But something about her had burrowed itself into his brain, and that wasn't part of his game plan.

His phone rang from the bedroom. He ignored the first ring until he remembered only his sister had his number. He closed the fridge and marched to where his phone lit up his cardboard box table, surprised at the local area code.

"Hello?" he answered, making his voice gruff as if the call had wakened him.

"Magee?" asked a familiar, annoying voice.

Brooke. Of course she'd dug out his contact information.

"It's not Monday, so I'm going to hang up now," he grumbled.

"We've got a dead body," she interrupted. When he didn't reply right away, her voice rose in frustration as she continued, "Remember? You're a cop?"

"I'm a detective," he corrected, his hand tightening on the phone. "And as a detective, I investigate. I don't respond to the scene. Let the cops process it first, and then—"

"You obviously haven't read your job description. *We* process the scene. You and me."

He shook his head.

"I'm not on the clock—"

"There is no clock, asshole. Welcome to being a small-town *detective*," she muttered.

He sighed. "You're just going to keep calling me until I show up wherever this dead body is, aren't you?" he asked.

"No. You'll just turn off your phone. I'm going to bang on your apartment door until you answer," she returned.

He rubbed his eyes. She'd do it too. If she had his phone number, she had his address. He straightened his shoulders and stretched his head from side to side. He was mostly sober, but if she got too close, she'd probably smell the alcohol on his breath.

And so what? a grumpy voice argued in his head. *You were off duty. Nothing wrong with having a few drinks. Or twelve. Or having sex with a stranger.*

He might have groaned, but he wasn't sure. He coughed to cover it, just in case.

"What do you know about the dead body so far?" he asked, giving in.

"Just that the local crime family is involved. I'll swing by and pick you up," she said, that smugness back in her voice. "Although you could probably walk to where it is."

Fifteen minutes after she called, Brooke held up the yellow plastic tape across double front doors that read **Do Not Cross**.

"You're kidding, right?" Quinn asked.

He'd met her in front of his apartment and walked with her one and a half blocks down the street.

"I don't kid," Brooke murmured.

The Steeltown Public Library was a historic house set back from the road on a bit of a hill. He hadn't noticed it on his drive into town yesterday, but if he had, he sure wouldn't have pegged it as a likely murder scene involving the local crime family.

Jesus, has it really only been a day? he wondered to himself as he followed Brooke into the library's small foyer.

Despite Brooke making him think they'd be processing the scene, there were two uniformed officers and two other people.

One pair stood to the left of the entrance, and the other was farther back to the right, behind a bookcase of children's books.

The first cop spoke to an older man who had a death grip on a black garbage bag. He wore gray coveralls and kept running a hand over his thinning hair, his expression shaken.

The other man wore a crisp suit and a sullen expression. Quinn recognized him right away from the altercation they'd had over littering.

The cop talking to him gestured intermittently with his hands, one of them holding a notebook and the other a pencil. The man's mouth made the sharp movements of one-word answers. He appeared calm, almost bored. As if answering questions about a dead body in a public library was all in a day's work. But Quinn could tell by the tension in his shoulders that he was pissed right the hell off.

"That guy looks familiar," he said to Brooke, who also looked at the pissed-off guy.

"Marko Olynyk," she murmured.

Of course it was. Whatever minuscule gin buzz he had disappeared.

"Where's the dead guy?" he asked.

"This way," she said.

She led him through a circular space with a bright red carpet and low, curved bookshelves. On top sat a selection of picture books with colorful covers. One that caught his eye had a yellow duck running down a plank with the word "Ping" on the front. The irony of death so close to innocence was not lost on him.

He had a good idea who they were going to find before she spoke, and he braced himself for the seeing a dead body relatively soon after seeing his last. At least he wasn't the one who'd laid this guy out.

Brooke walked toward a hallway. On either side were rooms with windows that faced the main library. The one on the left was dark, the one on the right, closest to the children's section, was lit up.

"Oleg 'Legs' Olynyk, sixty and head of the Olynyk crime family, which comprises his oldest son and several cousins. Although proof they're blood relatives is dubious," Brooke explained, standing at the open door and looking inside.

Quinn looked past her first, noting two more rooms before the metal door at the end of the hall. A red **EXIT** sign was lit up above it.

Brooke stepped inside the room, moving along the window to give him room to enter.

He walked inside, then tapped her arm.

"Give me your notebook," he said, waiting patiently while she rolled her eyes and handed it to him.

"I'm sure you need a pen too," she scoffed, handing him that as well.

He ignored her, flipping to a blank page and making note of everything he'd seen since entering the library.

"Did your boys make note of the vehicles parked outside?" he asked Brooke.

"Of course," she replied.

He glanced around and made a simple drawing of the room and where everything was. Then he braced himself to check the body, one foot of which he could see under the table.

On the far wall, he saw a mist of red at table height. He walked closer and crouched down. He saw the track-suited body of the older man he'd seen yesterday. He lay on his side on the floor. Strangely, the chair had fallen with him, so it looked like he was still sitting in it. The foot that was out of sight was hooked around the thin metal of the chair leg.

"Well," Quinn said, standing up. He rubbed his jaw with the back of his hand, then made more notes. As he wrote, his heartbeat picked up. When he noticed his hand shaking, he shoved both the notepad and pen into his pockets.

This wasn't Seattle. *Breathe.* First of all, he hadn't been the one pulling the trigger. *Breathe.* Second, it was just another criminal. *Breathe.* Steeltown was probably better off without the lump lying on the mossy green carpet of the library's study room.

When his breathing calmed, he walked closer to the body.

"So this is Olynyk," Quinn said, glad that his voice sounded normal. "What kind of crime was he into?"

"He owns a couple of strip clubs outside of Seattle. Pete's Place a block over and a place called the Buzz Bar down by the old mill. Pete's Place is legit, but the Buzz Bar is a dance club that virtually nobody goes to, so it's likely just a laundering operation. But his big business is drugs. His son started it years ago, dealing pot before it became legal. But he started lacing it with a heroin called Krokodil."

"Never heard of it," Quinn murmured, staring down at the body.

"It's a Russian synthetic made of desomorphine. The deso is made from codeine and different organic solvents," Brooke explained as she rounded the table in the other direction.

"You know a lot about it," he commented, his eyes fastening on the upper teeth of the deceased Legs Olynyk. The bottom jaw was... gone.

He turned back to face Brooke, who was still staring at the body.

She nodded in a musing way. "I went to school with a friend who overdosed on the poison Marko sold," she said.

When he walked past her to stand by the door, she stepped closer to the body. She pulled out a pair of rubber gloves and crouched down beside it.

"Marko still dealing?" he asked, glancing out the window. He knew who that was.

"Not for years. He's got a network now," she said, reaching to touch something.

"Don't disturb the scene until the crime scene photographer gets here," he said, but she turned and smiled at him.

"You mean me?" she asked and pulled a shiny red Olympus out of her pocket. "Don't stress. I took a course in crime scene photography and spent a month moonlighting with a county coroner."

"I'm not stressing," he said, then rubbed his neck. It was a lie. He wouldn't be surprised if his blood pressure was 300 over infinity.

He heard the buzzing of the camera, both with and without a flash.

"I'll let the coroner move the body. He'll let me take more photos when he does that," Brooke said.

He watched her as she took pictures from various angles, then stepped back when she walked around the table to take more from the other side. He appreciated her thoroughness while cursing his bad luck.

Nothing this serious was supposed to happen in this town, but then, he hadn't done more than a simple search of jurisdictions with the least amount of crime. Since they'd been sending the serious cases to another county, it skewed the results. But now that they had a bona fide detective on the payroll, these cases would come to him.

He watched Brooke continue to take photos, backing out of the room when she shooed him away.

"You're good," he said, realizing he was going to rely on Brooke more than he thought.

"Thanks. I don't want to make any mistakes that might come back to haunt us at trial," she murmured, continuing to bathe the scene in camera flashes.

He frowned.

"Assuming we find the guy who did this, you think it will make it to trial?" he asked, thinking of the gang-related killings that had happened up in Seattle. There was a street justice that handled most of the cases before suspects were even brought in for questioning.

Except for when they pulled a gun on a cop, he reminded himself. But then, hadn't he dealt out his own justice that day?

Brooke looked at him with a knowing expression. "Let's go outside," she said and walked past him, pausing when he didn't follow.

She raised an eyebrow, and he pointed into the room.

"What? You don't want the dead guy to overhear our conversation?" he asked.

She narrowed her eyes at him, then tipped her head toward the two interrogations taking place at the front of the library.

"See the old guy? That's the janitor from the museum next door," Brooke explained in a low tone, drawing his attention to the man in overalls. "He was working and heard something unusual, according to what he told Kramer."

"And Marko Olynyk?" Quinn asked, lifting his chin toward the son of the deceased.

"He says he was down the street when he heard the same something. Says he saw a girl running out of the library and down the sidewalk. He chased her, but she got on a bus before he could grab her," Brooke explained.

Quinn looked at Brooke, willing his expression to remain curious and not panicked.

"A girl?" he asked as a twinge of dread pinched his stomach. "What's a girl doing out so early in the morning?"

"That's what Phillips said he told him," Brooke replied with a shrug. She angled her head toward the two men in question. "Marko tried to get the janitor to agree with him, but the janitor was too shaken to say much more than, 'I heard a sound.'"

He nodded as he looked at the four men talking. He tried to look wise as his brain clicked through the timeline of his encounter with someone he'd also thought was a girl at first glance.

"How long ago was that?" he asked.

"Maybe an hour, give or take," Brooke said.

"Did he describe this 'girl'?"

"Well, that's the interesting thing. He says he knows her," Brooke answered. "And if he's right, then I sort of know her too."

This jerked Quinn's gaze to Brooke. "Who is it?"

"Lena Kozek. Well, Galyna is her full first name. She's the daughter of Olynyk's former hitman," Brooke explained. "Deceased hitman, that is."

Quinn arranged his expression into a look of interest even though his diaphragm tightened to force all the air out of his lungs.

The officer questioning the janitor appeared beside Brooke, thankfully drawing her attention away from his now-sweating face.

"There are some security cameras around the place," said the officer, looking from Brooke to him.

Brooke swung her gaze back to him and smirked. "You're the lead, Detective Magee," she said.

He cleared his throat and tried to look detectivey.

"Contact the security company and have them forward whatever was recorded for the last twenty-four hours. And fingerprint the whole place, including that back door," he said, pointing to the door under the exit. "And you." He pointed at Brooke. "Go back there and photograph everything, including whatever's out on the street."

When the two did as he ordered, he fought the urge to lean against a wall and hyperventilate.

He didn't know if he was more disturbed to be investigating a murder or that he'd slept with the accused killer who was also a hitman's daughter.

Chapter Thirty-Four

Thomas

Thomas lay back on the bed's polyester coverlet, not caring what horror story of bodily fluids might have been left on it. He stared at the water stains on the motel's ceiling. The brown rings almost matched the pattern on the slick polyester coverlet.

For a grunt agent like he was, it was a step down. For a grunt who'd gotten on his boss's bad side, it was better than he expected.

He flipped his phone over and over as he stared at the brown stains. Sleep had eluded him on the plane, and he was still no closer to it.

What if I don't go to Steeltown? he thought. He turned the idea over in his mind the way he slowly flipped his phone. He knew this was just Duncan's evil way of making him suffer before he got his termination slip with his next pay stub.

What if he stayed right there in this depressing motel? Duncan wasn't really expecting him to make a "significant contribution" to the case. He was expecting him to fail.

"So, what if I don't even try?" he asked the ceiling. The brown circles seemed to shrug at him, and he wished he'd packed his martini ingredients in his suitcase. A toast as his career crashed and burned in this miserable motel room at the end of a SeaTac runway seemed fitting.

He stopped flipping his phone and started swinging it by a corner and catching its narrow body between his fingers.

But what if he went to Steeltown? What if there was a way to watch the girl crash and burn instead? He could avoid Main Street and the memories that he was sure still lived there. He could avoid Marko, who would recognize him on sight.

He kept swinging the phone as he considered that idea, then almost jerked it into the air when it bleated with his sister's ringtone.

"Hey, what are you doing awake?" he asked instead of greeting her.

"Working, unfortunately," she said with a long groan. "Legs is dead."

The three words had him jackknifing off the bed. "Legs is *what?*"

"Dead," she confirmed.

"Holy hell," he said, dropping back to sit on the edge of the mattress.

"They're still investigating, but word is, they're looking at your girl."

"Holy *hell!*" he exclaimed again, getting to his feet to pace.

The depression of just moments ago evaporated, leaving his brain firing with purpose.

"Was she arrested? Did she do it?" he asked.

"Not arrested, and how should I know?" his sister replied tiredly. "There's another call coming in. This is a shitshow. I've got to go, Tom."

"Let me know if they arrest Lena."

"I will."

"Actually, I might come up there," he blurted, his pacing taking him to the grimy window that looked across a road at a sparse group of evergreens. Roadside garbage littered the edge of them like urban snow.

"What? Why? *Don't*," his sister commanded, sounding frazzled.

"I'm already in Seattle," he replied.

There was a pause, then a frustrated sound followed by an angry curse.

"Why?" she demanded when she ran out of F-bombs. "Dammit, Tom, you said you were handling things from back east."

"Things got... complicated. But don't worry, I'm here with my boss's permission," he said, which was the truth.

"Why do I think you're lying?"

"I'm not sure, and I gotta say, it's hurtful, Bella," he tried to joke.

She didn't laugh.

"If you come up here, something's going to go wrong, and you'll be in deep—"

"Don't worry about me," he said, only for Bella to snort.

"That's your favorite line, except you keep doing things that *make* me worry," she replied. "Whether this woman killed Legs or not, it's game over for her. She'll either be arrested or have a mysterious 'accident,' courtesy of Marko. He'll never let his father's death go unaccounted for. Just like someone else I know."

"Now you're getting it," he agreed in a hard voice.

"Is there anything I can say to get you to let this go?" she asked.

He switched the phone to his other ear, imagining being back in Steeltown. He pictured seeing Lena in a jail cell, facing charges. He could do that without even driving down Main Street. He thought ahead to the story he could weave for his boss. Maybe this could all end with him getting his revenge *and* keeping his job.

"Tom!"

"What?"

"I said let this go. It's over. Whatever revenge you wanted, you got it."

Bella was wrong. He didn't just need to get it, he realized. He needed to *see* it.

"I'm coming up there," he said stubbornly.

"I don't understand why," she argued.

"If nothing else, to see my sister," he replied and walked over to his bag. He tugged out the plastic evidence bag.

"Tom," she said in a warning tone. "You can't snow me with this fake surge of brotherly love."

He held up the bag and looked at the bloodstained hat. A weariness came over him, and he gave up trying to weave a lie she'd believe.

"I'm probably days away from losing my job," he confessed and heard Bella groan on the other end of the line. "If it happens, I'd rather be close to family."

Bella was quiet for so long, he wondered if the call had dropped.

"Close to family, my butt," she finally said with a dry chuckle. "You just want to see Lena go down."

He opened the closure on the bag and pulled out the hat, letting the bag drop. His thumb found the stiff seams where the stain was.

"You're right. I do. I really want to see that happen. But that's another reason I want to be close to family," he admitted and ended the call before Bella could say anything to make him completely lose his composure.

Chapter Thirty-Five

Lena

I rode in the back of Vas's car with a yowling Bruce Willis on my lap. Vas couldn't find any kind of carrier, then said we had to pick up someone named Valerie before he took me to where I wanted to go. He was surprisingly unsurprised when I told him about going to the apartment.

"Figured" was all he said.

Valerie turned out to be Vas's girlfriend.

Valerie lived in a tiny stuccoed cottage closer to Steeltown proper. It had a crooked chimney and a scabby front yard that looked like it had once dreamed of being a lawn. Vas leaned to look through the passenger window at the house, then gave a short honk from the Caprice's horn.

A light in the house turned off, and the front door opened.

Valerie had a curvy body packed into what looked like a short pink nurse's uniform. The kind of outfit that you'd buy at Halloween with the label "Slutty Nurse." She wore her streaked hair in a multi-colored beehive. A pink visor with **The Bold Bean** embroidered on it sat above her forehead. Perched between the words **Bold** and **Bean** sat a curvy coffee bean with long lashes. A mirror image of Valerie.

"Hey, baby," she greeted Vas when she yanked open the passenger door. She gave me a quick glance before squirming across the Caprice's front seat to nestle her round body against Vas.

"I know I saw you at dinner, but I've missed you," she purred.

"I missed you too, baby love," Vas crooned back, and then they made out for a good minute.

Just a day ago, I would have made gagging noises and cracked a joke.

A day ago? I thought in wonder. It felt like a year ago.

Anyway, I was just glad Vas had somebody who cared about him. New York Mike would have called that soft or heckled me for growing a heart. And so what if something had sprouted in that general area. Vas had his life, and I had mine, so far, and maybe I thought that way because picking up the case that rested by my feet had sparked something.

"This is my cousin, Galyna. Or Lena. I'm going to drop her off downtown," Vas explained.

Valerie looked me over, those lush lashes lowering and rising as she took in the rumpled sundress and bulky coat I'd thrown over it.

"So you're the one causing all the trouble, mm-hm," she murmured.

Vas pulled away from the curb, did a three-point turn, and headed back to town.

Bruce Willis mrowled soulfully from my lap before I could ask her where she heard about me and trouble.

"You have a caaaat!" Valerie gushed, twisting to peer over the seat at Bruce Willis crouched on my lap. "He doesn't look or sound happy."

"I don't think he's used to being around people," I replied. Then, because I wouldn't be me if I didn't throw a little sass into the mix, I added, "Or to all the sucking face."

Valerie looked at me, blinking so much, the eyelashes created their own windstorm. Then she guffawed in a way I couldn't not love.

"You're okay for a cat girl," Valerie said, adjusting her visor. She turned back around and plastered herself against Vas as he drove, speaking more to the roof of the car than to me. "I'm more of a dog person. If I didn't have to run the Bold Bean, I'd have three little Frenchies. God, those little things are adorable."

"Valerie runs and *owns* the Bold Bean," Vas clarified with pride. "Best coffee in the state. Even better than Starbucks."

"It's different from Starbucks, but the Bold Bean definitely has better Wi-Fi than any place in town. But that's still a very sweet thing to say," Valerie murmured, then started making out again, but this time with his neck.

I waited for the one-sided make-out session to slow down before I asked, "Where did you hear I was causing trouble?"

"Mrs. Tazia's got her cabbage rolls in a twist over you," Valerie said, a nonanswer to my question. "Says you're stirring things up."

"Did you talk to Mizbee?" Vas asked calmly, but he started twisting the steering wheel like he was wringing out laundry.

"She mentioned it yesterday afternoon. She dishes the dirt for free soy lattes and the fact that I saved her life."

That caught my attention.

"How'd you do that?"

"She kept complaining my milk was off, which is something I'd *never* allow to happen. I suggested she was lactose intolerant. I switched her to soy, and she's been grateful ever since. Anyway, I heard about you yesterday," Valerie finished.

"That was right after you showed up on our doorstep," Vas said, craning his head to speak at me in the rearview mirror.

I thought about that, remembering the women who had been visiting Auntie Korinna when I'd shown up. And then the meeting tonight.

"They must have been talking about me at the community center," I said to him.

His eyes widened. "I swear, I didn't hang around to listen in. They never let me, anyway," he vowed.

"So is it true? You're an assassin?" Valerie asked.

Geez, did Mizbee blab everything to anyone, lactose-intolerance death notwithstanding?

Valerie's lashes fluttered, and when I didn't answer right away, she twisted all the way around to face me.

"Are you?" she whispered, her flamboyance honed to a cautious tone.

"Will it get me a free mocha frappé with extra whip?" I asked, picking the most expensive drink I could imagine.

"Absolutely," she breathed.

"Then, yes. Well, I was trained to be one. I've only had one job, and it was a long time ago," I said.

"Trained?" Valerie asked, gripping the seat back. "Wait. A long time ago? How old were you when—"

"Baby love, those are questions you shouldn't be asking," Vas said nervously. "And you. Don't encourage her."

"I'm not," I replied.

"She's not," Valerie insisted, then raised an eyebrow at me. "Extra vanilla shots if you tell me who your job was."

Bruce Willis yowled, the pitch of it so piercing, it forced one of Valerie's long-lashed eyes to squeeze into a pained squint.

I looked down and saw my hands were clenched around Bruce Willis's shoulders. I loosened them, and the pitch of his complaining lowered to a less tear-inducing level.

"I can't say. It's against the assassin rules," I answered, hoping my expression looked lighthearted.

If she only knew.

Vas grumbled something under his breath, and Valerie turned away with a sigh.

Instead of going on about me being an assassin, she switched to a discussion about sleep. How she lived on five hours of sleep a night because one day her hustle would turn the Bold Bean into a chain to rival the other coffeehouses that dotted the county, and on and on and on.

"How do you like your coffee? Because if you like bold flavor with none of that acidy bitterness, you'll fall in love with my product. It took me months to talk my bean supplier into—"

"Uh-oh," Vas groaned, breaking into her monologue.

He slowed the car to a crawl. A cop with his signature cop hat was talking to the driver of the car in front of us.

I pulled my jacket tighter around me and hoped my raggedy cat would hide the very recognizable dress.

"What's going on, Officer?" Vas asked when it was our turn.

"Got an incident on Main Street. Are you a resident?" the man asked, flicking a glance at Valerie, then back at me.

I lifted Bruce Willis to face the officer, his furry body hiding half of my face. I smiled with the side of the mouth he could see, hoping I looked as innocent as possible. He frowned but looked back at Vas.

Whatever had happened on Main Street, it had to involve Marko. And if Marko had wanted to catch me earlier, he must have described me to the cops. I kept my face buried in Bruce Willis's smelly fur.

"Uh, sort of," Vas replied, his voice steady. "But I don't need to use Main Street."

The cop nodded and waved Vas away. Vas rolled up the window, and then he eased the car off to the right and down a narrow alley.

I'd never wanted to hug anyone, but if I could have, I would have hugged Vas.

"Thanks," I murmured, and since I still held Bruce Willis with both hands, I ran the cat's right paw over Vas's short hair. Hopefully, he'd take it the way I meant it.

"No problem," Vas said, and I caught a hint of pride in his eyes in the rearview.

Vas drove from one alley to the next until we were behind the apartment building.

"What's the plan?" he asked after putting the car in Park. Valerie slid a little away, and they both turned to face me.

"I don't think I should tell you," I said, pulling my backpack on and figuring out how to grab my bag, the saxophone case, and Bruce Willis without getting clawed to shreds.

"What? Why not?" Vas said. "You can trust me. I'm family."

"Plausible deniability would be my guess," Valerie replied, nodding sagely. "You do you, girl. Vas, text this woman my number. I'm ground zero for Steeltown gossip. If you need info, you text me."

Vas took his phone out and grumpily texted Valerie's number, making my phone chime.

"She's right. I don't want you to get into trouble, especially with your mom," I said.

"I guess," Vas said, but there was still a stubbornness in his expression.

"Take care, little assassin," Valerie said, winking a huge eyelash at me. "Don't kill anybody unless it's in another town. Everyone in Steeltown is a customer."

I climbed out of the car, hauling everything with me while keeping a growling Bruce Willis tucked under my arm.

I could hear Valerie's hearty laugh as Vas pulled away.

I stood in the back alley, looking up at my old living room window.

My apartment, I thought, gripping the saxophone handle.

I wished my dad was with me.

Technically, I was returning home, but there was no sentimentality in the thought. I didn't trust the whole idea of "home." For starters, home needed to be a place where I was safe. Not just physically, but legally. And that meant dealing with some unfinished business.

Chapter Thirty-Six

Lena

Keeping a yowling Bruce Willis squeezed under my arm, I set the sax case down and flipped open the latches.

My heart raced as my fingers brushed along the top edge. I lifted a corner just enough to see the blue velvet of the interior, black in the dim light.

There, tucked against the receiver assembly, was a round metal disc. I pulled it out, and a chain with two keys came with it.

I re-latched the case and stood up, my fingers finding the worn gold key that would unlock metal door.

"I used to live here, buddy," I told Bruce Willis, flinging my bag through the open door, then picking up the sax case.

Bruce Willis stopped squirming and just hung on my arm like a sack of meat. Maybe he sensed he had a new home.

I stepped into the dark hall, the door behind me self-closing and sending a familiar boom echoing through the lobby ahead.

"Mrowl!" Bruce Willis yelled, reverting to his old self and digging his claws into my waist. He pushed off and sprinted down the hall.

"Second floor, first door on the right," I called after him and pressed a hand against my waist. I hoped the scratch wouldn't leave a bloodstain on my dress.

I grabbed my stuff and headed for the stairs.

My home.

I put my hand on the newel post and looked up the dark stairs. Even though I'd been here a couple hours before, it felt different. And not just because I'd been mostly drunk then.

With the cop, it had been a musty old apartment building. Now, distinct smells hit me, buried like gold in my Lysol-infused memory.

Mrs. Clovis dropping off cabbage rolls and turnip stew. I loved the first and hated the last, but my dad made me eat it to be nice.

Then there was the potato varenyky Mr. Honchar made every Tuesday afternoon. On Wednesday mornings, he'd leave two wrapped in a paper towel on a plate outside his door. I'd run up to the top floor after school to snatch them up.

I wondered if he still lived there. Unlikely. He was ancient even back then. Had Mr. Honchar ever wondered why I stopped showing up on Wednesday mornings? Had he ever come down and stopped to knock at our apartment door, listening with his ear pressed against the heavily painted wood to see if I was home? That was a sad thought.

I took the stairs slowly. Since I wasn't pushing a drunk guy, I took time to notice how curves were worn into the edge of the steps. My fingertips found the pockmarks on the handrail where chipped paint had been repeatedly painted over, then chipped again.

When I got to the top, I saw Bruce Willis hunkered down beside our apartment door, watching me.

"You must be a mind-reading cat," I murmured.

I shook the keys in my hand, feeling the narrower metal of the second one slip naturally between my thumb and forefinger. I slid it into the top lock and unlocked the deadbolt first, then the doorknob lock.

Bruce Willis scooted inside as if sucked in by gravity, disappearing into the dark apartment.

I followed him in and closed the door. I reached for the light switch but never got the chance to flip it.

In less than a second, Bruce Willis yowled like he'd been stabbed. A clattering of claws headed in the bathroom's direction.

I'd gone from standing near the door to crouching against the wall several feet away. I don't know where my bag ended up, but my fingers were on the latches of my saxophone case, ready to assemble my weapon.

"Galyna" came the gravelly voice of my father, and I went from crouching and ready to assemble my gun to sprawling back against the wall.

"Dad?" I gasped.

A murky shape in the dark kitchen slid into the dim glow that came from the living room window. He floated closer to me, his hands shoved into his pockets, his shoulders hunched.

His head angled toward the saxophone case, and though I wanted to ask where he'd been, why he came back, and what he was doing there, I asked, "Look familiar?"

In the dark, his features looked like crudely drawn lines, and the ones that comprised his mouth bent up at the corners.

"Of course. I made that for you," he replied.

"You're still around," I said.

"Yes," he replied, sounding resigned.

Maybe he was still here because I had to tell him what happened. He couldn't just find out about it when I had.

"Let's sit down," I said, grabbing the sax case and heading to the kitchen table.

He dissolved, then reappeared in the chair he always sat in. His trousered legs were elegantly crossed, and his hands rested on a knee, overlapping at the wrists.

I pulled out the chair I always sat in and set the sax case on the table. I weighed telling him about his death against the job I still had to do and opted to start with the second. It would give me something to do while I thought out how I would broach the subject of me killing him.

I went back to the door and flipped on the lights. Sliding off my backpack, I returned to the table.

"What's this you're doing?" he asked with mild interest.

"Work," I replied.

I unzipped the backpack and pulled out the laptop and its portable charger. I connected the charger to the laptop and watched the red light come on and start flashing. I gave it a few seconds, then opened my laptop's lid.

"When you disappeared, I thought you'd... you know, figured out how to cross over," I said, typing.

"No," he replied, picking at the crease in his pants.

"So where did you go?"

"I went away because it was... hard to see you in that dress. Your mother's dress," he said and glanced toward the fridge.

I looked down at the dress, which was a lot more worn now than it had started out.

"I'm not big on dresses, but I... kind of like this one," I admitted. "I'm sorry that it makes you feel bad to see it."

"Not bad," he said, the words so gritty, they were hard to make out. He tipped his head from side to side as if weighing what he was really feeling. "Maybe... lonely. Yes. Lonely."

"I don't know how being dead works, but couldn't you try to find her—"

"She's in a much different place from me," my dad said, turning toward me but not making eye contact. "I'll never see her again. But I see her in you."

"You do?" I asked, sitting up.

Was it bad that I wanted to hear more about her despite my corpse dad looking like she was the last thing he wanted to talk about? Or was it worse that I was stalling about telling him I'd shot him? Because I was pretty sure once he knew that, his spirit would either move on to the next stage or decide to haunt me for life. He definitely wouldn't tell me anything I wanted to know about my mom.

"She had a smart mouth, like you. And she didn't like stupid people, also like you. But she had a soft heart for broken people. And she loved you, despite who your father was," he said, and his gaze finally swung to look at my face. It wore a sadness I'd never seen before.

"Let's get something straight. You were a solid dad," I said, and he smiled in that way people did to humor you when they didn't agree with you. "You think you shouldn't have taught me how to kill people, but maybe there are people in the world that need killing."

My spit ran out as I thought about the one and only person I'd killed.

"I was the best father I could be to you. Except for letting you eat macaroni and cheese. I've had time to look at those ingredients, and I don't think it's actual food," he said, some of his old energy back in his voice.

"Dad, I, uh, have to tell you something."

"Go ahead," he said, straightening in his seat and lowering his leg to plant both feet on the floor. He slapped his knees and took a deep breath. "You know who killed me. I'm ready to hear it."

"I did."

"You did what?"

"I killed you."

"Don't play games. It was Legs, wasn't it? He carried a monstrous gun that I doubt he'd ever fired, but if he was in the building across the street—"

"No, I mean *I* killed you. It was me. I pulled the trigger and my gun misfired."

He stared at me, and I could tell, even though his eyes were shrunken so far back in his head that they were hard to see, that he was replaying the scenario in his ghost brain.

"Nemaye. If that is true, and I doubt it for two reasons, I wouldn't be here," he insisted. "No. Nemaye." He shook his hand at me in a flat karate chop to emphasize the words.

"It's true. I even remember it. I pulled the trigger, and there was an explosion, and then you were lying on me, bleeding," I said, but he was vigorously shaking his head, which pissed me off. "Honestly, I'm a little insulted you don't believe me."

"Be insulted. You're wrong," he said; then he folded his arms and glared at me with disdain.

"Why am I wrong?"

"First, I bought you that AK because it's small and has a reputation for not misfiring. Second, if it misfired, it would have killed you and only wounded me. And I'm certain that if you really had killed me, or were responsible for my death, I wouldn't be back here. If someone had to kill me, I would have chosen you. That would have given me peace," he finished, his body rigidly righteous as Atticus Finch in his closing arguments.

I, on the other hand, slumped back in my chair. Call me loopy, but his words made me want to cry.

"You'd choose *me* to kill you?" I asked, the bucket of shame I'd dumped on myself suddenly evaporating. "Really?"

"Of course," he stated. "So. Tell me what you found out."

I still felt a little weepy but sat forward and tried to piece together the day. Having gotten drunk in the middle of it, I felt like my memory of it had gotten a little soggy.

"I don't know if I found anything useful, but I hacked into the library and downloaded about fifteen minutes of data. There's probably nothing there, but I set up a path so I can tap into it again," I said, but my dad just stared at me blankly. "I should be able to scrape together enough information to get the FBI off my back."

I went back to my keyboard and opened a few windows to check on the data I'd copied, but the connection was worse than horrible.

"Crap," I muttered, holding up my phone but only seeing one flickering bar no matter where I held it.

"What?" my dad asked.

"My connection sucks."

"Connection for what?" he asked. My dad had never trusted technology and even questioned our phone line.

"Connection to the Internet. I set up a script to mirror the data packets from the library and also to record the IP so I could get back in. The problem is, I need a solid connection to access my Swiss server where I saved everything. And I don't want to waste time poaching someone's Wi-Fi—" I glanced at my dad, who looked completely lost. "Never mind. I set something up to tap into everything that happens at the library without having to be there. Now that I'm on Marko's radar and something is obviously going on—"

"Stop," he demanded, holding his hand up. "You're on Marko's radar? How? Why?"

He got up and started pacing the floor.

"He almost caught me setting up my computer near the library. That's when he told me I'd shot you, then later—"

"He told you that you shot me?" He halted right in front of the table, staring at me with confused, hollow eyes.

"Yeah. He said he saw us go in the building and followed us upstairs. He was there and saw it happen, and then he took me—"

My dad's booming laughter caught me off guard. He laughed so hard, he bent backward, then had to brace his hands against his back, probably so his disintegrating spine wouldn't snap in two. Now that I'd envisioned the possibility of seeing that happen, I was grateful he'd done what he had to in order to prevent it.

"It's not funny," I complained, but he continued to laugh.

He even looked at me and pointed, laughing even more.

"You're laughing, but I was really upset," I yelled at him. Geez, my dad could be an ass.

"Don't you understand? If Marko was there when I died, *he* was the one who killed me," he explained, wiping at tears that actually looked more like greenish goo.

"Marko was the one," I repeated, staring blankly at my monitor. "Marko?"

"Tak, tak," he insisted, holding his hands out to me. Yes, yes.

Finally, grudgingly, one of the several windows I'd opened on my computer changed from fuzzy static to a view of a desk and bookshelves. One of the video feeds from the library.

There, his neck tattoo barely visible, stood Marko, making angry movements at the police officer standing at his side. Behind him, two people wore papery, mint-colored bodysuits and went in and out of view into a room.

"That one always spent too much money on clothes," my dad grunted from where he'd moved into position behind me.

I opened other windows on the computer, trying to assess how much data I'd grabbed. I could tell from several of the folder names some of it was cell phone data from whoever "borrowed" the library's Wi-Fi. Even better. I could imagine all of Legs's people using the library's data.

Whatever I'd collected, it didn't matter. I had some data, and some data would have to be good enough to solve my felony problem.

I grabbed my backpack and checked the pocket, sweat popping out on the back of my neck when I couldn't find it.

"C'mon," I muttered, scratching deep into the pocket where I was sure I'd put the piece of paper. It had to be there.

"What are you doing?" my dad asked.

"Trying to find my get-out-of-jail card," I joked.

"What card does this?" he asked, but I shook my head.

I sagged when my fingers found it.

I pulled out my phone and dialed the number on the card, waiting through three rings until a woman's voice answered. Voicemail.

"Who are you calling?" my dad asked, which made me miss what the recording said before the beep.

"Hi. Uh, this is Lena Kozek. Tommy... Thomas gave me this number. Tell him I have what he's looking for."

I ended the call and looked into my father's stern, decaying face.

"What is this person looking for?" he asked me.

"Dirt on the Olynyks. It will help me with my felony problem, and then I can help you with your undead problem," I said. "Since you seem stuck here."

"I don't know that it's such a problem," he said with a shrug, then gestured toward me. "I'm enjoying myself. If this is my fate, it's not so bad."

I looked at his face; I wasn't sure, but I thought his skin looked more cracked than before.

"You look like you're falling apart. Don't you want to move on?" I asked, but I felt sort of good about what he'd said.

Other than him looking like a horror movie, I didn't mind the idea of him staying. Having family, and I meant family that actually wanted me around, felt pretty cool. I made the choice right then to stop thinking he was a manifestation of my orphaned psyche and accept him like a real dad.

"What is peace? I haven't known peace my whole life. Why would I find it when I'm dead?" he asked.

I nodded.

I was about to tell him that if he was happy, I was happy, as long as I didn't have to clean up after his decaying face, when a tingle skittered up my spine.

I slammed the laptop shut and turned to face the doorway. I didn't know how I knew, but someone was out in the hall, leaning against the door and listening.

Chapter Thirty-Seven

Quinn

Quinn stopped breathing, not moving in case taking his ear off the door made any sound. He'd been listening to a voice in the vacant apartment that apparently wasn't vacant anymore.

He'd looked forward to taking a long hot shower after spending close to an hour at the crime scene. He'd watched Brooke coordinate the investigation and fought back the excitement that flowed through him.

Detective work wasn't being in the line of fire; it was dealing with what happened later. It was safe and involved using his intelligence and intuition to solve a puzzle.

So much for early retirement, he thought, but the voice went silent once the coroner had shown up. He'd gone into full detective mode and realized he relished every moment, even the discussion of the bullet wound—more like a massive hole than a wound—to the victim.

When he'd shot the man in Seattle, it had been self-defense. Everyone assured him the internal review would confirm it. He'd been proclaimed a hero. The man had been firing on police, and the mayor himself had said he'd saved lives by taking a life, and a bad one at that. That the mayor and a state senator had sons who were connected to the man Quinn had shot was conveniently left out of the press release.

When his colleagues congratulated him on the killing, he hadn't felt like a hero. He'd seen the hole his Glock 19 had left in the man's neck. It had been a fluke that his bullet had nicked his jugular, which spouted blood in time with his heartbeat. *Beat-stream-beat-stream*, the red arc ebbing lower as the heart slowed and eventually stopped.

In the library, standing with the coroner over Legs's body, he had been catapulted back to that day. He'd expected it, braced for it, and watching the coroner examine the corpse had brought some memories back. But it hadn't hit as hard as he thought it would.

Now, though, with his ear pressed against the door, he knew the voice he heard was Lena's. His pancake-art-making hookup was in that apartment, and it froze his feet to the floor.

Brooke had admitted she knew Lena—Galyna Kozek, her full name—in elementary school, which made his connection to Lena even more complicated. He wouldn't say anything to Brooke until he figured out if he had to.

He thought of the pancake he'd wrapped. A very specific and detailed pancake. Was Lena really an assassin like Brooke had hinted? Had he had sex with a murderer?

He watched his fist rise and hover to the right of the peephole. He heard something and stilled his hand.

Rustling. Then the scrape of a chair. Then a murmur, something like, "It's a long story."

He pounded on the door, then jumped back when the door jerked open.

Lena stood there, her pale face staring at him defiantly.

He checked her hands, which were visible and not holding a weapon. The blue-and-white checkered dress, looking a thousand years old, was engulfed by an oversized jacket. Her hair was mussed, her body tense.

He scanned the dark apartment behind her, but none of his senses yammered a warning to his brain.

"Are you alone?" he asked, just to be sure.

"That's an odd thing to ask," she replied, her face scrunching into a disapproving expression. "How about, 'Hello, neighbor!'"

"You live here?" he asked with a frown. He thought it was more likely she'd broken in.

"Yeah," she said, folding her arms. "You caught me. I live here. I mean, I own this place. I kind of just found out about it, if you're wondering why I didn't mention it earlier."

Her voice was calm and her body still, but her eyes shifted from side to side.

"You just found out, huh," he stated, feeling cop mode settle over him.

"My aunt told me about it when she kicked me out of her place," she replied. Then she wagged a finger at him. "You kept me out past curfew, you bad boy."

"I...?" he half inquired, then reined in his composure. "You're the one who fell asleep."

"You're the one who coerced me into making pancake art," she retorted.

"Coerced!" he half shouted, then swiped a hand over his mouth and chin. "I seem to remember someone criticizing my heart and eagerly stepping in to show me how it's done."

Her mouth quirked up at the corner, and an annoyingly adorable light flickered in her eyes.

"I'll give you that," she said, then looked him up and down. "What happened to the fluffy housecoat?"

"I got called in to work," he answered and hooked his thumbs into his pants pockets. Time to put aside thoughts of an adorable neighbor and treat her like the alleged killer she maybe was.

"Right. Work," she murmured, sweeping her gaze over his clothes again. "I thought you were a cop. Am I right? You're a cop?"

"Something like that."

She half turned toward his apartment and pointed in the rough direction of the library. "Are you working on whatever's happening over there?"

"Yeah," he said, then rubbed a hand over his neck. "I need to ask you to come into the station and give a statement."

"You do, do you? Why is that?" she asked and refolded her arms. She looked to the side, and her eyebrows jumped together in a frown.

Without asking, he pushed the door open and looked inside, his internal radar giving a beep. He scanned the wall and the dark bedroom to the left but saw nothing.

"What?" she asked, watching him warily.

"It seemed like you were looking at something," he said.

"Well, now you know I wasn't. Why do I need to give a statement?"

"Because you were in the area during the time of the... incident," he replied.

She compressed her mouth, then moved her lips from side to side as if contemplating his request.

"What kind of incident was it?" she asked.

"I'll tell you at the station."

"Why can't you tell me now?"

"Because I said so."

"Is that the official Steeltown Police Department's position? Because Mr. Star Wars Pancake Maker says so?"

"Yes, actually."

She examined him once more, then glanced to the side again. He swore she gave a nod, and he looked at where her eyes had darted.

"What are you looking at?" he asked.

"Just my guardian angel," she said with a smirk and spun on her boots to walk to the table. She picked up her laptop and a cord and shoved them into her backpack. Then she grabbed a large case and walked back to where he stood. "Are you going to press charges, or will I be able to come back here?"

"I don't know yet. Are you going to confess to some crime?" he asked.

"Highly doubtful, but I don't want to disparage your interrogations skills," she replied, giving him half of that upside-down smile he didn't want to like.

"It's likely you'll be released if you cooperate."

"Good. I adopted a cat, and unless there are a few mice in this place, I'll have to come back to feed him."

He was about to reply, but she pushed past him, the hard case banging into his knee with an unexpected heaviness. Then she grabbed him by his coat and pulled him out of the doorway.

"Hey," he complained as she slammed her door shut and locked it. "You don't need to bring all your stuff."

"Yes. I do" was all she said before she marched down the stairs.

So much for a shower.

Quinn watched Lena settle into the chair at the small table. They were in the closest thing the Steeltown Police had to an interrogation room—an empty office beside the stairs that led down to records.

She put her backpack on the floor and the case upright between her feet.

Her face was tight even though she leaned back in the plastic chair with a loose-limbed confidence. His gut told him she was projecting a casualness she didn't feel, but was it because she'd committed murder or because nobody liked being brought in for questioning?

Brooke sat across from her, all the assuredness she'd had at the crime scene gone. The woman fidgeted with her notepad, dropped her pen twice, and paused several times to reposition a thick file she'd lugged into the room with her.

He walked behind her and leaned against the wall between the women. He glanced at the tab on the file. **Kozek, Ilya**.

"Where were you—" Brooke started, breaking off when Lena leaned forward, lacing her hands together on the table.

"You look familiar," Lena said.

"What?" Brooke asked.

"I've got it!" Lena shouted, slamming her hands flat on the table. "Third grade, Mrs. Remnick's class."

Brooke sat up so quickly, Quinn swore he heard a vertebra crack.

"Uh," Brooke muttered, her face stiffening.

"I'm right, aren't I?" Lena asked, then looked at him with a wondering shake of her head. "This girl... I mean, woman, led a squad of girly-girls to bully me."

"We didn't bully you," Brooke denied, but Quinn noticed a pink flush flare in her cheeks. "You made Marisa Thompson cry, and we thought—"

"That it would be okay to shove me around at lunch," Lena finished, hands in the air as if it was a natural conclusion.

Brooke looked down and turned the blank page on her notepad over to another blank page.

"We were stupid kids, okay?" Brooke murmured, clasping her hands on the notepad and looking up at Lena. "I'm sorry that happened."

Lena shrugged, all the sarcasm leaving her expression.

"Fair enough," she agreed, then held out her hand. "So accept my apology for kicking your ass on my last day of school."

"You didn't kick—" Brooke attempted, staring at Lena's hand.

The expression on her face told Quinn she was trying to determine if shaking Lena's hand would alter the power dynamics of the interrogation. Quinn didn't have the heart to tell her Brooke had never had the power from the minute Lena sat down.

"I punched you in the eye, you stayed on the ground.... Is it coming back to you yet?" Lena asked with genuine curiosity. "Anyway, let's shake and make up. Then you can ask me all the questions you want."

Brooke's face reddened, and when her eyes slid to his, he shrugged toward Lena's outstretched hand.

"Fine," Brooke said, grabbing the hand in a shake that was more like a jerk.

"Okay, what's your first question?" Lena asked, sweet as pecan pie.

"What's your connection to the Olynyk family?" Brooke asked, making a note on the pad.

"I don't have one," Lena replied.

"Wasn't your father an employee of Mr. Olynyk?"

"Maybe."

"Maybe?"

"Maybe, as in it's possible," Lena elaborated as if Brooke was unaware of what the word "maybe" meant.

"Don't you know what your father did for a living?" Brooke asked.

"Well, he bought me toys at Christmas, so I guess he could be—" Lena suggested, breaking off as her eyes widened. "Holy crap, you cracked the Santa Claus case!"

Brooke's lips pressed together, but she otherwise kept her cool.

"Wasn't your father a hitman for Legs Olynyk?" Brooke demanded, some of her old starchy self finally showing up.

His eyes moved to the thick file, a tension taking hold in his gut.

"Is that what it says in that mountain of a file?" Lena asked, her voice shifting down in tone. She laced her fingers together on the table.

Brooke put a protective hand over the file, and his gut churned harder.

"That, and a lot of other things. Your father was brought in for questioning several times."

"Does that folder say who shot my dad? Because I have an interest in an answer to that," Lena said.

He wasn't sure if he should be more disturbed that he'd slept with a killer's daughter or an actual killer. He mentally willed Brooke to get on with the important questions.

"Your father's death is a cold case that nobody's really following up on," Brooke said, careless cruelty in her voice. "But it's believed that his own boss arranged for his murder."

"Sounds like *someone's* following up on it," Lena suggested, sarcasm drenching the words.

"Did you have a grudge against Legs Olynyk?" Brooke demanded, mirroring Lena as she laced her fingers together. "Is that why you came back to Steeltown?"

"I don't know the man, so... no," Lena answered.

"Where were you from approximately midnight until 12:30 a.m.?" Brooke continued.

"Having sex with a stranger," Lena answered, and he felt his cheeks warm.

"Do you have any contact information for this stranger so we can corroborate that?" Brooke asked, picking up her pencil.

"The kind of strangers I have sex with aren't required to show me their ID. Hence the term stranger," Lena replied with sweet sarcasm. "What kind of strangers do *you* have sex with?"

"I don't... that is, I never—" Brooke sputtered before Lena talked over her.

"You could ask Mr. Dad Cop over there. I'm pretty sure he knows him," she said, giving him a smug look.

That caught Brooke off guard, her shoulders jerking back in surprise.

"You—" Brooke said, glancing at him over her shoulder.

"I was with Ms. Kozek from the late evening until after midnight," he acknowledged and walked around Brooke to take up a position on the other wall, still between the two women.

Brooke swiveled her head to follow him.

"You were *with* her?" she asked in an almost-gasp. "With *her?* Why?"

"Uh-oh," Lena mused, her face scrunching into false sympathy. "Am I raining on someone's crush parade?"

"I—no! But... what—" Brooke stammered.

He held a hand up, but before he could speak, Lena rolled right along.

"It's pretty simple. I hooked him with some *Star Wars* trivia. Between us girls, that's pretty awesome foreplay for him. Then we did the nasty, and he cooked me a midnight breakfast thing before I took a not-that-shameful walk of shame," Lena reeled off, then perched her chin on her hand and looked at him with fluttering eyelashes. "Did I miss anything... Snookums?"

"Midnight... breakfast?" Brooke mumbled, her eyes widening before jerking back to look Lena over.

"You might have left off the part where you killed Legs Olynyk," he suggested, swiping a hand across the back of his hot neck.

The only satisfaction he got was watching her eyes dilate after he spoke.

The chin, the hand... her whole body went rigid as the shock of his words registered.

His gut told him the one thing that made him feel better about having slept with a suspect.

She didn't do it.

Chapter Thirty-Eight

Lena

Geez, if I ever needed a poker face, it was right then.

"Legs... is dead," I stated, impressed at the calm in my tone. "I bet my aunt's old lady friends are happy."

"Nobody's happy about murder," Brooke admonished, leaning over the table. "You didn't answer Qui—Detective Magee's question."

"He asked me a question? It sounded more like a statement," I said. Focusing on needling Brooke diverted me from the shock that still echoed along the surface of my skin.

Legs was dead, and I was here because they thought I did it. Although, on the plus side, it was a felony I *wasn't* guilty of.

"Did you kill Legs Olynyk tonight?" Brooke demanded, a manic undertone to the question.

"Legs Olynyk, the slimy crime guy who works out of a library? I would think the head librarian would have killed him herself years ago."

Brooke sneered at me. "The librarian's a man."

"Good detective work," I whispered. "But to answer your accusation, no. I didn't kill Legs."

Resentment boiled in Brooke's eyes, and it made me want to both gloat and bawl. She'd been incredibly mean in school. Her apology from two seconds ago was something, but no way would it wipe out the torment she'd put me through. When I explained the punch in the eye to my dad, he'd patted my back and encouraged me to keep defending myself against bad people.

Only now, this woman thought *I* was the bad people, and I had no physical way to prove my innocence other than with the only guy in the room.

"Who saw you after you left Detective Magee's apartment?" Brooke asked, back to business with her notepad.

"Let's see. I left after pancakes," I mused, pursing my lips as I thought. "Then I got on a bus. Oh, Marko Olynyk might have chased after me on the street."

"Why would he do that?" This came from Quinn.

"That's a good question. You should ask him," I said, then gave Brooke an innocent smile I knew she would hate. "Let me know what he says. He looked pretty upset when he was chasing me down the street."

"We've talked to him, and he says *you* killed Legs. That he caught you in the act," Brooke said. Her face was serene, but I could see the bully lurking underneath. She was loving this.

"Really. Interesting. So... if I killed his dad, and he witnessed it, why didn't I kill Marko?" I asked.

"Because your vendetta was against Legs," Brooke answered.

"My vendetta?"

"Legs had your father killed," she replied, glancing meaningfully to the thick folder as if it were the body of my father.

I could imagine my dead dad rolling his eyes at this if he'd been in the room. He'd get a kick out of this interrogation when I told him about it.

"Is that the file on my dad's murder?" I asked, wondering if there was a way I could get a copy.

"This is his criminal record. The case file on his murder is separate," she explained like I was a police rookie who should have known that.

I hated her smug expression, but I buried the urge to slap it off her face. Instead, I mirrored her posture and her crap-eating look. I leaned back in my chair and gave them a dose of keeping my mouth closed.

I glanced at Mr. Pancakes, but he was frowning at Brooke.

"Is the Kozek case really still open?" he asked.

Brooke's jaw tightened.

"As far as I know, it is. It has nothing to do with Legs's murder, though. Kozek's murder happened over ten years ago," Brooke explained patronizingly.

A surge of warmth bubbled up as I watched Quinn frown more deeply. At least someone was on my side who wasn't a ghost.

He looked like he was about to say something more when voices outside the room distracted all three of us.

They started as angry chattering but switched to outright yelling in just a few seconds, and then loud footsteps rang against the floor. Footsteps that got my attention like a gun fired in the air.

The door burst open, and a goddess with expensive blonde hair and a billowing brown coat stood in the doorway like Galadriel from *The Lord of the Rings*. Her mouth opened, and I was positive she was about to proclaim, "All shall love me and despair."

And I did love her once I found out who she was.

"This woman is my client, and she will not say another word!" she proclaimed, her eyes on fire as she pointed a red, manicured nail at me.

Hell yeah! I wanted to shout, but I also wanted to be cool, so I just nodded knowingly.

Quinn looked confused, but Brooke looked confused *and* pissed. Even better.

"Conflict of interest, Bella. Which means you have no legal right to be a part of this interrogation," Brooke protested.

"As of one hour ago, I have every right. Legs Olynyk is no longer my client. Neither is the organization or any family member," she stated. "Are you charging her?"

"Ms. Kozek is here voluntarily to make a statement—" Brooke said, but Quinn cut her off.

"No. We're not charging her," he said.

My awesome lawyer's expression didn't change. She just rotated her pointing hand palm up and waved at me. "Let's go," she said.

I jumped to my feet, threw on my backpack, and hugged my gun case against me.

"I'm going," I agreed.

She pointed the way out of the room, glaring at Quinn and Brooke as if she was conducting a jailbreak. And I guess she sort of was.

"My car's right out front," she said, close behind me.

The few officers in the main office watched us with wide eyes, which was impressive for three in the morning.

We pushed through the double doors, and I saw a sleek car parked halfway on the sidewalk.

"You weren't kidding about out front," I said.

She strode around the front of the car while I climbed in, noticing the car was still running.

"We need to—" she said, but I cut her off.

"I imagine there's a lot *we* need to do, but *I* have something I need to do first," I told her. I unzipped my backpack and pulled out my laptop. Five windows popped open, and I tethered to my phone's Wi-Fi.

The tumbling emotions of the last hour dropped away, and all my next steps materialized on a checklist in my mind.

My lawyer stared at me, and then her eyes shifted to my laptop's screen.

"All right. Where do you need to go to do whatever you're doing?" she asked.

"First, let's start with what I should call you," I replied, setting up a data transfer before looking over at her. "Besides an *actual* guardian angel."

She pursed her lips, then looked somewhere in the dashboard's vicinity.

"I'm Arabella Palmer. You can call me Bella," she said. She gripped the steering wheel, then tapped one of those long nails on the leather. "You know my brother, though."

Arabella Palmer. Palmer, Palmer.... Something snapped in my brain. Of course I knew her brother!

"He's Batman," I whispered, awed. When she frowned at me, I clarified, "Tommy."

"Yes. Tom," she corrected, but her mouth moved in a way that told me she got it when I called her brother Batman.

"Well, what I have to do involves him. And me now, I guess. We should—" I said, but she cut me off.

"Let's go see him," she said, then pulled on her seat belt.

"Go see him?" I asked, sure I'd misheard. Unless she planned on driving me across the country.

"He's in town."

My mind equalled blown.

Chapter Thirty-Nine

Thomas

Thomas stared through his windshield at the sky over Rob's Harbour. It had lightened to a smooth indigo, signaling the arrival of dawn in another hour.

He'd parked his rental car at the end of Main Street, blocks away from where his life had gone to shit. Looking at the sidewalk and then at the bench further down was a surreal feeling.

He was back home, a place he'd sworn never to be, staring at a street he'd vowed never to walk on, reliving a past he thought would be buried after sending Lena back.

His phone rang with a familiar ringtone.

"Yeah," he greeted in a gruff voice.

"I'm with Lena. I just picked her up from the station," Bella stated.

"With who?" He was positive he'd misheard.

"Lena. She's my client," Bella clarified in a stiff voice.

"She's your *what*?" he demanded, reaching for the green hat on the seat beside him. He clenched it in his fist. "How is that not a conflict of interest?"

"I quit the Olynyks and represent Lena now," she said.

He clamped his mouth shut, otherwise he'd be sputtering inanities. Bella didn't speak, either, as if she knew he needed to collect himself.

"You know what my plan was, and you still—" he attempted.

"That plan is over as of right now, so take a breath and tell me where you are," she said.

He glared through the car's windshield at the empty street. The bus bench where he'd last seen his father sat in a pool of light from a streetlamp. It was the last time he'd seen his dad and the last time his father had seen him.

A few feet from the bench was where the green trilby had rolled into the crime scene photos he'd seen. The trilby he now clenched in his hand.

"Representing Lena," he repeated, the last bits of his plan crumbling in his mind. His sister was no longer on his side. "Why?"

Bella let out a long sigh.

"You do what you think is right, and I do the same. We just have different ideas of what's right," she finally replied. "I think you and I need to get on the same page."

He huffed.

"What happened to wanting to be with your family no matter what?" she demanded, and he heard the sharp edge of anger in her voice.

"I don't remember saying 'no matter what,'" he grumbled.

He heard a high voice mumbling in the background, and his spine stiffened. It was her. The woman at the center of this mess.

"What's she saying?" he demanded.

"Something about brotherly love," Bella murmured. "Where are you?"

"I'm around," he said. "Where are you?"

He heard Bella's muffled voice ask, "Where are we going?" and an answering murmur.

Bella gave him the name of a place, and he ended the call. He looked at the phone, then threw it on the seat.

So this was how it would go. Betrayed by his own family. There was no other way to look at his sister taking Lena Kozek on as a client. She was too good-hearted for this to be a devious move to help him get justice.

He was about to turn the key in the ignition when a movement at the end of the street stilled his hand.

A shadow separated from darkness on the left, an orange glow of light illuminating a harsh profile. Thomas recognized the arrogant, slumping posture and the way he lowered the cigarette and flicked ashes from it with his thumb.

Marko.

The man rolled his shoulders, then sauntered across the empty street, walking right up to the curb in front of the bench Thomas had just been staring at. He blew a plume of smoke upward, and the streetlight turned it into a white cloud over his head. Then he looked down at the bench.

Something about the way he stood there, satisfied, made Thomas's stomach sour. It was a sharper feeling than when he'd first seen Lena and more acidic than hearing Duncan's promise to fire him.

There was a time when Marko had been Thomas's boss. He'd called Thomas his best salesman.

"Tommy, son, I'm upping your percentage," he'd told him and named a number that was three times what his dad's cop salary paid. An amount that made the words "Tommy, son" a little bit easier to take.

"Not only that, but you'll be your own boss. Prove yourself, and it could put you in the inner circle," Marko had told him.

"I'm all in," he'd replied, excited and nervous. Screw school and rules and scraping by on his parents' dismal salaries. He would be his own man, calling his own shots, and all at the age of only eighteen.

"Good boy," Marko had said, slapping him hard and emitting a strange laugh. "You just have to meet my man. He'll be right out there tomorrow, wearing a green hat. Pass that test, and everything's golden."

Only the man in the hat hadn't been a drug connection. And he definitely hadn't been expecting to meet *him*.

Thomas started the engine.

He put the car in gear, letting the transmission start it rolling. He didn't pull into the road, just kept the car moving along the curb. The tires rubbed against it here and there, the curbside debris crunching under the tires.

Marko half turned when Thomas was a hundred feet away. Then he fully turned when the car was fifty feet away. The man stepped onto the curb with a glossy shoe when the distance got to thirty feet.

Thomas flipped on his high beams, smiling when Marko reared back and shielded his eyes. He glimpsed a rumpled white shirt under a dark jacket, a spatter of dark spots between the lapels. Then a tattoo around the man's neck. Then he saw the smirk.

That crooked know-it-all twist of a mean mouth that used to make Thomas laugh along with him now made him press his foot down on the accelerator.

Thomas must have come within a foot of the man before he veered away from the curb and accelerated around the corner. The time to settle scores had arrived, and he wouldn't watch it from a distance. Whatever his sister and her new client had in mind, he would make sure it involved taking Marko down.

Chapter Forty

Lena

I thought I was having a nervous breakdown. I mean... come on.

A talking corpse and sleeping with a cop notwithstanding —now I seemed to be the prime suspect in a murder. Then I get a free lawyer, but that lawyer turns out to be Batman's sister?

It's an amazing story for the grandchildren I won't live long enough to have.

I looked at the sleek blonde driving the car. I thought about pinching her to see if she was real but opted for a verbal check instead.

"You're *really* Tommy's sister?" I asked. "And really a lawyer?"

Her jaw clenched as she took a sharp corner. I braced my arm against my door and steadied my laptop.

"Really, I'm both," she said, checking her rearview and compressing her lips.

I looked behind us, but I didn't see any headlights, just the purple dawn filling the sky.

"Why are we going to the Bold Bean?" Bella asked.

"Best Wi-Fi in the Pacific Northwest, from what I've been told," I replied. "Any chance you could take these corners in a way that doesn't make me barf?"

Her eyes shifted to the open computer on my lap, then back to the road.

"Any chance you'll tell me the truth about whether you killed Legs?" she asked.

"I didn't kill him. I never even thought of killing him," I answered, then groaned when she took another sharp corner.

"Sorry," she said and at least slowed down. "Why do you need good Wi-Fi? Isn't your phone tethering?"

"I need to pull a metric crap-ton of data from Switzerland as fast as I can to get your brother off my back," I explained. "There's a slim possibility I could tell you who killed Legs too."

She braked suddenly, forcing my body against the locked seat belt. I gripped my laptop so it didn't smash into the dash.

"Hay-seuss Christi!" I complained.

"Sorry. We're here," she said and eased the expensive car into the driveway.

The small trailer with a neon sign that read **The Bold Bean** sat in the middle of an empty lot. A gravel path led from the road to encircle the business.

Bella steered the car to the left, the rutted ground making it dip and bounce almost worse than her sharp corners.

"God, please just stop the car," I groaned, rolling my head dramatically.

"I guess here is as good as anyplace to park," she murmured, unbuckling her seat belt.

I pushed the door open and climbed out, then slung my backpack on and grabbed the saxophone case while holding my open computer steady in one hand.

"Let me take that," she said, pointing to the case I held.

"I got it," I said and walked to the trailer, leaving Bella to close my door and lock up.

"Welcome to paradise!" Valerie greeted when I walked into the small space. She stood behind the counter on the left, holding her hands up. "I knew you'd make it eventually."

I grinned. It felt great to have allies. I definitely thought I'd be needing as many as I could get.

"Glad to be here," I answered.

"Are you ready for that mocha frappé?" she asked, then waved a rag at me and started moving behind the counter.

"You know it," I agreed. "What's the password for your awesome Wi-Fi?"

"Latte100, capital L. But if you need superfast, go to Bold Bean Private. The password is Ki$$MyA$$, one word, title case, and all the *s*'s are dollar signs," she said and winked a feathery lashed eye at me.

"I feel like I could have guessed that," I said, standing by the counter while I followed her directions on the laptop.

"You," Valerie said, and I caught her giving Bella a disdainful look. "You have extra-hot, extra-foam chai latte written all over you."

"I'd actually prefer some green tea, if you have it," Bella replied, but I could tell by the way her hands clenched, Valerie had probably nailed it. And by the way Valerie's eyebrow shot up, I knew she thought so too.

"It's been a slow morning, but you're just in time to meet one of my regulars," Valerie said and angled her impressive hairdo toward the back of the small coffee hut.

There, sitting hunched over a steaming mug, was a wizened old woman.

"Mizbee," I whispered, instantly reverting to my ten-year-old self who'd caught trouble for digging in her rose garden for Lord knew what. I straightened my posture, but I couldn't do much else since I had to balance a laptop, my gun case, and my backpack.

"Galyna Kozek," she greeted, her voice suggesting a gravelly surprise. Her eyes flickered to the chair in front of her and back to me. "Come and sit with me. You," she said and looked at Bella, "can sit over there."

Mizbee cast her eyes at the table closest to the counter. There were only six tables in the place, all of them crowded close together. Unless Mizbee wrote me notes, anyone in the shop could overhear us, but I knew her gesture meant something else. It was a power move, and for some reason, I was being included in the inner circle of the Blue Hair Mafia. Or sucked into it, I guess. After all, I was a suspect in the murder of said mafia's number-one enemy.

Bella compressed her lips but sat at the table Mizbee indicated.

"Now. You." The blue-haired woman looked me up and down. "You've been busy tonight."

Mizbee's mouth and forehead were so wreathed in wrinkles, her face looked like a walnut. Though only her mouth moved, it had a ripple effect that made her whole face swim. I didn't think I'd ever been this close to her, and though the strange motion of her face was a distraction, the sad gleam of her eyes told me I was in for some hard truths.

"You could say that," I agreed, lowering myself into the chair across from her.

I slid out of my backpack and put it and the sax case on the floor under my seat. I set the laptop on the table between us. I tapped a few keys to start the data transfer, then lowered the lid to half-mast. A sizzle of goose bumps up my arm told me things were about to get real serious.

"Sleeping with a police officer is a... bold decision," she murmured.

I shrugged. She wasn't wrong, and trying to explain nervous horniness to a woman who looked days away from disintegrating seemed like a waste of time.

"He's a detective, apparently, but you're right," I said.

Mizbee nodded, rotating her white coffee mug back and forth as she studied me.

"I didn't know what to think when you showed up on your aunt's doorstep," she said.

"I didn't expect to be there," I admitted, feeling some of my old resentment bubble up.

"Do you know your aunt wanted to take you in after your father was killed?" she queried in a scientific tone. She was probing me, curious to see how I'd react.

This was a test, and I knew it. But instead of figuring out how to pass it, I let her see all the emotions going through me. This was a time for the truth, and her words were boots to my heart.

"I didn't know that," I said, uncaring that Mizbee's family was historically the crime family of Steeltown before Legs stole power. And the Breziaks stole it from someone else, and so on, and so on. The problem was, she'd stolen something from *me*. The right to have a family. "That's a harsh thing to do to a little kid—separate her from her blood family."

She stared at me, her mouth twitching a little. "But the right thing."

"Did my aunt tell you that?"

"I was there when Marko dropped you off," she replied, squinting at me and creating a whirlpool of movement on her forehead. "In the house, out of sight, but there."

I let that sink in, willing memories of that day to come back. Opening myself to whatever bits of my past my brain wanted to dish up. Now that I was open to it, my brain was ready to dump it all out.

The memory of snuggling against my mom, the soft fabric of her favorite dress against my cheek belonging to the dress I now wore. The trips to practice shooting on Copper Ridge with my dad. My father destroying my mother's photos out of grief. Potluck visits to my aunt's. The history of the Breziaks.

Then other flashes came to me, like tiny embroidered flowers augmenting a vyshyvanka shirt. Why paska and ham were never on the potluck table. Fighting with Vas and losing every time until the day I won. Me going back to school and enjoying my new tough persona around Brooke until I got kicked out for that punch.

Lastly, me on a plane, alone and heading to New York. Me believing I'd shot my father. Then learning I could just... forget.

I'd buried the past so expertly that it didn't exist until a certain corpse came back and cracked it wide open.

"You were there," I repeated, pushing into that memory. Feeling it come alive around me.

Dead grass under my feet and my aunt pulling the saxophone case out of my hand. A twitch of the curtains that I'd thought was Vas. It wasn't.

"I convinced her it was too dangerous for you to stay," Mizbee said. "You'd just shot a man, and it was only a matter of time—"

"No, I didn't," I said, ready to explain what corpse Dad had already told me about Marko.

"You did," she said and waited patiently while my mind buzzed around that fact.

My dad told me that I hadn't killed... him. Wait. He said I hadn't killed *him*. I slumped in the chair. He said I hadn't shot him, but I distinctly remember pulling a trigger.

"Hm," Mizbee grunted, her mouth denting in at the corners. Her next words jerked me in a new direction. "I knew your mother."

My mouth opened, but nothing came out. All thoughts of killing evaporated. Here was something I really wanted to hear.

"She was a lovely girl who had to grow up too fast. Korinna wanted her to leave, too, after it happened, but she refused," Mizbee said, finally picking up her mug to sip at her coffee.

"After the shooting happened?" I asked, confused. Was the old lady losing it? My mom died of an aneurysm when I was four.

"After what Legs did to her," Mizbee said, her eyebrows coming together. "Didn't Korinna give you your mother's diary?"

My feet froze against the sax case under my chair. I hadn't totally forgotten there was something else in there—I'd just *mostly* forgotten.

I wanted to wait until I was in a place where I could cry and not have anyone see me. Of course, then the whole hookup murder thing had happened, and, well, here I was.

"She mentioned something. I haven't read it yet," I replied.

Mizbee grunted and sipped again. Then she set the mug on the saucer and pushed it to the middle of the table. Its edge made a dull *clink* when it tapped against the laptop.

"I suggest you look through it," she said, looking me over again. "And bring your policeman detective to the potluck on Sunday."

"Why would I do that?" I asked, more to mask being caught off guard by the turn in the conversation than to be argumentative.

"You come to the potluck because, despite everything, you're family. And you bring this man because he's a certain someone in your life now," she said.

"How do you know he's a certain anything?" I asked.

"When will you stop being surprised that I know everything that goes on in this town? We had a meeting about it earlier with your aunt. About what to do with you," she said.

I waited for her to finish, but she just stared at me with a tiny smile pulling up the corner of her mouth.

"And what was the consensus?" I asked, which only made her smile widen.

"Bring that wiener dish you used to make," she said, waving her hand regally. "It was... unique."

Now I gaped at her.

She leaned toward me, sniffing delicately, and the wrinkles on her face twisted into regret. "Maybe take a shower too," she added.

Then she slid off the chair and walked past me, patting my shoulder as she did.

I dragged out the sax case and shifted myself into her now-empty seat so the wall was now behind me. I flipped open the latches and lifted the lid, holding up a "just a minute" finger at Bella when she got up. She sat back down.

Lying on top of the velvet-shrouded AK parts was an elastic-banded book. It was worn with age but seemed to glow with an urgency that made my heart glow right along with it.

On the cover, in writing that could have only been my mother's, it read "My Diary."

Chapter Forty-One

Quinn

Quinn listened to Brooke rant, first about Lena, then Bella, then the Olynyks, before he waved a hand in front of her.

"I want to look at this file," he said, picking up the thick Ilya Kozek folder and tucking it under his arm. "Once you're less pissed about all the people you know who are elitist pricks, let me know if you think there are any viable suspects. Other than Marko," he said.

That got her attention.

"You think Marko did it? He idolized his father," Brooke said, but Quinn was already moving away. "Those two went everywhere together—when Legs left the library, that is. Why would he kill his own father?"

"Why, indeed? Why don't you look into it while I go through this?" he said, flicking the folder with his finger.

He intended to go to the chief's office but instead pulled open the door to the basement file storage. He wanted the privacy. Brooke could handle all the excitement of the murder, which had brought in most of the department's cops to mill around upstairs.

Something about Kozek's murder stuck with him, and if it didn't go away after reading through Ilya's file, he'd probably want to dig up everything on the Olynyk family. Might as well be close to where the digging would happen.

He flipped the light switch and walked down the stairs, the overhead lights buzzing as they came to life. A small table was at the base of the stairs, and he laid the folder on it. He scraped a chair out to sit, then flicked open the cover.

Inside was a photo of Ilya Kozek, steely eyes staring back at him. Beside it was the photo of a young girl.

Lena.

Galyna Adeline Kozek. Age unknown, which he found interesting. He studied the photo, comparing her to the woman who'd been upstairs.

The photo showed a young Lena with streaked blonde hair cut just below her ears. Bangs lay in a precise line high on her forehead. Her expression, which made Quinn smile, was resentful. Maybe it had to do with the purple smudge on her left cheekbone. He laughed, wondering if it was evidence of her encounter with Brooke. The generic background made him think it was a class photo.

He unclipped Ilya's photo and held it beside the girl's. The no-bullshit demeanor and steely glare were the only similarities. Maybe the hair color too.

Quinn flipped to the earliest record at the back of the folder and read forward.

A few misdemeanors, but the bulk of the paperwork looked like cops pulling him in to shake him down about the Olynyks and their various businesses. In the transcribed interviews, he could pick up on Kozek's personality. Sometimes he just repeated the questions back, and his answer was noted as "Mr. Kozek shrugged." Sometimes Kozek just said, "No effing comment," repeatedly.

One interview caught Quinn's attention. All the questions

focused on Olynyk's drug business. The description of Kozek differed from the other statements.

"'Mr. Kozek appeared to be angry. He folded his arms and said something in Ukrainian before replying that he knew nothing about that and that we should talk to Marko,'" Quinn murmured aloud.

When Quinn finally got to the top page, which contained the details of Kozek's murder, it was the briefest page of the whole folder. But one detail leaped out at him.

"Ilya Kozek was killed after assassinating Officer Wallace Bradford," Quinn murmured. "Officer Bradford was investigating a drug ring at the Steeltown High School run by Legs Olynyk. There were no witnesses. A tip about a member of Seattle's Petrov crime family being in town that day was called in, but no caller information was noted. No Petrov family member was found in town."

Quinn sat back in the chair. "Wallace Bradford," he said.

He looked around, then found a small computer on a corner desk. He dragged his chair over and pushed the Power button. The screen came to life with the record management portal graphic and a single field asking for his badge number.

Taking a chance, he typed in his Seattle badge number. After a pause while the computer thought about it, a welcome window appeared.

He searched for Bradford's name. The cursor blinked several times, then spit out the file location. Aisle two, shelf four, item 327.

A few minutes later, he'd dropped Bradford's file beside Kozek's. The two were similar in thickness even though Bradford's only pertained to his murder. Not especially surprising, given he was a cop shot in the line of duty and Ilya was a criminal.

Quinn opened Bradford's file and read through it. After four pages, he pulled out his phone and started dictating notes.

Bradford's file contained more details regarding Kozek's crime scene than Kozek's file did.

There was a drawing of where both Bradford's and Kozek's bodies were found. Kozek's was around the corner from the library on the third floor of an apartment building, while Bradford's was across the street from the library beside a roughly drawn rectangle labeled **BENCH**.

A line marked the trajectory of the bullet from Kozek's outline to Bradford's body. A note was made about the caliber of Kozek's gun and that it had been recovered at the scene and booked into evidence. They'd also catalogued a bullet casing. Just one.

He learned the bullet found in Bradford's head matched the caliber of Kozek's gun. Then he found an evidence disposal notice. A handwritten one, which was not standard in any police department he'd ever worked in. It noted that Kozek's gun had been destroyed two weeks after the case file had been opened, another anomaly. Holding evidence for a minimum of ten weeks was the norm.

"There's no autopsy report for Ilya Kozek," Quinn dictated into his phone. "Check with the coroner to see if it was completed but not forwarded to the department. See if residue was noted on his hands or body or if the coroner even requisitioned the test."

He tapped the Stop button, keeping his next thoughts to himself.

He doubted there would be an autopsy report. There was enough evidence that pointed to Kozek, so why waste more city money on testing?

He flipped to the tabbed pages where the evidence photos were. There lay Bradford, sprawled facedown with a wet, seeping hole in the back of his head and his hat a few feet away. Another photo near the pavement level showed his right eye, bloodshot but wide open. As if shocked at what had happened.

A last photo looked like it was taken inside a building. It must have been the landing near Kozek's body.

It was a close-up of the casing for a .47 or bigger bullet. It had rolled into a corner and was surrounded by the narrow baseboard on a linoleum floor. He looked closely at the photo.

Something had been etched into the metal cylinder, the oxidation and dents almost fully obscuring it.

"Huh," he murmured, then tapped the Record button on his

phone. "Kozek's shooter etched a symbol into the casing, along with—"

He rotated the file to get a better look.

The letter *K* had been etched above crosshatchings of lines and shapes that surrounded the casing.

"Along with the letter *K*. For Kozek?"

He stopped recording and dialed the number for dispatch.

"Who's processing the library?" he asked.

"Officer Miller. Do you want me to put you through to him?" dispatch asked.

"Yeah," he replied. The call clicked, then rang.

"Officer Miller," the man answered.

"Are you still processing the scene?" Quinn asked.

"We're just packing up. The coroner's done. Should we leave the tape up?" he asked, but Quinn ignored him.

"Did you bag any bullet casings?" he asked.

"Uh, no, I don't think so. But we fingerprinted the whole place like you wanted. Even the outside of the back exit door," the officer said, his tone nervous.

"Did you check the floor for anything?" he asked.

"Uh, Lopez might have. I can check—"

"Never mind. Bring everything back to the station but leave the tape up for now," he replied.

"Will do," Miller said, and Quinn ended the call.

He gathered the files and was halfway up the stairs when the door slammed open, startling the shit out of him.

"You'd better check this out," Brooke said and stood back when he walked past her.

He rounded the corner into the office and saw a cluster of people outside the front desk. A number of off-duty cops stood on the inside of the desk, nursing coffees and trying not to make eye contact with the people.

"What's this all about?" he asked, noting that many of the faces belonged to older women. One belonged to a Black man with dreadlocks who waved when he noticed Quinn was looking at him.

"We'd all like to give statements about the killing," he called out, then pointed to the officers. "We have important information, but they're ignoring us."

"What the hell," he mumbled, then waved at the stunned officer to let the people in.

They crowded into the space just inside the door, shuffling to let a small woman in shiny shoes and a rumpled tracksuit step out from their group.

"My niece, Galyna Kozek, had nothing to do with the murder of Legs Olynyk," she announced, then lifted something to her mouth. She vaped a long stream of smoke toward the **No Smoking** sign and smirked at him. "Are you a detective?"

"Uh, yeah. Yes," he replied, rattled by the way she swept her eyes over him.

"So, you're the boyfriend," she murmured.

He didn't like the knowing look in her eyes and liked Brooke's annoyed sigh even less. Did everyone know he'd had sex with the prime suspect?

"Boyfriend is a stretch," he replied and pointed the woman to a desk. Brooke left to deal with the rest of the crowd.

Lena's aunt strolled to the desk, blowing another puff of vape steam in his direction.

"Is one-night stand a better description?" she asked, sitting in the plastic chair opposite him. "I don't know what young people call it."

"It sounds like you know what your niece was up to tonight. Which puts her very close to the crime scene," he began, opening a drawer to hopefully find a pad of report sheets. Instead, he saw a Glock in a duty holster surrounded by paperclips and pens.

He took it out and placed it on his desk, staring at it. It wasn't his job to find the cop it belonged to and reprimand him, especially when the sight of the gun torqued his anxiety to the point where words wouldn't come easy.

"Is that supposed to intimidate me?" Lena's aunt demanded, blowing her next mouthful of steam at the gun.

"Maybe it's to reassure you," he replied.

"Huh," she grunted, her expression very not reassured.

He grimaced and stood up just as a red-faced cop hustled over.

"Sorry about that," the man said, taking the gun and retreating.

Quinn fell back into the chair. Since he was officially on duty, he'd need to get his own firearm issued, ideally before he left the station.

He swallowed, noting the calculated look the aunt gave him and gave her a steely glare back. It didn't faze her.

Opening another drawer, he finally found a notepad.

"You think *you* can reassure me? This is *my* assurance," she said in accented syllables. She leaned forward and pulled up the leg of her tracksuit. Strapped to her calf was a black leather case containing a small gun, probably a .38. Embossed on the case was a neat pattern of symbols. Grapes and a cross and—

"Stop looking at my leg," the woman chided as she dropped her pant leg. "Now write this down. Galyna was with me at home all night. All. Night." She tapped the blank paper with each word.

He heard murmuring from the crowd standing behind her, all of them nodding. He had a feeling everybody was going to claim Lena was with them. All. Night.

Chapter Forty-Two

Thomas

Thomas pulled the rental car up beside the only other vehicle in the parking lot. He reached for the door handle just as his phone buzzed.

Great. It was Duncan.

"Yeah," he answered, resigned. He'd forgotten about the precipice his job was hanging from.

"Nice to see you're up early. What is it there, five?"

"Close. Look, if you're calling to fire me, just get to it. I'm meeting my sister and—"

"I heard Olynyk's dead. That true?" The question came out like a statement without a hint of anger or annoyance in his boss's tone.

"From what I understand," he said and sighed. He had new plans that dovetailed nicely with being fired. Now it sounded like it might not happen.

"That changes things. The New York office is lighting up with a lot of Danchuk chatter, and the Seattle office called to say the guys watching the Petrovs out there are seeing the same action. Where are you right now?"

"In Steeltown," he replied.

"Good. You think your girl was involved?"

"I'm about to find out, I think," he said.

"Okay, then. Find out. Talk to anybody involved and see what links there are to either family. Word is, there's going to be a turf war for the Pacific Northwest with Legs gone. Since I've got a man on the ground there—" Duncan paused, his sneering tone filling the car. "—I've been told to do everything I can. No screwups. Understand?"

He gripped the phone. The idea of quitting crossed his mind, but he pictured himself serving popcorn at the local theatre and bit back the words he wanted to say.

"Understood," he said instead.

His boss beat him to ending the call, and he slid the phone into his breast pocket. Then he picked up the hat and put it on before heading into the coffee hut.

Bella stood up when he walked in, but he scanned the small café until he spotted *her* at the back. She was mostly hidden behind an open black case.

"Tom," his sister greeted, tugging his sleeve when he didn't look at her right away. "What the hell is that?"

She looked pointedly at the trilby, her expression saying she knew what it was but was hoping he would lie about it.

"Dad's hat," he replied. The time of hiding from anything in the past was over.

He pointed for her to sit back down, then slipped into the seat opposite her.

"What's going on?" he asked.

"Do you remember the Breziaks?" she asked.

"Vaguely. The Olynyks took over from them back in the day," he answered, movement behind the counter catching his attention. A woman in a towering beehive stared him down.

"Drip coffee, black," she called out like an accusation, then set an ivory mug in front of him before he could answer.

"Tazia Breziak was just in here having a one-on-one with Lena," Bella explained. "From what I could overhear, she's the one who wanted Lena sent to New York."

"So?" he asked and sipped the black liquid.

The taste shocked him. Velvety, but strong. It tasted nothing like the sludge he choked down back at the home office on the rare occasion. He looked over to see Beehive staring at him. She read his expression before giving him a knowing smirk and going back to whatever baristas did between customers.

"So," Bella drawled, jutting her chin out in frustration. "She's not exactly sending Lena away this time. Back in the day, Legs didn't just take over. He killed Tazia's father to force the issue. Golan Breziak was a straight guy for a crook, and to many people in town, his daughter was royalty. A kingmaker. Or in her case, a queenmaker," Bella murmured.

He glanced over at Lena. Her eyes moved back and forth in quick bursts as she read something he couldn't see behind the case.

She looked different from just a couple of days ago. For one, she was wearing a dress. A stained dress, but a dress. For another, she'd aged about ten years. She also looked like she'd think about your question instead of shooting back an immediate insult.

"You're saying Tazia Breziak is naming Lena Kozek the next head of Steeltown organized crime?" he murmured and watched Lena's eyes close as she leaned back. He looked at his sister.

"Maybe. Although... it could just be a straightforward potluck—" Bella stopped, sitting up straight as she stared at Lena.

Thomas looked back to see what caught her attention.

Lena's face had paled, and when her eyes opened, they shone, staring about five feet above the barista's beehive hairdo. Then her eyes dropped to his so quickly, it sprayed goose bumps across his neck and shoulders. He shifted uncomfortably as if he could sense Lena reading something in his eyes.

"You lost me at potluck," he said, glancing back at Bella.

"I heard Tazia invite her to a potluck. For that crowd, sharing food like that is more than a get-together. It's paying tribute to a new leader, like how it used to be in the old days before killing became a way to seize power."

He sipped more of his coffee before saying, "Sounds like a weird custom, but I'll take your word for it."

The goose bumps had receded, but he could still feel Lena's eyes boring into him.

Or, he thought, risking a quick glance at her, *boring into his hat.* Why did she care about his hat, though?

"What's your story?" Bella asked, nodding at him. "Still have a job?"

"Surprisingly, yes. The dead-end Kozek murder has unexpectedly turned into finding what crime family is going to fight for power in Steeltown. The New York Danchuks are lighting up the wire taps, talking about it, and apparently the Petrov family in Seattle is getting chatty about it too," he said.

"Jesus," she murmured and pressed her hands against her cheeks.

"Why the shock? You were the Olynyks' lawyer."

She quirked an eyebrow at him. "If I had a dollar for every time I stopped them from telling me about some crimes on their to-do list, I'd be a billionaire," Bella muttered.

"Now she's your client, and if what you said about Breziak is true, then she's in the middle of a shitstorm," he said.

"I think we're *all* in the middle of it with no way out," she groaned, glancing furtively at Lena the way he had. "What's your next move?"

"My new mandate as of two minutes ago is to question everyone related to Legs's murder and find out who the competitors are," he replied, thinking back to Marko standing near the bench. "But I think I know who wants to take over Legs's place."

"Marko? If the Danchuks really are chattering, he's going to get swatted like a fly," Bella said. "Maybe Lena too. And maybe quicker than we can pay our bill and get out of here."

"Marko's the heir. He won't give up without a fight. And from what I remember, he likes to fight."

They both looked over at Lena, who looked down at her lap. To Thomas, she seemed vulnerable. He didn't know what her involvement was, and Bella wasn't likely to divulge anything. Wise face or not, Lena didn't look like someone who knew how to face off with mobsters.

Chapter Forty-Three

Lena

I could have listened in on my lawyer and the Batman's conversation, but the throbbing in my head dragged a buzzing curtain across my ears. Although the green hat distracted me for a moment.

That green hat....

I shook my head and picked up my phone.

Yo, I need your help, I texted to the only people I trusted anymore.

After a few seconds, they replied.

Name it, replied Brick.

Same, JP answered next.

Check your Proton accounts, I typed and opened a window in the Control Panel to access the encrypted mail server.

I gathered the downloaded data, compressed it, and uploaded it to a new directory on my Swiss server. Then I typed up an email with what I needed and fired it off.

With any luck, they'd be able to synthesize the video data faster than I could. I could hack into live streams, but putting the raw data back into something usable was something I'd only ever done once, and it took me days.

"Bella, do you have a Proton account?"

"A what?" she answered.

"An encrypted email account. I'm going to have some friends forward you footage from the library."

That sure as hell perked Batman up, which stirred something in my stomach again as I looked at him wearing that hat.

"You have access to that?" he asked.

"Don't answer that," Bella told me, pausing before smacking Tommy hard. "You're investigating the Olynyks, remember?"

"I'm going to set an account up for you. Your login is soapdish.proton.me...," I said, typing in the random email address, then thinking up an equally random password. "Memorize them and don't write them down."

"Soap dish? What... never mind. Okay," she said, squinting her eyes closed as she mouthed the email and password over and over.

"I texted you a link," I said, and Bella pulled out her phone and started tapping.

"Now for the serious stuff," I said, putting my phone away.

I looked down at the slip of paper that had fallen out of my mom's diary. The book was personal. Too personal to read in a coffee shop with a bunch of strangers, although Valerie was really growing on me. I made a mental note to tell Vas not to screw that up.

No, after I saw what the paper was, I especially didn't want to read anything. That embossed document told me all I needed to know about what I had to do next.

"Don't freak out," I called up to Valerie, "but I'm going to assemble my gun."

"That's fine," she called back. "You need a refill, hun?"

"No, thanks," I said with a smile. Leave it to Valerie to roll with weird crap.

I looked down at the items in the saxophone case, but it was useless to pretend I wasn't the one who was freaked out.

My hands shook like I'd had eight cups of straight caffeine instead of the one frappé. No reason to go overboard, though that was kind of what I was planning on doing already.

"What do you mean, assemble a gun?" Tommy asked, sliding out of his chair and walking to stand over me.

I focused on the black gun parts in front of me and not what was on his head. I hovered my hands over the case. When I saw my fingers tremble, I closed them into fists.

"It's part of getting ready for battle, Tommy. As an FBI dude, you should be familiar with that," I replied.

"Don't call me Tommy," he grunted.

"It's too late to change," I replied.

"Battle with who, exactly?" he asked, stepping up beside my table. "Jesus."

"Not Jesus, but definitely somebody with a God complex," I muttered and looked up to see him staring at my AK pistol.

"Oh my God," muttered my lawyer, who'd followed Tommy to stand on the other side of the sax case. "What are you going to do with that?"

"Here's the plan," I said, stretching my fingers out. Nope. Still shaking. I pressed them flat on the table. "Some friends are helping me assemble data I captured from the library today. Audio, video, and other ones and zeroes. That's all I can do for the FBI, and if you're the kind of FBI guy who doesn't lie, it should be enough to drop your felony threat."

A weird expression spread over Tommy's face. It told me he was exactly the kind of FBI guy who lied.

"But if you don't drop it, you can deal with my lawyer," I said, tipping my head toward Bella. "Maybe you guys can settle it the way brothers and sisters do, with a good old Rock-Paper-Scissors."

I stood up and shook my hands out. It would take a year for my nerves to go away, so I decided... screw it.

I stared at the pieces in the case, then touched the soft velvet where they were nestled. The second I touched the metal, though, my hands moved, the muscles dancing a long-forgotten choreography.

Pull the initial pieces out. Wrap the trigger spring. Insert that, then slide in the hammer pin. Trigger assembly next.

My hands just moved—no remembered instructions necessary. I could tell from the dry feel of the metal that it hadn't been properly cleaned after its last use, but that shouldn't be a problem. I wasn't planning to actually fire it. At least I didn't think so.

Its last use. My hands completed the assembly as my mind flew back to that day.

That green hat.

"Is that yours?" I asked Tommy, not looking away from what my hands were doing but needing to know.

"What?"

"The hat," I replied.

"It was my father's," he answered, touching the brim.

"He didn't have it for long, though," Bella said and reached over to snatch the hat away. "The only time he wore it was when he was meeting someone for a case he was working on."

"How do you know that?" Tommy asked, his eyes fastened on the hat. I could tell he didn't like her holding it.

"When you wouldn't let this thing with Lena go, I tracked down Gabe and talked to him."

"Who's Gabe?" I asked, clicking the magazine into place, then cradling the gun loosely, the barrel pointed down.

Both Bella and Tommy looked at the gun, then up at me.

"Don't worry, I'm pretty sure I won't be firing it," I promised, then nodded at Bella.

"Who's Gabe?" I asked.

"Dad's partner," Tommy answered, looking over at Bella. "Why did he talk to you? He wouldn't talk to me when I called him after the whole... thing."

Bella's mouth opened to answer, but then her eyes watered, and she clamped her lips together.

"Let's talk about this later," she said, then looked down at the hat she'd turned over in her hands. One of her fingers hovered over a black splotch, and I swallowed.

That had to be blood. My trigger finger tensed against the metal receiver, safely away from the trigger but definitely in a ready position.

I'd put that blood there.

"Let's talk about *everything* later, because there's more to that hat than you know," I said.

I swung the backpack on, then slung the gun strap over my right shoulder. I closed the case and snapped the clasps shut. I wasn't thrilled with all the luggage I was carrying, but since I refused to let any of it out of my sight, there were no alternatives.

I grabbed the sax case and smiled when Bella backed away to let me pass.

"Thanks," I said and winked at her.

She just shook her head. "Good Lord, this is not how I pictured this weekend going," Bella muttered and rubbed her forehead.

"Be safe, people," Valerie called when I got to the door. "Fresh scones will be ready to go in an hour. They sell out fast, so be warned."

I stopped, and Bella plowed into me.

"What the hell?" she complained, then grunted when her brother walked into her back.

"What's the holdup?" he muttered.

"What kind of scones?" I asked.

"Blueberry lemon and maple walnut," she replied, hooking a thumb behind her where two trays of dough blobs waited.

"Save a maple walnut for me," I told her.

"I don't save things, not even for young ladies holding guns," she replied, her mouth twisting into a know-it-all grin.

"I'll pay triple," I promised, then grimaced. "Rather, my lawyer will pay triple. The FBI guy might have frozen my bank accounts."

"Now you're talking," Valerie replied, making a *tsk* sound and pointing a finger at me. "Where y'all heading?"

"To the library," I replied, and her look got serious.

"You be safe, young lady. You promised three times my scone price, and I'm going to hold you to it."

"I'll be as safe as I ever am," I replied and pushed the door open.

"Oh, boy," Bella muttered.

"Good God," Tommy grunted.

"That's good enough for me," Valerie said and waved as we walked out the door.

Chapter Forty-Four

Quinn

Quinn walked the twelve blocks to the library, hyperaware of the newly-issued gun on his belt. He hadn't fired any gun in weeks, and he had no plans to fire it today. But if he was forced to, he would. He could shoot without intention to kill, maybe hit Marko in the arm. Or the foot. Because if anyone forced him to shoot, it would be Marko.

Main Street was coming to life even though it would be a while before the shops opened for business. As he walked by Halloran's, the need for a couple shots of gin made his drinking hand twitch. Something to steady his nerves. Or something to give him some nerve. Maybe it was the same thing.

"Dammit," he muttered, keeping his walking pace steady. He would go into the library sober and do his job. The job he didn't really want to do despite picking it out personally. The job he couldn't let Brooke do, instead telling her to stay at the station and talk to the growing crowd who kept streaming through the door.

Somehow, Lena had gotten the entire town to defend her. Even though her cousin, Vasily, had said she hadn't lived there for ten years.

Quinn crossed the street and started up the library sidewalk, the yellow police tape sagging against the faded stucco of the building.

Lifting the tape, he pushed open the front door.

"Sir," greeted an officer inside the small lobby.

"Anyone inside?" he asked, surprised anyone was here.

"No. Mr. Olynyk went out—I mean Marko Olynyk, that is, not the... you know, not his dad—"

"I know. Where did Marko go?"

"He left an hour ago."

"Did he say where he was going?"

"Uh, I believe he mentioned going to have a smoke, sir," the officer said.

"Right," Quinn said and pushed open the inner door to go inside.

Nobody had mentioned how screwed up it was that a crime family operated out of a library. That men to whom life meant nothing sat just feet away from books about ducks and giant peaches.

Then he thought about the moms and grandmothers who'd shown up at the station, ready to defend Lena. Maybe they knew exactly what went on where their children and grandchildren gathered for story time.

He walked to the back, where Legs's "office" was.

Everything, from the crooked table to Legs's toppled chair, had been put back in place. A hole in the far wall, likely where the bullet lodged after it had torn Legs's jaw off, showed where it had been dug out by the forensics people. A large square of carpet, no doubt full of blood and brain matter, had been cut out as well.

Other than that, it looked like a standard reading room.

Quinn put himself where he thought the shooter would have stood and held out an invisible gun. At that range, most casings from shots fired would go up or up and to the right. But the table was there, with nothing against the far wall.

He crouched down and scanned the carpet under the table just to be sure. Then he walked around the table and did the same from a different angle.

It was very possible the shooter pocketed the casing before he left, but if the shooter was who he suspected, he believed he'd be in a highly emotional state. Likely too hyped or angry or excited to look for a casing.

Quinn walked back to where the shooter had to've been standing. If the killer had angled the gun…. The memory came back to him. Who had welcomed him to Steeltown with a sideways shooter stance? A right-handed stance, meaning the ejection would go to the left.

He looked at the low bookcase near the door, stepping closer and dragging it away from the wall. A fake fern on top tilted, and he gripped the edge so it didn't topple off.

There was nothing behind the bookcase. He crouched but saw nothing underneath either.

Running his hands on top of the books and stacks of paper, he came up empty. Then, just to be thorough, he picked up the fake fern.

There, gleaming under a fake frond, was a hollow piece of gold metal. He pinched it out of the pot, not having to look hard to see the etched design on its side.

"Ah, thank you for finding that for me," murmured an accented voice, low but still startling.

Quinn held his breath, grateful that he didn't gasp or jerk around.

"You're welcome, but this is evidence," Quinn said, turning to look at the man leveling a gun at him. "Interesting way to show your appreciation."

"There's a killer on the loose, or haven't you heard?" Marko murmured, stepping into the room while keeping the gun trained on him. Trained on his forehead, to be exact.

"That's a gorgeous piece. What is it?" he asked.

Marko smirked.

"It was a gift. From my father, many years ago. It's been in his family for a long time," Marko said and waved the gun to prompt Quinn to move back.

Quinn did, stepping backward until the gun stopped waving. He didn't like that he was now standing in the hole left by the missing carpet.

"That's nice work," he commented, keeping his hands where Marko could see them but pointing his casing-free hand at the etching on the side of Marko's gun. "I bet it matches that tattoo on your neck."

"You're pretty observant for a *cop*," Marko spit, his free hand reaching to his collar automatically. He adjusted it, the motion giving Quinn a clear look at one marking. A match to the casing. He would have held the metal piece at arm's length to compare it if he hadn't been sure Marko would shoot him.

"Actually, I'm a detective," he corrected, returning Marko's smirk. "The observing thing comes in handy when you're trying to solve a murder."

"I can solve it for you. Lena Kozek killed my father. I bet you'll find that casing matches her gun."

"Her gun? What gun would that be?" he asked.

"That's for you to figure out, *Detective*," Marko sneered. "I bet that bitch has guns stashed all over this town."

Quinn's hands wanted to clench into fists at the word "bitch," but he forced them to stay relaxed. Emotions weren't his friend in this situation, and he was pretty sure "bitch" was the nicest thing Marko had ever called a woman.

"Her father was my father's hitman, after all. I'm sure he trained her well. Why else would she come back to town except to murder my father?" Marko asked.

"That's a good question, now that you mention it. Why *would* she murder your father?" Quinn asked reasonably.

"Revenge. She thinks my father had something to do with her father's murder," Marko said. "I set her straight, though."

"Oh yeah? What'd you set her straight about?"

"I told the slut that she killed her father," Marko replied. "She didn't mean to, but—"

Marko's voice droned on, but it was static in Quinn's ears. Bitch was one thing. Slut? That sent the blood pulsing through his veins.

His vision narrowed on Marko's eyes, waiting for his moment. When it came, Quinn was on him.

He was pretty sure his feet left the ground when he leaped. His left forearm batted Marko's gun arm up, while his right fist, holding the casing tight, connected in an uppercut with the man's jaw.

Then they were wrestling on the ground, with Quinn winning, since he was on top and had Marko's gun hand braced over the man's head. Winning until a gunshot made them both freeze.

"Am I interrupting an intimate moment?" inquired Lena.

Her words sounded far away, the blast from the gun she pointed at the ceiling dulling all sound. A fine shroud of dust drifted around him and Marko in a drywall cloud. He squinted and looked over his shoulder.

Lena still wore the dress he'd first seen her in, her skinny legs braced in their black boots and her elbow propped on her hip, pointing the very real version of her pancake up at the ceiling.

Behind her, like a corporate version of the Avengers, appeared Bella in her classy lawyer clothes and another guy in an expensive suit. Like a pair of jarringly beautiful superheroes, the two had to be related.

If the other two were Avengers, Lena was an avenging waif, and damn if it wouldn't have been a turn-on in any other situation.

He was about to make some comment about her gun when he noticed her eyes were black, all pupils. He didn't like what that look meant.

As the ringing in his ears faded, he thought about how he was between two people holding guns, while his remained holstered. He didn't like that either.

"Nice to know this gun still fires," Lena said, dropping the tip of the gun and catching the hand guard, then holding it trained on him and the piece of scum still under him. "Maybe roll off my brother so I can shoot him."

Chapter Forty-Five

Lena

Saying the word "brother" made something click into place for me. Something strange and uncomfortable, but seeing the shock on the two men's faces was grounding. I wasn't the only one coming to terms with the psychological grenade I'd just tossed into the room.

Quinn's face lost all muscle control, falling into a kind of droop like he'd had a stroke.

"Brother?" Quinn mumbled, rolling off an enraged Marko but keeping a chokehold on Marko's gun hand.

"What kind of bullshit is this?" Marko spit out, trying to jerk his hand free of Quinn's iron grip.

"Not so fast," I negated, stepping closer but keeping clear of his feet. I wouldn't put it past him to sweep the leg.

"I'd cuff him, but I don't have my cuffs with me," Quinn said, shifting to keep his grip firm.

"No need," I said, lowering my gun to point at him. "You can let him go."

Quinn hesitated, then did as I asked. He immediately jumped up and pulled his gun out to point it at Marko, who knew better than to get up off the floor.

Marko, to give him credit, didn't shoot me right away. He rotated his wrist, then slowly lowered his arm until his gun pointed at me.

Fun. A standoff.

Thomas stepped up on my right, drawing his own weapon.

A shuffling noise behind me drew Marko's gaze to the doorway. Then came the unmistakable rasp of metal on leather.

Guns drawn. Hell yeah!

"What the hell are *you* all doing here?" Marko demanded, his hand tightening on the gun.

I didn't need to look to know Auntie Korinna, Tazia, and more of the blue-haired granny squad had filed into the room.

The awareness of the situation swelled under me until I felt suspended, watching it all play out below me. I had to say, it was a powerful feeling.

In my mind's eye, I saw the women behind me look uncomfortable but determined. My aunt's face was particularly pale but focused on the scene in front of her. Without a doubt, she'd have my back no matter what I did.

Something faltered in Marko's expression, and I shifted from being suspended to...

* * *

...back to right freaking now

"Galyna," purrs Marko on the other end of my gunsight. "Think about this," he reasons. No more raging Marko. He's calm. Friendly, even. "Killing is so final, family or not."

"Family," I repeat, my tone hinting that I'm open to contemplating what he's saying. But my finger tightens on the trigger, and I can see his pupils shrink to pinpoints.

"Tak, rodyna," he says with a nod. Yes, family. "We have much to talk about, and I can't talk if you shoot me."

"I don't need to talk," I tell him, lifting the gun to sight the barrel between his eyes.

He smiles, shrugs, and then his expression smooths into pure hate, and his gun arm stiffens.

"So who will shoot first?" he muses, his eyes flickering to all the players in the room.

It's a solid question, since there are so many guns in the room, but Quinn interrupts.

"What's going on here?" he murmurs, his Glock hand shaking a little. He grimaces and clamps his other hand around it to steady the gun.

"About the brother thing?" I ask.

He glances at the row of people behind me.

"Sure, let's start with that one," he murmurs.

"I have a piece of paper that says Legs is my biological father," I reply. "Bella, do you wanna get the paper out of my pocket? The right one."

I swirl my skirt a little, unwilling to move my gun's sight one millimeter off the space between Marko's eyebrows.

"Okay," she murmurs behind me, and she retrieves the paper.

"Read the part about my father," I say, watching Marko scowl at me.

"Certificate of Live Birth...," Bella reads, murmuring some other details. "Father's name, Oleg Olynyk."

"That's bullshit!" Marko shouts, his gun wavering to move from person to person. "You faked that, and you're all in on this."

"Looks pretty legal to me," Bella replies.

"And you're a bitch traitor," he yells at her, a little white blob of spit forming at the corner of his mouth.

"She's just cutting her losses with you," I tell him. "But if it makes you feel better, she's still representing somebody in your family."

His face flushes, and I laugh, knowing it will piss him off. Knowing it will have him aiming only at me, which he does.

His movement also makes Quinn move. He steps away from me but closer to Marko. Then Tommy does the same to my right.

"You all—" Marko accuses, his eyes frantically jumping from gun to gun as his own weapon shakes.

Crowding behind me is a pack of grannies, the muzzles of everything from a .22 rifle to an antique Colt poking into my peripheral vision.

Marko pushes himself into a sitting position. His hand wavers as he tries to keep all of us in his sights, and when we all take two steps forward, two perfect rivulets of sweat run down from both temples.

I swallow. With so many guns in the room, the chance that any of us, especially me, will leave in a body bag is high. Very high. Mount Everest death-zone high.

"Before things get out of hand, let's think about this," I say, stepping forward. It makes Marko's arm jerk toward me, but he doesn't stop twitching.

"Lena, what the hell—" Quinn mumbles, but I ignore him.

"Before two minutes ago, this gun hadn't been fired in years. I mostly just want you to confess to killing my father. And then maybe I can compromise. Just shoot you in the leg or something."

There's a confused mumbling around me, and I realize my mistake.

"Sorry. I mean confessing to shooting my fake father, Ilya. Not your—our—dad, although you should probably confess to that too," I amend, and the mumbles break into several, "Ahs" and "Rights."

"I didn't kill anyone. Not your father, or my father, or anyone who was a fake father—" Marko grumbles, confused.

Before I can reply, Quinn steps up beside me. His right hand, gripping the Glock, is shaking, and he's raising his left fist in the air. If it this is some new cop move, it's lost on me.

"I have proof that you killed both men," he says.

"You do?" I ask, shifting slightly closer to him for reasons I don't want to explore at the moment.

"I'm pretty sure of it," he replies, shaking his fist.

"Is that righteous indignation or some Jedi trick?" I muse, catching a flicker of smugness in his eye when he glances at me.

"Just good old detective work, thanks to that fern back there."

"The idiot left evidence hanging around? God, how embarrassing. Even more so because it's family, and—"

"Shut up!" Marko roars. "You just confessed you're going to shoot me. Now I can kill you in self-defense."

"No, I confessed that I was going to wound you, which is—"

Everything happens in a breath.

I can't explain how I know he's about to shoot me, unless it's the subtle movement of the lines around his mouth and a steadying of his gun hand.

A calm drops over me. I know for a fact that this is my training bubbling to the surface. I might not see him, but I feel my corpse dad hovering behind me. He's not there to critique or help, but to admire, and it fills me with the steely confidence I wish every living soul to experience once in their life.

Three-days-ago Lena would have either passed out or puked. The me in this moment takes a step closer to Marko's big-ass gun and matches him with my intent.

"Then it will be a race to see who shoots first," I agree. Then I sight my gun to his kneecap and squeeze.

A screech and an explosion ring through the room, and Marko jerks back in reaction, his knee twitching and blossoming in a red flower, his gun flying up and shooting a hole in the ceiling close to the one I put there.

It's a miracle everybody doesn't fire. They jump and jostle and mutter, but they all stay gun-calm.

As for me, I adjust my sight to find his other kneecap.

"...tap into the live feed," booms a familiar voice through the library's PA system. "Now try the camera outside first. It's the one that had the audio working."

God love him, it's JP.

"Do you think this library has an adult section? Like triple X, because I want to tap that camera first," enthuses another voice.

Of course it's Brick.

Geez, I've never been so happy to hear my Neanderthal friends' voices.

"Guys?" I ask, not hiding the wavering in my voice. "We're hearing you loud and clear."

"Who's that?" Brick asks.

"It's Lena, asshole. We must've tapped into the library's PA system," JP mutters. "Hey, Lena. Sorry we're late."

"What the hell is going on?" Marko yell-whimpers from his sprawl on the floor. One hand clearly wants to hold his knee but hovers above it instead. I can't blame him; it looks pretty gross.

"I'll have to echo that," Quinn murmurs, looking around the room like he's searching for God.

"It's a long story, but they're the ones who are unscrambling the data I... diverted from the library's cameras," I explain, staring Marko dead in the eyes. "Diverted from the moment I was reunited with my scumbag brother, here. Remember that, bro? From earlier today?"

"You... what?" he stammers, and I can see the tiny cogs in his tiny mind grind as he tries to understand what I'm telling him.

"You didn't tell us we were deciphering a snuff video," Brick said, his words booming around the room. "Some dude straight up wasted an old man."

"Can you guys access whatever camera is in this reading room?" I ask, checking all the corners until I see a tiny round lens tucked against the ceiling. "That's where we are."

"Dammit, my team was supposed to do that," Quinn says, then scans the ceiling for the speaker and faces it. "You got the murder on video?"

"In disgusting technicolor," Brick enthuses though the speakers.

Quinn keeps his gun trained on Marko, and I realize he's still holding his fist in the air.

"What's up with your hand?" I break down and ask.

"The evidence I found links Marko to the deaths of both men," he says, and like effing Hercule Poirot, he lowers his hand to reveal a bullet casing.

Just as I'm trying to figure out how to high-five him without shooting him, the booming of guns shakes the room.

Chapter Forty-Six

Lena, about 8 hours of loose ends later...

Yes, it's later. And yes, I'm still alive.

Everybody's still alive despite about ten guns going off. Here's what happened.

One of the grannies, who couldn't see what Quinn was holding, got curious and moved to get a better look. She stepped on the foot of the granny next to her, who accidentally squeezed her trigger. That caused two more grannies and Tommy to discharge their weapons.

The final tally had Marko taking two more hits (not serious, I was told) and the ceiling taking four. I dropped to the floor after the first granny shot, escaping everything except being handcuffed, since I shot Marko's knee out.

My hotshot lawyer got me out, but not before I got an awesome nap in. Marko is at the hospital under armed guard, and Brooke, bless her heart, is looking after the reopening of Ilya Kozek's murder by filing the new evidence Quinn uncovered.

But right at this moment, I've got something else in a death grip. My foil-wrapped wiener-filled casserole is making my biceps cramp.

The only other things I'm bringing to the potluck are my keys, a folded piece of paper, and the hope that none of Marko's goons will show up.

Oh, and Quinn. Speaking of which...

"Quinn!" I yell, kicking his apartment door with my boot. The motion lets the air swirl under my dress. Yes, I'm wearing the same clothes. At this point I'm thinking my outfit is the real guardian angel in all of this.

"Coming," he says, his voice muffled. "What time is it?"

"Time to go."

"No, exactly what time is it?" he calls out.

"My hands are full. What does your Death Star clock say?" I yell back, not without a bit of spice. It's a special family occasion and he's going to make me late? Nuh-uh.

"It says 4:12 a.m."

"Then it's very broken."

The door jerks open, and Quinn stands in the doorway, looking panicked. And looking very dorky.

"Which is why I need to know the time," he explains, smoothing down a faded pair of cargo shorts and twitching the front of the blue-and-green striped shirt he's wearing.

"You're wearing that?" I ask, doubting my idea to arrive at my aunt's with him.

"It's my least-wrinkled shirt," he defends. He runs a hand over the front but looks behind himself. "I could change—"

"No, I'm talking about the shorts," I say, raising my eyebrows at the khaki cargo shorts he's got on. Just below his knee is a big square bandage taped into place. Right, add a deflected bullet to the day's injury total.

"It's a potluck, and my phone says it's in the eighties," he says. He looks at me with scorn, but I can tell he's second-guessing his bold shorts move.

"They're fine. Let's go," I say and take a step back. "Wait a second. Where's your dish?"

"What dish?" he asks as he steps outside and closes the door.

"Whoa, whoa, whoa. It's a potluck. You're supposed to bring something in a pot. Or a dish." I lift the casserole like a flash card, hoping he'll make the connection.

"You asked to borrow my only dish," he says with a shrug.

"Yeah. To make my dish. *My*. Dish," I explain. I lift the dish again, since he seems to miss the point.

"I also gave you the macaroni and the wieners," he points out, tilting his head to the side.

I'm wondering how many rounds we're going to go before I have to explain this isn't the date I'm pretty sure he thinks it is.

"I *borrowed* them. You didn't *give* them to me," I explain.

"I figured, what with the dish and the macaroni and the wieners, that, uh. It would be a sort of—"

"I thought so. What is it about guys—" I start, but then his phones buzzes.

"Hang on," he says, checking the phone but holding up his hand at me like he's directing traffic. "It's my sister. Hey, Patricia."

I drop my shoulders and give him a look, but he just shrugs at me.

"Yeah, everything's great. I'm actually on my way out, so…. Yeah, it's fine. The job is great, the apartment's fine, everything's good."

Instead of inching to the stairs, I decide to mess with him.

"Tell her how you took down a big-time crime boss," I whisper loudly and jump back when he covers the phone and shushes me.

"She thinks I don't start work until Monday," he whispers.

"So bring her up-to-date. Here," I say, shove the casserole against his chest, and grab his phone. "Patricia? Yeah, this is your brother's neighbor. He had to start work early, and he arrested—"

Quinn is vehemently shaking his head, and I take pity on him.

"He arrested a real bad guy in town," I amend.

"He did? Well, that's just like Quinn. What's your name?" she asks.

"Lena," I reply.

"Well, Lena. If you're really his neighbor, can you do me a favor and keep an eye on him? He's the only family I've got, and he's pretty special to me even though he likes to keep most of the country between us," she says.

I look over at my dorky non-boyfriend and am embarrassed to say, the sincerity in her voice made me a little misty.

"Sure thing," I promise, ready to hand the phone back when she says, "And please make sure he doesn't get mixed up with that crime family. I heard they're the real bad news in Steeltown." There's a combination of disgust and worry in her tone.

"I'll do my best," I say, crossing my fingers and shoving the phone back at him.

I grab the casserole back and head down the stairs, thinking about the irony of the last eight hours. I was supposed to come back and infiltrate a crime family, and now it seems like I'm an heir to one.

"My sister was hoping I'd move closer to her," Quinn says as he tromps down the stairs.

"Yeah, I got that. Maybe you should," I say, leaning against the wall but looking pointedly at the bandage on his leg.

"And maybe I'm old enough to make decisions about my life," he returns, then stares at the casserole. "You'd think you'd feel sorry for me and let me co-bring this macaroni thing you made."

He looks at me with that kooky dad-face that absolutely shouldn't make me feel giddy, but it does.

"This isn't a couple's dish. This is *my* dish from *my* family recipe, and you and I are just friends," I say, then wink at him. "Plus, I sort of promised your sister I wouldn't get mixed up with you."

"We're already mixed up," he contradicts, holding the front door open and pointing to a dirty SUV.

"Because we had sex? That's in the past."

"Not that. I mean yes, that, but there's more to us being mixed up," he argues as he unlocks the passenger door and yanks it open.

"Like what?"

"We shared some things. I made you pancakes," he says after he gets in the truck.

"You made me an *approximation* of pancakes that I never ate," I reply. "I made you art."

"See? And I bet you don't make art for many guys, do you?"

I scowl. He has me there.

I don't know how to handle romantic stuff, and he's getting pretty close to guessing that I kind of, sort of, maybe like him *like that*. He's nothing like Batman, who makes my tongue sweat now that he doesn't want to incarcerate me. Quinn's reliable. Like... a really good pair of boots.

"I'll tell you what isn't art," I say and give him my best derogatory look. "Those shorts. Now let's get to this potluck and hope nobody shoots us, okay?" I suggest and nod down the street where so much crap had just gone down.

Chapter Forty-Seven

Lena

Quinn spends the entire drive convincing me that sharing the macaroni-and-wiener concoction on my lap isn't a date, but the sight that greets us when we turn onto my aunt's street stops me in midnegotiation.

"What the hell," I murmur, seeing cars parked along both sides of the road and clusters of people walking down the street.

"Is there more than one potluck going on?" Quinn asks as he eases the car down the narrow corridor.

"Not that I know of," I reply, glancing at the people as we pass them. Every group is holding some sort of pot or dish, and more than a couple of them get this excited look on their face and wave at me.

"Do you know those people?" Quinn asks.

"No," I say, not sure if waving back is a good idea.

Quinn pulls the car seven houses past my aunt's before we find a place to park. As I juggle my backpack and the casserole, he jogs around the car to open my door.

"Thanks, I—" I start, but like a jerk, he grabs the macaroni dish and jumps back.

"Hah!" he declares and jogs away, blindly following the other people toward my aunt's backyard.

I scan my mental insult folder, but you know what? It's kind of sweet that he wants to share ownership of my dish, and maybe letting people think we're together isn't such a bad thing.

"Fine," I yell as I slam his door.

He stops and waits for me, but when I don't grab the dish back, he relaxes.

"From the look of things, I think you're coming back home as a conquering hero," he says, gazing around at all the smiling people.

Home. I will have to revise my opinion of that word now that I'm back in my old apartment. Now that I seem to be welcome at my aunt's place.

"I guess so," I say. "Although I'm part of a different family now."

I stop walking, letting that roll over in my mind. My aunt is still my family, but my father no longer is. And yet he's still the only family I want.

"What?" Quinn asks, taking a few more steps before stopping to look at me.

"I guess I'm realizing it doesn't matter what a birth certificate says. My dad was still my dad, despite my DNA marking me as an Olynyk," I say. Then I have to look away because a bubble of something hot and face-twitching overwhelms me.

"Hey, it's okay," Quinn murmurs, and I feel his arm go around me.

I nod, but I'm not okay. Instead of joking or moving away, though, I decide to let that soppy wet stuff overflow my eyes.

"Hm," he mumbles and awkwardly pats my arm.

I roll my face into his shoulder like he's a giant eye blotter and get myself under control.

"Thanks," I say, then make a grab for the casserole. He's too quick, though, and holds it away.

"Nice try," he says, walking toward my little Auntie Korinna, who's striding toward us. "We made this!"

I laugh, then laugh harder when my aunt looks skeptically at the dish.

"Over on those tables. Put it with the other salads," she directs, and Quinn winks at me, then disappears around an overgrown cedar.

"Lena," my aunt says, and her face wiggles.

Then mine wiggles, and then we're both hugging each other like saps.

"I know Vas took you to your apartment. That means you're staying in Steeltown," she announces in her bossy way, pulling a ball of tissue from inside her bra strap. She dabs her eyes, then passes it to me.

Gross at it sounds, I don't even hesitate. I grab it and swipe at my eyes.

"I guess I am. I didn't really come here for a job interview. I lied about that," I admit, and her entire face does an eye-roll. "But I talked to a drunk guy at a bar, and there might be something for me at a bank."

"I imagine there are several options for you," she says and links her arm through mine to drag me into the crowd of milling people.

Vas appears and puts his fingers in his mouth, giving a screech of a whistle. Then my aunt elbows him aside.

"Our guest of honor has arrived!" she announces, and the look on her face makes that bubble threaten to overtake me again.

Instead, I look around at those hundred strangers who are now cheering for me. Me! Even little kids who were just chasing a dog stop and clap their hands.

It's too much, and I scan the faces for any I might recognize, and wouldn't you know? I catch Mr. Batman and his sister strolling over.

"Thanks for springing me from jail," I tell her. "Hey, can you still be my lawyer if I'm an Olynyk?" I ask her.

She looks doubtful for a long moment before she smiles.

"If you want me, you got me. Although I'm dubious you can afford me," she says.

"I'll figure that out later. I just need to know if Tommy, here, still wants to arrest me," I say, and I look at the tall man beside her.

He's staring at me like he thinks behind bars is the best place for me, but at least he isn't wearing the green hat.

"I need to put our contribution on the table," Bella says with a grimace, holding up a plastic bag with dinner rolls in it. "I've been told there's a food hierarchy that Mrs. Breziak oversees."

We all look over at the food table where Mizbee is directing the placement of food among the overflowing platters and bowls with the air of a general. Bella and her store-bought roles are going to get a scathing "end of the table"—I'm sure of it.

Bella leaves, and Tommy moves to stand in front of me.

"Will you *ever* not call me Tommy?" he asks, but he already knows my answer, so I don't have to say anything. "We should talk."

"Probably," I agree.

Instead of talking, though, he takes my arm and points to the far side of the Airstream.

I feel a little guilty that his touch makes my arm tingle. It's not fair that a government agent should be so good-looking.

"There never was a felony charge," he says once we stop out of earshot of the crowd. "I just needed leverage to get you here."

"I knew something stank with your blackmail," I almost yell, but then he smiles, and I sort of back down. Okay, I fully back down.

"Yeah, well, I had some warped idea about you being a loose end I needed to get rid of," he says. "But now that everything's out about who killed my father, and with Legs dead and Marko in jail, well... I should probably try to put all of that behind me," he explains, looking at the side of the trailer and then flicking part of the rusted metal trim with his thumb.

I nod, thinking how easy it would be to leave it at that. I could just pretend I didn't know it was his dad wearing that green hat. Or that when I pulled the trigger that day, that it was *his* dad I shot and not my own dad. Who wasn't even my real dad!

Geez, that's a lot to follow.

But even though that's the easier way out, I know it's not the *right* way.

"My father didn't kill your dad," I tell Tommy, and his gaze flickers to mine. "I did. He was my father's mark, but I was the one who pulled the trigger. Then Marko killed my father and... well, the rest of it is kind of a blur. Honestly, a ton of my life is still a blur. But I know with zero doubt that I was the one who killed your dad."

I brace myself for his rage. I watch his pupils contract until they are pinpricks in his sapphire-blue eyes. Those eyes give me another reason to feel bad that I'm about to make him hate me all over again, if not arrest me right on the spot.

Then something amazing happens.

Chapter Forty-Eight

e sighs. A very long, defeated sigh. A sigh that empties his whole body until he's almost collapsing against the trailer.

If I were the kind of person who runs, it'd be the perfect scenario to get the hell out of there. Except this weary guy in front of me doesn't look capable of arresting or chasing anybody.

He opens his mouth, and the words that come out shock me.

"I was there that day, you know," he says, and now it's my turn to let out a long breath.

"You were there," I repeat.

The skin around his eyes wrinkles, giving his face a haunted look. It's like he's disappearing inside himself as his brain travels back to that day.

"I was supposed to meet my new supplier. Marko said it was a promotion from the seller at the high school to manager."

I can't stop my head from jerking back.

"You were one of Marko's sellers?" I burst out, then slap a hand over my mouth. Two grannies look over, and I wave at them with a weak smile.

"I was the king of Steeltown High," he replies with a heavy dose of cynicism. "I was so good at my job that Marko said it was time to step up. I was going to negotiate a buy with this new supplier. He said the man would be wearing—"

"A green hat," I finish.

"A green hat," Tommy agrees, looking right through me. "That's what Marko told me. And he told my dad that his dealer would be looking for a guy in a green hat."

"So Marko screwed you, your dad, me, and my dad," I mumble, feeling bad for everybody.

"Marko always thought it was hilarious that a cop's son was his best seller. I thought so too. What an asshole I was," Tommy says, disgust filling his expression.

"I'm guessing your dad didn't know he was meeting you?" I asked.

"No idea until he saw me," Tommy mutters, his voice cracking at the end. "The look in his eyes when he did—"

Tommy can't finish, the words strangled.

I look away from his trembling lips, poking at the trailer's trim like it's the most amazing thing I've ever seen. It gives Tommy enough time to compose himself and continue.

"That's when he realized his son was a drug dealer. Right before he was shot." He tries to smile through his twitching lips. "Every day I live with the memory that that was his last thought. I thought getting rid of your dad, then you, and all the connections to that day would make this guilt go away. I even toyed with changing my name, but it didn't matter. None of it helped."

"Jesus," I can't help whispering, and though it's probably pointless, I mumble, "I'm sorry."

"Yeah, well," he grunts, then blows out a long breath.

"If it makes you feel better, I won't fight against you arresting me," I offer, and it's true. "I'll admit to everything. Maybe your boss will give you a promotion or something."

"I could give a shit about my boss. Or my job. Or that you just admitted to being a murderer. Nothing could make me feel less like the scum I am for what I did to my father. For letting an animal like Marko make me idolize a criminal instead of the man who put a roof over my head," he groans and rubs his palm across his forehead.

I'm trying to think of something comforting to say, but this is a situation I don't find myself in very often. Being nice to someone. Then something over Tommy's shoulder moves.

I squint, trying to make it out. Then I realize why I'm struggling.

There, half transparent by the trailer door, leans my corpse dad with a hand on his hip and that little creepy smirk on his face.

Then I know what to say.

"Hey," I tell Tommy. When he ignores me, I give him a solid punch in the shoulder.

"Ow, what the hell?" he says, rubbing his arm and looking at me with more annoyance than self-pity.

"Wherever your dad is, I think he's forgiven you for being a scumbag son, okay?" I say.

"What would you know about it?" he asks.

I see my dad roll his eyes in annoyance, and it makes me laugh.

"I know something about the afterlife. Let's just leave it at that," I replied.

Tommy looks like he wants to say more, but Quinn walks up to us and gives Tommy a heavy whack on his back.

"What's the good news, Agent Palmer?" he demands cheerfully.

Quinn, with his dad haircut and sad cargo shorts, looks me dead in the eye and grins at me. Damn, if my heart doesn't speed up. Just a little.

"I got called into the station. What time do you want me to come back and pick you up?" he asks me.

"I can take her home," Tommy volunteers.

"No, I got this," Quinn insists, puffing out his chest in his dumb shirt.

"It's not a big deal," Tommy assures him.

He's not puffing anything out because he's already just big and imposing. I know, surprising for a government agent kind of guy, am I right?

Something in my stomach flips, though, as I look at both of them. Crap, this was the closest I would ever get to two guys fighting over me, and I wanted to remember it.

I finally nod at Quinn. "You go on." Then I look at Tommy. "I've got a way home, but thanks."

My corpse dad steps through both men and turns to face them.

Both Quinn and Tommy shift on their feet as if trying to figure out why they suddenly feel a weird vibe.

"I'll see you later on, then," Quinn says to me uncertainly, then gives Tommy a hard look, as if to blame him for the spookiness.

"What?" Tommy asks defensively, then huffs and stomps past Quinn.

It makes me laugh. Then I cackle, stopping only when Quinn stares at me.

"You're one weird woman, do you know that?" he asks, then walks away in his own huff when I just keep laughing.

"Good job, Galyna," my dad tells me even though he's still glaring at the two men's backs.

"Having two guys like me?" I ask.

"Telling that man that you killed his father. He deserves to know the truth," my dad says. "Now you have a bigger decision to make."

I look at him in confusion. I thought my decision to say no to both men just now was pretty strong.

"A big decision about what?" I ask him.

"Have you seen what's over on that table?"

"The food table? Aside from my amazing casserole, no. Why?" I ask.

He looks at me with a knowing look.

"Only the most important dish at one of these things," he says.

It sinks in, and my upper lip breaks out in a sweat, making me wish I had a shot of Fireball on this hot day.

Suddenly I know who I have to talk to next, and I know the kind of decision my dad's talking about.

Chapter Forty-Nine

Lena

I give the table a quick scan, but before I can spot it, Mizbee materializes beside me.

"Marta brought her holodets, but she used chicken in the jelly instead of pork, and it's a little—" Mrs. B. shrugs and turns her hand back and forth in a meh gesture. "Who am I to tell her how to change her recipe?"

I couldn't care less about the holodets, to be honest. The super-traditional dish uses pig's hooves, so in my opinion, the chicken is a step up.

I glance back at the table, searching for that one dish, only to be distracted by the varenyky. Those are my favorite depending on what's inside. Cabbage and chicken? Fine. Tart cherries and cottage cheese, however? Chef's kiss right there.

"I brought this," Mizbee says in a solemn voice and clasps her hands together as she walks to the end of the table.

I follow her, knowing exactly what she is about to show me and knowing what it will mean.

There, sitting majestically on a colorful platter, is a golden, braided paska bread. It's huge because inside is a clove-studded ham. How she did it on short notice, I have no idea. But then, how does one's father come back from the dead to haunt/annoy his daughter?

"That's a paska ham," I say like an idiot, pointing at the meat, then looking at Mizbee

"It is."

"Ham *in* a paska, not ham *with* a paska," I clarify because the impossible act of creating a perfectly cooked ham inside a gorgeous loaf of bread is a feat.

"That's right."

"And it's not Easter," I state, looking at her pointedly. I want to be very clear about what this hunk of meat in fancy bread means. I want her to know I know, and I want her to say it out loud.

"It's not Easter," she agrees.

I think about what everyone in this small community of people knows about the anointing of the heads of The Family. That the Olynyks had never been welcomed by the Breziaks in the traditional way. That way was staring me smack in the face right now.

"Mizbee," I say, shaking my head at what she is about to ask me. I'm sweating all over now, too, which I don't do elegantly, but I'm not embarrassed about it either.

"Call me Tazia like the others do," she invites.

"I don't think I can," I murmur, pressing my hands to my cheeks, feeling like a kid.

"Lena. Galyna. Galyna Olynyk," Mizbee says, squinting up at me thoughtfully.

"I think I'd prefer to stick with Lena Kozek," I say.

"I can see why," she allows. "That doesn't change the fact that we want you to lead the organization. The Family."

"Ahhhh, you know... I don't know," I sigh, rubbing my neck and shuffling my feet.

"You don't need to know. *I* know," Mizbee says and takes one of my hands in hers and pats it. "You didn't need to do what you did this morning, but you did. You didn't need to come back to Steeltown after all this time, but you did."

"Yeah, but that was... not for the reasons you think," I say.

I hear a hissing noise, and my father hovers into view right beside the ham. He's blowing air through pursed lips to let me know he thinks I'm a moron.

"Why are you talking yourself out of this? You're made for this job," he says and leans over the paska. "Ah, what I wouldn't give to taste this. Tazia had a way with cured meats."

"What I think," Mrs. Call-Me-Tazia says, "and what the other women agree with me about, is that you should lead The Family. The true organization, not with the drugs and the killing that the Olynyks did," she says, then makes a *tsk* sound. "The *other* Olynyks, I mean."

I rub my neck again, then notice the other grannies have gathered around. Auntie Korinna is the last to arrive, but she pushes through the circle to stand by me, taking my hand out of Mizbee's grip.

"Give the girl some space, all of you," she scolds, searing them all with a look.

Their faces pull into accepting frowns, and they move a few paces away. They pretend to look at the clouds, the trees, one another, while not wandering too far away that they can't listen in. Even Mizbee backs away, although she ends up standing right inside my dad, who is still trying to smell the paska ham.

"Lena. Lena, Lena," Auntie Korinna says, holding my hands and looking at me in a way that my brain doesn't catch on to, but my gut does. "There's a saying my... *our* mother taught us. 'In a pack of wolves, even a fish can run.'"

"Are you say-aying," I stammer, her expression kinder than I'd ever imagined her being. "Are you saying I'm a fish?"

"You're our fish," she confirms, then shrugs her shoulders up to her ears. "Or maybe we're the fish and you're our wolf."

I huff a couple times as I look at my aunt. My aunt. My family. Although don't for a second think I didn't love being the wolf.

"But you get to choose this time. And I will make sure you have the time to make the decision that is right for you. I want you to stay. In your apartment, or here, with us," she says, giving a sharp laugh as I glance at the trailer. "No, not the trailer. Whether you accept Tazia's offer or not, you're welcome in my house. But it's your choice."

She squeezes my hand every time she says "you," and I blink hard and fast to keep her clear in my vision. Damn emotions.

"Thanks," I mutter.

"All right, everybody, let's eat, huh?" my aunt calls out.

The ladies rush forward, waving me away from the table so they can fuss over stacking a ridiculous amount of food on a plate for me. Each portion's a scoop from their own dish until they get to the end of the table where the ham is.

Mizbee brandishes a huge knife, then slices into the golden-brown end of the paska, the ham inside glistening and pink. She expertly lays it on top of the mountain of food like a blanket being tucked around a fat baby.

She hands off the knife and takes the plate, approaching me like she's the Archbishop of Canterbury about to crown me.

Everyone gathers around, murmuring and chatting like it's no big deal, but I know deep inside what this is. It's a Very. Big. Deal.

I look around the crowd. Vas gives me a thumbs-up while Valerie claps her hands together and shouts, "You go, girl!"

Tommy and Bella look confused, while my dad, still standing near the ham, looks pleased.

"This is your moment, Galyna. This is who you are, but your aunt is right. *You* get to choose," he says.

I look at the woman in front of me and accept the plate from her. But I know that's not enough.

"Tazia Breziak, I accept," I say, and damn if my voice doesn't ring out a little like Galadriel's.

"Nova krov!" Tazia calls out, clapping her hands. New blood!

"Khorosha krov!" everyone answers, even me. Even my father.

Everyone but Tommy and Bella knows what the response means. *Good* blood.

And damn, if I didn't feel *good*!

But WAIT! I know what you're thinking. What about Damon? What does he think about everything that's happened?

First of all, calm down. Breathe. Are you good? Great. Second, I've got you covered with Damon. Scan the code and you'll get access to the BONUS CHAPTERS for Damon AND a final conversation with my dad AND a little something-something for Quinn.

See you in the bonus...

Books by Nala Henkel Aislinn

Hitman's Daughter Novels

Pancakes & Handguns (July 2024)

Double Tappuccino (Spring 2025)

Baking & Entering (Fall 2025)

Blunt Force Shawarma (Spring 2026)

Maple Cove Sweet Romance Series

Small Town Shepherd (Sam's story)

Beauty and the Bulldog (Vi's story)

Foxhound Foes (Matt's story)

Billionaire Beagle (Olive's story)

Westie Bestie (Quinn's story)

Second Chance Corgi (Eliza's story)

Pomeranian Princess (Jackson's story)

Professor Pug (Hannah's story)

Terrier Trouble (Pastor Pete's story)

Cranberry Hill Inn Series

Operation Vengeance (**FREE** prequel)

Blueprint for Love (Katy's story)

Deadline for Love (Summer's story)

Recipe for Love (Carson's story)

Spark of Love (Rally's story)

Race to Love (Cassie's story)

Christmas is Love (Garrett's story)

Magic at Snow Fox Lodge (Sweet Christmas Series)

Billionaire's Christmas Wish (Only 99¢)

Billionaire's Christmas Baby

Billionaire's Christmas Auction

Billionaire's Christmas Tale (Pre-Order 99¢)

To be part of the naming contests, freebies, and giveaways, **please visit https://www.subscribepage.com/l4m3s1** and join my email list!

About the Author

 Nala has been writing all her life, but when she was hired to ghostwrite a romantic trilogy that received five-star reviews, she realized bringing funny, complex characters to life was her true purpose.

She is the author of the contemporary sweet romance series Cranberry Hill and Maple Cove, as well as the Christmas-themed series, Magic at Snow Fox Lodge.

If you like a good laugh along with a hearty dose of heartfelt love story, join her newsletter for freebies and giveaways by clicking here to join her newsletter reading club!